Volume 19 of
The Hansen Series:
The Rogue and the Rose

REDEEMED

Book One:
Stefan & Blake

Kris Tualla

The Rogue Redeemed is a work of fiction. Names, characters, places and incidents are products of the author's imagination or are used fictitiously and are not to be construed as real. Any resemblance to actual events, locales, organizations, or persons, living or dead, is entirely coincidental.

Published in the United States of America.

© 2019 by Kris Tualla

ISBN: 9798730889804

*This book is dedicated to
Diana Gabaldon
whose "Outlander" series
and "Outlandish Companion"
prompted me to sit down
and "try to write a novel"
thirteen years ago.*

Chapter One

January 10, 1845
Cheltenham, Missouri

"Arrested?" Nicolas glared at Stefan, who sat on the other side of his father's battered oak desk. "For what?"

Stefan tried to sound unconcerned. "For murder..."

"Murder!" his father bellowed.

Sydney, the only mother he had ever known in his life, gasped softly from her upholstered seat nearby. Her hand covered her mouth and her eyes widened. She shot a startled gaze at Kacy, who had slipped inside Nicolas's office and now stood still just inside the doorway, with her hands clasped behind her.

Kacy caught Stefan's gaze and her expression hardened. His baby sister was obviously disappointed in him.

Join the crowd.

"I was innocent, of course! It was all a misunderstanding!" Stefan turned to his adopted older brother for support. "Leif! Tell him!"

Leif faced Nicolas with an apologetic expression that Stefan angrily recognized and thought of as: *you know how he is.*

"Someone tried to pin the murder of a working girl on Stefan by leaving a bloody dress next to him when he was asleep," Leif gave Nicolas the short version.

Nicolas scuttled his hand through his thick but graying blond hair and returned his attention to Stefan. "Where in the hell were you sleeping?"

Stefan felt his face heating. "Outdoors. By a river."

"In December?" Nicolas snorted. "Are you daft?"

"He—*we*—didn't want to bed down in the brothel," Leif offered. Judging by the cautious look on his face he knew the declaration, meant to be helpful, would certainly bring more questions.

Nicolas's brow lowered and his dark blue eyes turned stormy. "So, what? You were whoring?"

Stefan scoffed. That particular accusation was rich, coming from his father.

"Like *you* never did?" he challenged.

Nicolas recoiled, his face reddening at Stefan's impertinence. "*What?*"

"He has you there, Nicolas," Sydney reminded her husband softly. Clearly his mother was trying to calm the growing storm.

Stefan shot her a grateful look and grabbed at that straw. "Exactly! And Aunt Rosie is like a member of the family now."

Nicolas's fists hit the top of the desk. "We are not talking about me!"

Sydney stood, her hands clasped in front of her still trim waist, and quickly changed the subject. "Is that why you boys were not here for Christmas?"

Boys?

Stefan was thirty-one and Leif was thirty-six. They had not been counted as boys for nearly a decade and a half.

Stefan smiled sadly at Sydney. "Yes, *Mamma*. I am really sorry."

"We came as soon as we could," Leif confirmed. He waved a hand toward their sister. "At the least we are here in time for Kacy's birthday."

"Her name is not Kacy," Nicolas growled.

"Pappa, stop." Their brave younger sister stepped further into the room and addressed Sydney as well as Nicholas. "I like the nickname—I always have. Those are my initials and my name honors both of your mothers."

Nicolas snorted and opened his mouth to speak when his daughter cut him off.

"In fact…" She paused as if pondering the wisdom of her next revelation. "I never mentioned it, but I went by Kacy the whole time I was in Philadelphia."

She shifted her gaze briefly to Stefan before she gave Nicolas an apologetic shrug. "And before you say anything else, I plan to use it in Washington as well."

Stefan startled. "Washington?"

Kacy faced him fully now. "I am moving to the Capitol with Pappa and Mamma when Pappa returns to the Senate."

That was a surprise. "Why?"

Stefan had not seen his parents for years—not since Nicolas was elected as a United States Senator from Missouri, and his parents moved to Washington D.C. Both of them had aged far more than he expected since then; his father's face was heavily lined and his mother's once-black hair had turned solidly gray. Clearly life in the eastern city was harder than in quiet little Cheltenham, Missouri.

Maybe Kacy going with them is a good thing.

"I have an education that is wasted here, to be honest," Kacy continued, talking more to her parents than to her brothers. "And I want to do more with my life than sit out here in the west with no prospects."

No prospects?

For the first time it occurred to Stefan that, as of tomorrow, his twenty-five-year-old and strikingly beautiful little sister was already considered an old maid.

Why has no man swept her up?

"Well, I am glad you boys are here now." Sydney broke into Stefan's thoughts and he turned to face his mother.

She stretched out her arms. "I have missed you both terribly."

Stefan gladly stepped into her comforting embrace. At six-foot-three just like his father, her head tucked neatly under his chin. "I love you, Mamma."

"I love you too Stefan, you know that." She released him and reached for Leif.

Leif wasn't as tall as Stefan and Nicolas so his cheek pressed against Sydney's hair. "I love you, Sydney."

"And I love you." When she stepped back, she looked pointedly at Nicolas. "Will you finally greet your sons?"

Nicolas rose slowly. Stefan realized with a jolt that it was more age than reluctance that affected his father's movements. Nicolas rounded the ancient desk and held out his hand.

"I am glad to see you both, do not mistake me."

Stefan nodded as he gripped his father's hand. "Yes, sir."

Nicolas shook Leif's hand, but his eyes were fixed on Stefan. "And this conversation is not finished."

January 13, 1845

Three days later Stefan and Leif once again faced Nicolas across the worn desk. The office door was closed.

Nicolas leaned forward and clasped his hands together. Stefan stared at the evidence of arthritis in his father's thickening knuckles, again reminded that his once invincible father was aging.

"Is this behavior of yours getting you anywhere, Stefan?"

Stefan's gaze jumped to his father's eyes. He had a good idea what his father meant, but asked anyway.

"Behavior?"

"Do not play stupid, son. You are a smart enough man." Nicolas glanced at Leif, then his dark gaze pinned Stefan's again. "Where are you going in life?"

"I am—well, *we* are—investigating various business

ventures." That sounded responsible enough.

"What business ventures, specifically?"

"Well—"

Think quickly—what would his father approve of?

"Do you have money to invest?" Nicolas pressed.

Stefan did at one point. Until his recent misadventure in the Saint Charles brothel, where he was slipped some sort of drug and woke up to a bloody dress, empty pockets, and a stack of debt slips from the poker table with his signature unsteadily scrawled across them.

Stefan tried to act nonchalant and hoped Leif would back him up on this slight misstatement, which omitted the gambling debts. "Due to the false murder charges and the lawyer's fees to prove my innocence, I admit that I am short at the moment."

Nicolas nodded, unclasped his hands, and leaned back in his big leather chair. "I suspected as much."

Stefan felt a jolt of unexpected hope. "Does that mean you will help me out?"

Nicolas crossed his arms over his still impressive chest. "I do plan to help you out, Stefan. But not in the way that you are expecting, I do not believe."

Stefan's hope deflated. "What do you mean, Pappa?"

Nicolas turned his attention to Leif. "It is time for my son to grow up. I do not mean for what I am about to say to affect you as well, so you may decide for yourself what to do next."

Leif nodded. "I understand."

Anger surged in Stefan's chest. His grieving father ignored Stefan for the first six years of his life. But within a year after he started acting like a real father, and giving Stefan a mother by marrying Sydney, Nicolas adopted Leif.

While Stefan was thrilled to have a brother, the older boy began traveling with Nicolas in his first political campaign, while Stefan was forced to stay at home and go to school. Ever since then, there was a bond between his father and Leif that Stefan felt unable to match.

Nicolas looked at Stefan again. He sighed and his

expression softened a little. "I love you, son. I always have, even when it seemed that I did not."

Stefan's gaze dropped to the desktop and he waited.

"Will you look at me?"

Stefan somberly regarded his father from under his brows.

"I am not going to give you any more money."

Stefan's head jerked up. "What?"

"Starting now, you are on your own financially."

Stefan's jaw slackened. "But—"

Nicolas held up his hand to silence his objection. "There are no buts, Stefan. You are in line to inherit this estate one day, and I need to assure myself that there will still be an estate waiting for you."

Stefan looked to Leif for support, but his brother did not look at him.

"Two families besides ours rely on this estate for their livelihood. You know this," Nicolas continued, hacking away at Stefan's hope that he might somehow be able to renegotiate the situation.

Of *course* he knew that. Their estate foreman Jeremy McCain, and his wife Annie who was now their housekeeper, had been with them for over twenty years. The same was true for former slaves Jaqriel—Jack—and his wife Sarah, who were the farming foreman and Kacy's nanny respectively.

"I do, but—"

"There are *still* no buts." Nicolas uncrossed his arms and leaned forward, resting his elbows on the dark oak expanse of the desktop. "I need you to show me that you can be responsible for what I expect to pass on to you—*before* I give it to you."

Stefan glared at his father. "Is that a threat?"

"Not a threat, son. A condition."

"Condition?" Stefan growled.

Damn. I sound just like him.

"Yes, a condition." Nicolas shrugged as if this was the most normal thing in the world for him to decree. "Go out and make your way however you see fit. When you have succeeded, come back and show me."

Stefan's hands were shaking with anger. He curled them into fists. "And then?"

"And then I will reinstate you as my heir."

"You *already* changed your will?" Stefan shouted. He jumped to his feet and jerked a thumb in Leif's direction. "Is *he* your heir now?"

Nicolas shook his head and spoke calmly. "No. Kirsten is. She is as yet unmarried and, if she remains so, she will need to be taken care of."

"And if she marries?" Stefan demanded.

"I expect you to have made solid progress by then. If you have, I will change my will back." Nicolas stood, using the support of the desk to push himself upright. "Until then, you are free to pursue any avenues open to you."

"And Leif?"

Nicolas looked at his adopted son. "That is up to you, Leif. Do you want to stay here and oversee the estate? Or do you want to cast your lot with Stefan?"

Stefan turned to face Leif with his hands still fisted. He held his breath, waiting to see what his brother would choose. How would he survive without Leif's constant companionship in their various misadventures?

Misadventures that must now come to an end.

Leif rose to his feet as well. "I know that living life as the gentleman of this estate offers many comforts and advantages, and I sincerely thank you, sir, for the offer."

Stefan's body went limp.

No no no.

"But I feel I can best serve you by sticking close to Stefan." Leif clapped a hand on Stefan's shoulder and the weight of it was almost more than he could stand. "I have great confidence in what he and I might be able to accomplish together, and I look forward to building a fortune of my own along the way."

Nicolas flashed a crooked smile. "Well said, Leif."

Of course.

Leif is perfect.

"Is that all, Pappa?" Stefan croaked.

Nicolas's expression was both sad and resolved. "Yes, Stefan. That is all."

Stefan turned stiffly to face Leif. "Let's pack up. We can make it to Saint Louis before dark."

*****

"I understand, Stef. Please do not worry about me." Kacy stopped her own preparations for departure and hugged Stefan tightly. "And I am so glad that I got to see you, brother. I miss you so much when we are apart."

Stefan guessed that Nicolas had not mentioned the changes in his will to his sister, and he was not about to inform Kacy of her currently elevated status.

"When do you leave for Washington?" he asked when she let go of him.

"Two more days." Kacy grinned but her eyes glittered with unshed tears. "And it takes less than two weeks by train to get there, now."

"To be honest, I am glad you are going with them," Stefan said carefully. "Keep an eye on Pappa. He has gotten... older."

"I know. I see it, too." Kacy's smile dimmed. "But I intend to take this chance to make more out of my life than I have been able to thus far, being stuck out here in the woods of Missouri."

Stefan felt a surge of hope at her words. Maybe his sister had no interest in the estate, even if Pappa wanted to give it to her.

Kacy moved her embrace to Leif. "I love you too, brother. Take good care of him, will you?"

Stefan bristled, knowing he was quite capable of taking care of himself.

Why does everyone think I am not?

Leif held her close mumbled into her hair, "Always."

When Stefan knocked on his parents' open bedroom door, his mother turned teary eyes on him. "Coming to say goodbye, I wager."

"Yes, *Mamma*." He assumed she knew all the details of what Nicolas had done. Throughout their marriage his parents routinely discussed everything before making any decisions— from sailing to Norway to candidate for kingship, to sending Kacy to live in Uncle Gunner's house and attend college in Philadelphia.

Stefan crossed the room. "I am sorry our visit was so short."

Sydney wiped her eyes. "It cannot be helped. Your father must get back to Washington."

"I am glad Kac—*Kirstie*—is going with you." Stefan flashed his sincerest grin. "I do think it will be good for her."

And hopefully she'll find a husband there.

Quickly.

Sydney smiled past her tears and winked at Leif. "I agree with your sister. I think the nickname you gave her is cute and more than a little sassy, just as she is."

Leif chuckled. "She was feisty as a twelve-year-old, that's for sure."

"I cannot imagine where she got that trait," Sydney teased. She stood to hug Stefan. "Where are you headed this time?"

"Saint Louis for now." Stefan returned the hug. "We'll stay with Aunt Rosie for a couple days and see what sort of work we can find."

"Be sure to let us know where you end up and what you're doing." Sydney hugged Leif. "Do you have our address in Washington?"

Leif nodded. "Kacy gave it to us."

"And you can always send letters here, too."

Stefan dipped his chin. "Yes, *Mamma*."

He and Leif turned around and walked out of the room with the sounds of Sydney's soft sniffles trailing behind them.

Chapter Two

January 20, 1845
Saint Louis, Missouri

"A whole week of knocking on doors and answering advertisements, and we have nothing to show for it." Stefan pulled a chair away from the tavern's table and dropped dejectedly onto it. The worn wooden seat creaked its objection to such undeserved mistreatment.

Leif mimicked his actions and waved to the serving girl. "We will find something. We always do."

"It had better be soon. I am not sure how long Rosie's man will tolerate our presence." Stefan turned to the girl. "Pitcher of beer and a bowl of stew."

"I will have the stew as well," Leif said.

Stefan's fingers drummed on the tabletop as his thoughts rifled through his options.

When they showed up at Rosie O'Malley's large home on the outskirts of the city, she was thrilled to see them. The ex-Madame hugged them both—age had not calmed her boisterous personality one whit—and pulled them into the brightly lit foyer.

"Come in boys! A lot has changed since I saw you last."

Stefan smiled at his unofficial aunt. "You look good, Rosie."

She winked up at him. "It is due to the love of a good man."

As if summoned by her words, a middle-aged gentleman walked out of the nearest doorway. He was thick around the middle and a couple inches shorter than Rosie, but his expression was pleasant.

Rosie stretched out one bejeweled hand. "Thayer dear, come meet Stefan and Leif Hansen."

"Did you get married?" Leif blurted.

"No!" Rosie scoffed. "D'you think I'd give up everything I've worked so hard for all these years?"

Thayer smiled. "I was her accountant, you see. That is how we met."

"We are deeply in love and living in sin," Rosie stated without apology. "But I am otherwise behaving myself."

The pitcher of beer arrived and Stefan watched Leif pour two glasses. "Thayer is nice enough, but I think he would be happy to wave us goodbye."

Leif nodded and took a sip of his beer. "Hopefully we will find new opportunities on the board at the post office."

Stefan winced. "And hopefully they will be far away from Saint Charles. No one has come after me yet, but if they do, I cannot pay what they claim I owe."

When the men finished their lunch, they visited the privy before walking to the main post office. The cloudy day was cold and blustery, threatening snow.

Stefan pulled his collar closer around his neck. "I hope we can get to the stable and ride back to Rosie's before the storm hits."

"This should not take long." Leif ran up the four stone steps of the pillared brick building and yanked open the heavy wooden door. "And it is warm inside."

Stefan and Leif stood in front of the board and scanned the postings. They had already considered—and dismissed—most of what was posted there.

"This is new." Leif pulled a sheet down. "*Wagon Train Workers Wanted.*"

Stefan looked over Leif's shoulder and read out loud. "Leaving March first from Independence, Missouri to follow the Santa Fe Trail. Twelve weeks of employment guaranteed."

"Hostlers, Mechanics and Wheelwrights, Hunters and Sharpshooters, Doctors." Leif grinned at Stefan. "We could do this."

"And it gets me out of Missouri..." Stefan quickly warmed to the idea. "It would be an adventure, that is for certain. How do we apply?"

Leif looked back at the broadsheet. "The office is six blocks away."

Stefan laughed. "What are we waiting for?"

*****

There were a dozen men already waiting in the Westward Wagons office so Stefan and Leif each took a number and sat on the long bench to wait their turn.

Stefan quietly sized up the other men waiting and decided that he and Leif definitely stood out in the group, most of whom appeared to be city dwellers.

"We should not have difficulty getting this job," he said softly. "We both know horses, can shoot the eye out of a crow, and can build or repair almost anything."

Leif nodded. "The advantages of working the estate. I do not regret a single minute of those labors right now."

The line diminished slowly over the next hour with most of the men being turned away. Finally, Leif's number was called.

Stefan stood when Leif did. "I am next, so let's go in together as a team."

The wagon master looked surprised when the two men entered his office together. "What's this?"

"We are brothers," Leif answered with a grin. "We would like to work together."

The skeptical expression on the man's face proved that he noticed their lack of physical resemblance: Stefan's thick hair was auburn and curly, Leif's was ashy blond and straight. Stefan's eyes were bright blue, Leif's were dark brown.

And the adoptive brothers were of significantly different heights.

"I suppose any litter can have different fathers," he muttered. "Have a seat, gentlemen."

Stefan decided to ignore the slur. He needed to find a source of income soon, and this opportunity was in truth the most interesting thing he had ever come across. He smiled, nodded his thanks, and silently sat.

As the pair answered questions and listed their experience and qualifications, the wagon master visibly relaxed. "You two bring a very good end to a very trying day."

Leif dipped his chin. "Thank you, sir."

"I will take you both on." He slid a sheet of paper across the desktop. "Write your full names here, and then complete the rest of the information."

Stefan cleared his throat. "Might I enquire about the pay?"

"We provide meals along the way, plus fifty dollars a week paid every seven days after the wagons roll."

That's six hundred dollars.

Stefan tried not to look too happy at the generous salary. "Will we need any special equipment?"

"A sturdy horse, a good rifle with plenty of ammunition, and a warm bedroll to start."

Leif finished filling out his information and passed the sheet to Stefan. "What do we do next?"

"Show up at the Westward Wagons office in Independence by February twenty-first." He waited for Stefan to complete the roster then added. "Do not be late, gentlemen, or we *will* leave without you."

Stefan stuck out his hand. "We will be there, sir. You can bet on it!"

February 2, 1845

"Thank you again, Rosie." Stefan hugged their hostess. "Your kind hospitality was greatly appreciated."

Rosie did not argue the point. "You two be careful out there, ya hear?"

"Yes, Ma'am." Leif hugged her as well.

"And you wrote to Nick and told him where all you're goin'?" she pressed.

"I did, Rosie," Stefan assured her. "And I gave him the address for the Westward Wagons office in Independence in the event that he needs to get in touch with us."

Thayer stuck out his hand. "Best wishes, men."

First Leif, and then Stefan, shook his hand.

"Thank you." Stefan winked. "Take good care of Aunt Rosie, you hear?"

The brothers left the big house and mounted their horses, tied to the rail out front. The winter weather in Missouri was being typically ugly, spitting pellets of snow on a brisk wind.

Both men wore wool-lined leather coats, leather leggings over their trousers, sturdy boots with thick socks, hats, scarves and gloves. Their bedrolls were lashed to the backs of their saddles and their loaded rifles were settled into holsters at the front.

Stefan prodded his horse forward, glad to have such a powerful beast under him. The son of his father's grand Fyrste and his mother's beloved Sessa, Sterk—Norwegian for strong—had been given to Stefan when he turned twenty-one ten years ago.

Leif also rode a son of Fyrste called Heder—meaning glory—which he was given when he turned twenty-one five years before Stefan. The brothers had trained their colts under Sydney and Nicolas's tutelage and both were closely bonded with their mounts.

If they covered twenty miles a day, they would reach Independence in twelve days. To make certain they did not arrive late, the pair gave themselves an extra week to complete the journey.

"We cannot afford to lose this chance," Stefan stated. "So if we can cover more than twenty miles when the weather is decent, then I think we should."

Leif agreed and consulted the map. "In that case Chesterfield should be our first goal."

Now halfway there, the men dismounted to rest the horses. The day's early high clouds were now lowering. While the snow pellets had stopped, the air was dampening.

"It feels like the temperature is dropping," Leif observed.

Stefan agreed. "Let's keep moving."

Traveling across Missouri in the late winter was precarious. As they traveled west, Stefan and Leif did their best to find a town every night so they could eat hot food and sleep indoors, but at least a third of the time they found themselves hunkered down in the woods eating venison jerky for supper.

There was a solid reason for the timing of the wagon train's departure, however. If the convoy set out in early March from Independence, it would reach Santa Fe by mid May. That gave the settlers time to procure land and plant the crops which would feed them over following winter.

Stefan pulled the collar of his coat tighter, and reminded himself what was at stake in this venture.

Don't think.
Just keep moving.

February 14, 1845

The men lost time when a heavy sleet storm engulfed them in Marshall Junction, just seventy miles from Independence. Luckily, they were able to procure stable space for their horses, and then the brothers shared a room in Marshall's only inn.

Stefan sat by the window and watched the miserable scene

outside. "I suppose when this mess passes, the horses will be well-rested and fed enough to make up the time."

"And so will we." Leif stretched luxuriously in the upholstered chair in their cozy room. "I cannot complain one bit right now."

Back in the saddle two days later and eager to make up time, Stefan and Leif had fifteen miles behind them when they encountered a hunting trio of Indians. Both men reined their mounts to a halt and left their rifles holstered as the three natives approached.

"Greetings," Leif said in Sauk.

"Greetings," one man answered in the same language. "What is your purpose?"

Stefan watched in fascination as Leif conversed—albeit hesitantly—with the trio. He knew Leif had spent a lot of time with Annie, their half-Sauk half-French housekeeper, but he did not realize how much of her language he had learned.

When Leif smiled, nodded, and waved, Stephan knew that whatever concerns the Indians expressed had been assuaged.

"What did they say?" Stefan asked as the three men rode off into the woods.

"They wanted to know where we were going and why."

Stefan and Leif kicked their mounts back into motion to resume their journey.

"I did not know you spoke Sauk," Stefan said, trying not to sound petulant.

"I would not say I *speak* Sauk, exactly. But I was able to understand and make myself understood." Leif chuckled. "Did you see all my hand gestures? That definitely helped."

"Still. I am impressed. That might come in handy on the trail."

Leif shrugged, obviously self-conscious. "I have discovered that languages are easy for me. I spoke Norse first, then English. Annie taught me Sauk and said that Fox was similar." He looked at Stefan. "Like Norse and Swedish are similar."

Stefan blinked. "Do you speak Swedish?"

"Not well." He glanced sideways at Stefan. "How much Norse do you remember?"

Stefan blew a heavy sigh. "Not much at all, to be honest. I was only seven when I spoke it, and after we came home, and you learned English, I stopped using it."

Leif nodded. "That happens."

February 18, 1845
Independence, Missouri

Stefan and Leif arrived in Independence with three days to spare. They got directions from a tavern keeper and, after a quick beer, headed for the Westward Wagons office.

"May I help you?" a thin man behind the desk asked.

Stefan removed his wide-brimmed hat. "We are checking in. We have both been hired for the March first wagon train."

"Excellent." He pulled a ledger from a drawer in his desk and opened it. "Names?"

"Stefan Hansen."

"Leif Hansen."

The man made some notes, and then handed Stefan a printed flyer. "Here are your instructions and list of supplies. Training begins on February twenty-second. Meet here at eight o'clock in the morning."

"Training?" Stefan asked. "What sort of training?"

"Protocol mainly. And procedures." The man smiled. "Rules are important both to have, and to enforce, if we are to ensure the safety and successful delivery of our clients. And Westward Wagons is quite proud of our exemplary record thus far."

"How many wagons will be traveling?" Leif asked.

"We have twenty-nine scheduled at the moment, but that could change."

"And how many men working the train?" Stefan asked.

The man held up one hand and ticked his answer on his

fingers. "Two hostlers, two mechanics, three sharpshooters, and a doctor."

He lowered his hand. "And the Wagon Master, of course. He is in charge of everything."

Leif gave Stefan a satisfied look then addressed the thin man. "Do you know what we will be doing?"

"Not being Wagon Master."

Stefan's brow lowered. "Can you tell us anything else?"

"Nope."

Leif returned his attention to Stefan and shrugged. "I guess we will find out in four days."

Chapter Three

February 18, 1845
Kansas City, Missouri

Blake Somersby stood under a blustery winter sky and ceremoniously wiped her hands before she turned away from her father's fresh grave.

And it is finally finished.

She lifted her skirts and walked through the cemetery's dead, wet grass, knowing that her shoes would be ruined by the water, and that it no longer mattered. She had quite a lot to do in the next two weeks and no time to fret over useless shoes.

Blake had been planning her escape for years—ever since her father began his decline into dementia and the unbridled cruelty that accompanied it. Still single at twenty-eight because of her familial duties, Blake was ready to grab life with both hands and salvage what she could of her youthful dreams.

The first step was to empty the bank account.

*****

Blake smiled sweetly. "Yes. All of it, please."

"Are you sure that is wise dear?" the portly banker asked.

"It is a necessity, I am afraid," she replied, matching her tone to his. "You see I am leaving K-kansas City now that my father has p-passed away."

The man's brows leapt toward his receding hairline. "But where will you go?"

Blake held on to her temper, offended by the impudent question. "How long will this take? I have much to attend to, as you c-can well imagine."

Flummoxed by her ignoring his question, the banker cleared his throat and shifted papers on his desk. "Do you, um, have the death certificate?"

Blake removed the folded paper from her reticule and handed it across the desk.

The banker unfolded it and squinted at the document. "And a, uh, copy of his will, leaving the money to you?"

Blake handed that over as well. All of her plotting and planning had ensured that, when this day arrived, there would be no impediments to her becoming an independent woman with enough money to launch her in a new direction, far and away from this cursed place.

"This all seems to be in order." The banker squinted again as he looked at her over the top of the paper. "We are talking about a large sum of money. How will you transport it?"

Blake lifted the small leather satchel with a lock that rested by her feet, and set in on the desk.

"Please c-count it out in front of me."

*****

Blake stepped outside of the bank which her father had used for most of his life and drew her first free breath in over ten years. Packed in her satchel was nearly fourteen thousand dollars in cash, which she now needed to make secure.

She strode down the busy street running through the center of Kansas City, stepping over muddy puddles of melted snow, until she reached the office of the lawyer who helped her make what she thought of as her very own 'independence day' arrangements.

The double meaning made her smile.

I wish I had fireworks.

Blake stopped in front of the office, opened the front door, and stepped inside, wiping her feet on the mat by the door.

"I am here to see Mister Whittle," she announced to the receptionist.

The woman smiled her greeting. "He is expecting you, Miss Somersby. Go on into his office."

Mister Whittle stood when she entered. "Miss Somersby—how did everything go?"

"Smooth as silk, sir, thanks to your help." Blake set the satchel on his desk. "We shall c-count the money together, and then divide it up as we discussed."

"Excellent." Whittle walked past her to close and lock the office door.

When she raised questioning eyebrows, he gave her a quelling look. "We cannot be too careful, can we my dear?"

*****

An hour later Blake left the office with three thousand dollars in her reticule.

Of the nearly eleven thousand dollars remaining, Mister Whittle would keep half in a small safe hidden in his office—one to which only she knew the combination. The other half would be judiciously invested, with Whittle retaining a large enough percentage of the profits to ensure that he would do the best for her.

Blake thanked the lawyer profusely and promised to get in touch with him once she was settled. But even he did not know the whole truth about where she was going.

I am safer that way.

Blake walked a mile to the waggoneer's shop where she had placed an order a week ago, once she knew for certain that her father was finally dying. She needed a small wagon that could both handle the weight of her household goods and withstand rough use crossing the prairie.

"Hello, sir." Blake stepped inside the office. "Is my wagon ready?"

The waggoneer looked up from his ledger and gave a quick nod. "Yes ma'am. Just stretched the canvas today. Would you like to see it?"

Blake felt a surge of joy blooming in her chest.

"Yes, p-please."

The middle-aged man walked her out the back door to the covered workshop where the wagons were built. Several were waiting there, but hers was the smallest.

It is only me, after all.

The wagons all had wooden hoops that went from one side of the wagons to the other. Heavy white sail canvas, which was waterproofed with linseed oil, stretched over the multiple hoops which angled forward in front and backward at the end to protect the openings.

In a few short days, Blake would pack everything she required to start her new life safely inside, and then she would set off on her unknown journey to a brand-new life.

She walked around the wagon, running a gloved hand over the wheels and along the smooth sides. "It is beautiful."

"Once the bill is paid, you can leave the wagon here until your brother leaves." The man paused. "He is going on the Santa Fe Trail wagon train, I believe you said?"

Blake flashed a grateful smile. "Yes. He leaves on March first. Thank you."

She opened her reticule and, being careful to hide its full contents, fished out six fifty-dollar bills. "Here you are. Three hundred dollars."

"Thank *you*, miss." The waggoneer tucked the money

inside his jacket. "Will you be seeing your brother off?"

Blake made a sad face and bit her lower lip as if she was about to cry. "No, I shall say my goodbyes at home. I d-do not think I could withstand watching my twin d-drive the wagon out of my sight, without knowing if I will ever see him again."

"I understand. Maybe you will join him someday," the man offered hopefully. "In the meantime, what is the name I will be looking for?"

"B-blake," she replied. "His name is Blake Somersby."

February 20, 1845

Two days later Blake boarded a carriage which would carry its passengers the ten miles east to the town of Independence and the Westward Wagons office. Once there, Blake would pay eight hundred dollars for Mister Blake Somersby, bachelor, to join the wagon train leaving on March first for the Santa Fe Trail.

The costs were adding up, but Blake was fortunate enough to have inherited her father's small fortune.

How do families manage this otherwise?

As the eight-person carriage filled up Blake realized with alarm that her fellow passengers were also going to the wagon train office.

Why did I not think of that?

She should have worn a bigger hat. Or brought a little book to read. Anything to avoid being noticed.

Blake tucked herself in a corner, smiled briefly at the other passengers, and then turned to the window, praying that no one would try to engage her in conversation.

I could pretend to be deaf...

Her stakes were unsettlingly high at the moment. Blake could not risk being recognized as a woman when she drove her little wagon to meet the train, or she might be denied the chance to travel, and then all her machinations would come to naught.

A single woman had never driven her own wagon westward as far as she had heard—and she had been paying close attention ever since the idea came to her nearly four years ago. She knew she would have to hide her identity, and she berated herself for not thinking about that today.

I have to be more careful.

My life literally depends on it.

Blake leaned her head against the window and closed her eyes, hoping that no one would be rude enough to disturb her. At least while she was sitting down her unusual height was not obvious. Her five-feet-nine inches were both a blessing and a curse.

Conversation in the carriage was sporadic and most of it centered on questions like *how much wheat are you taking*, or *do you think we might encounter any savages.*

Blake's pulse surged at that possibility. It was the single most terrifying element in her escape plan, one she thought long and hard about before making this decision.

Indians had killed her mother in front of her when Blake was five, and the horrific images of her murder haunted Blake's nightmares for the last two dozen years.

Even now she suffered the aftermath whenever her emotions were stirred too violently, resulting in an embarrassing and frustrating stutter. She felt the hesitations looming when the banker started questioning her about her plans, but when she redirected the conversation, she regained control.

In the end Blake concluded that the prospect of living the rest of her life in her parents' dark house with the unhappy ghosts of the past was a far worse fate.

She just needed to stay calm in the wagon train office.

And buy a large hat before riding the carriage back.

*****

The hat was the easy part.

Explaining why the bachelor Blake was not there to pay his own way and sign his own contract was proving problematic.

"I-I am sorry. We d-did not know," she managed as she pulled the eight hundred dollars from her reticule. "C-can he sign the c-contract when he joins you?"

The wagon master looked at the impressive stack of fifty-dollar bills that Blake held out to him and quickly made his decision.

He grabbed the payment. "If he is not there when we pass through Westport, then that will be his problem. We will continue without him and this money will be gone. Do you understand?"

Blake nodded mutely.

"You sign here now." He pointed at the contract.

I sign?

With what name?

She could not sign *Blake*, obviously. She leaned over the desk and accepted the quill, dipping it slowly in the well and tapping off the excess while she scrambled for ideas.

Susan.

Susan Somersby.

Blake signed the contract and handed the quill over. "He will b-be waiting."

Then she spun around and marched out of the office before the wagon master could challenge her any further.

February 22, 1845

Blake vacillated between selling her parents' house and renting it out for additional income, seeing the positive results possible from either path. But with so little time left for her to complete her preparations, she decided to engage a rental agent for now, and deal with the house at some later date.

"It is fully furnished," she explained as she led the neatly dressed and balding man inside. "But it will require some repairs. My father's illness lingered and there was no one but myself to care for him."

Mister Fitzwilliam nodded his understanding as his evaluative gaze moved through the house without ceasing. "I can see to that."

"I will need someone to maintain the house as well," Blake continued. "How much do you b-believe I might rent it for?"

Mister Fitzwilliam's still-scanning eyes narrowed. "I would say thirty dollars a month as it is now, but at least forty when the repairs are made."

Blake nodded. "Your fee would be twenty-five percent of the rent, is that c-correct?"

He looked at her now. "Yes."

"That is acceptable." Blake stuck out her gloved hand. "I will put you in touch with my lawyer, Mister Jackson Whittle. He will handle my finances while I am absent, and will also ensure that the property is well c-cared for."

Fitzwilliam shook her hand and bowed a little. "I will do my best for you, Miss Somersby. I do have a reputation to uphold."

Blake smiled sweetly. "And that reputation is why I called upon your services."

As they walked to the door, he asked, "Do you know how long you will be gone?"

"No, I do not." Blake opened the front door. "Thank you and good day, Mister Fitzwilliam."

*****

With that matter happily settled, Blake set out on a task that she had greatly been looking forward to—shopping.

Not only was she going to be able to furnish her own

kitchen and be able to cook whatever she wanted, but a large part of her plan was to establish a business once she reached Santa Fe. A little restaurant for sure, and perhaps an inn as well.

Blake wandered through the Kansas City shops with a reticule filled with cash and felt like she was in a dream. Cast iron pots and pans, long-handled spoons and ladles, rolling pins, pie tins, bread tins, flatirons and waffle irons—the variety at her disposal made her giddy.

Blake even bought three cookbooks to feed her creativity.

I don't remember the last time I was this happy.

After arranging for her purchases to be delivered to her home the next day, it was time to buy new linens. Sheets and towels for her new home and her new life.

The last stop was the spice shop.

Blake breathed deeply when she opened the door and stepped inside. She closed her eyes and sorted through the mingled aroma, picking out specific ingredients.

"Welcome Miss Somersby," the proprietor greeted her adding, "My condolences at your recent loss."

Blake opened her eyes. "Thank you, sir."

She stepped forward. "I am here to stock my kitchen for a year, so I shall need everything tightly sealed. What would you suggest?"

"A year?" The man's eyes brightened at the anticipated magnitude of the sale. "Metal tins Miss, with lids that screw on. They will protect their fragile contents from both light and air."

"Perfect." Blake grinned. "Let's get started, shall we?"

Chapter Four

February 25, 1845

Blake pulled out every item of her father's clothing that she had been altering for the past six months and spread them out on the floor to take an accounting.

Two pair of woolen trousers.

Two pair of cotton-and-linen trousers.

Four white cotton shirts with stocks.

Eight pair of socks.

One pair of shoes.

One pair of boots.

One woolen jacket.

And a dozen wide strips of linen to bind her chest.

"I will need thicker socks to keep the shoes and boots on," she said as she began her next shopping list. "And a long leather coat."

Would she need anything more formal? Like a waistcoat?

"No. I am playing a simple bachelor of limited means," she reminded herself. "But I do need undergarments and a night shift."

Was that too risky—sleeping in a woman's garment? It could be if there was any sort of attack in the night.

Blake wrinkled her nose. "Fine, then. I will sleep in a man's shirt."

After all, her disguise would be discarded once she reached Santa Fe. She could bide with the three months, at the very most, for which she would be required to hide her feminine state.

But my undergarments will be my own.

Blake went to the wardrobe in her room and considered what to take along for her eventual transformation back to a female. She decided to keep the simple theme of her choices consistent, and not hint that she was relatively wealthy.

She selected four serviceable dresses, a petticoat, two corsets, three pair of stockings, one pair of shoes, and one pair of boots, and two nightshifts.

That should do.

And I can purchase more clothes in Santa Fe, if needed.

Necessity forced her to pack a number of rags for her monthly cycle—which she suddenly realized could not be washed and reused, but must be secretly discarded along the way.

Ugh.

She needed to add a small shovel to her supplies.

Blake went to the linen closet and pulled out a worn cotton sheet which she ripped into strips. Hopefully she would not use them all on the trip, because she would require a new supply once she arrived in her new home.

After a moment's thought, she tore up a second sheet, just to be safe.

Blake packed all her feminine items in one small trunk with the rags on top for easy access, and then packed the men's clothes in another.

Satisfied that she had not forgotten anything thus far, Blake headed back to the shops to buy the few items still on her list.

Just one question remained: where was the safest place to hide the one thousand dollars in cash which would go toward the purchase of her new restaurant in the center of Santa Fe?

February 27, 1845

Blake stood beside the corral and stared at the oxen. She had absolutely no idea which two animals she should buy. A pair of men leaning on the fence nearby caught her attention and she sidled a little closer to try and overhear what they had to say.

"I would think that if the animal is too large, it will be hard to bring enough grain to keep it fed."

I need to bring grain for the oxen?

I thought they would just graze.

Blake risked a glance in the men's direction.

"Oxen can eat the wild roughage that horses would starve on, remember," the taller one said. "That's one main reason they are used to pull the wagons."

Blake turned her face away from the men who stood about twenty feet to her left. So far, she learned to buy a smaller team and purchase grain to supplement their diet. Both of those things were extremely helpful.

"That one there hasn't been castrated. That is a problem if there are females in the line."

So I should get two small castrated males.

"The rules say no intact males," the taller one stated. "I wonder if that will be enforced?"

Definitely castrated.

"I hope so, or the hostlers might have a situation on their hands."

The men wandered off and Blake could no longer hear their startlingly helpful conversation. In case they might have noticed her, she waited until the pair turned a corner and were out of sight before she headed for the office to make her livestock purchase and ask about the grain.

There was far more to this adventure than she initially realized, and for a brief minute wondered if she should rethink her plan. But the gloomy thought of staying in that house, in this city, continued to push her forward.

February 28, 1845

Blake's trunks and crates were packed and delivered to the waggoneer's. She followed along to ensure that they were loaded into *her* wagon. There would be time later for her to rearrange their placement—and that would have to wait until the male version of Blake manifested himself.

Tomorrow at dawn her pair of oxen and sacks of oats would be delivered, and she would need to figure out how to hook the team to the wagon.

Surely the waggoneer will help me.

After choosing her team, Blake bought two pair of heavy leather gloves and lined them with a cotton pair. The thought of blisters reminded her that she had not packed any sort of medical supplies, so she scoured the house for anything she thought would be useful in the event of an illness or injury.

She found a leather pack at the back of her father's wardrobe and put the medical supplies inside that. Then she stopped and stared at the remainder of her father's clothes, still present in the wardrobe. After so many years of misery she had no sentimental attachment to them, nor any further use for them now that she had altered what she needed.

I suppose whoever leases the house can have them.

Blake returned to her room and her own wardrobe. She considered the remaining dresses, petticoats, and shoes. Her collection of cotton and silk undergarments beckoned, but she reluctantly stood her ground. If her wagon was searched for any reason at all, she could not afford to have such luxuries mixed in with her manly clothes.

The one trunk, separate from everything else, could easily be passed off as a gift—either for a female relative already in Santa Fe, or even as a trousseau for 'his' prospective bride.

Blake sighed heavily and turned away from the wardrobe. The burden of what she was about to do pressed heavily against her chest, and every doubt she ever had raised its ugly head and glared at her.

Am I crazy?

Blake plopped on the top stair, still holding the leather pack. The front door at the bottom of the stairs was both an opening and a barrier.

Can I really do this?

Throughout the exciting and challenging process of putting her plan into action, Blake had never allowed herself to worry—but at this moment, worry could no longer be denied. She was just half-a-day away from climbing aboard her wagon, loaded with everything she thought she needed, and leaving the United States of America to begin life anew in the Republic of Texas.

I do not even know how to hook up a team of oxen, much less how to drive one.

Panic zinged through her veins. Tears blurred her vision. She hugged the leather pack of medical supplies against her breast and pulled deliberate breaths in defiance of the fear which was trying to suffocate her.

God be with me.

Due to her unfortunate situation with her father, Blake had not been able to attend church in years—but that did not mean that her Sunday School training had been wasted.

Please be with me.

I cannot do this alone.

Tears ran down her cheeks. As the sun set and the house gradually grew darker, she remained, unmoving, on her perch. When all light faded, the truth bubbled to the top of her thoughts.

I cannot stay here.

I cannot waste the rest of my life.

I must be brave.

I must follow the path I have chosen.

If I do not, I will forever regret not doing so.

Blake climbed to her feet and set the leather pack at the top of the stairs. She went back into her bedroom and lit her lamps. There was one last thing she had to do.

*****

Blake examined her reflection in the mirror and was surprised by how large her eyes—which she always thought of as plain, unremarkable brown—now looked.

Long curling hanks of her wavy red hair blanketed her lap, victim of her sewing scissors.

There is no turning back now.

Only a couple inches remained rooted to her scalp and covering her head, but its vibrant color was not tamed. That was her next hurdle.

Blake retrieved a tin of brown shoe polish and a rag. She swiped the rag through the polish and worked the color through her short locks, not satisfied until the color darkened to auburn.

It matches the tall man from the corral.

She flashed a wry smile at her image.

"Hello, Blake," she said in a deep raspy voice. "Nice to meet you."

She stood and carried the tin of brown polish to the pack, still waiting at the top of the stairs, and tucked it inside.

*****

Sleep eluded her that night, and when she did doze, she dreamt she was awake. Lists tormented her as she mentally recounted every item she had packed. Twice she got up and stuffed an item in the pack at the top of the stairs.

What else have I forgotten?

Blake rolled onto her side, startled that she did not have to swipe hair out of her eyes. Then she remembered she didn't have those long locks anymore. Furthermore, they would take at least two years to grow back.

Should I buy a wig?

Blake groaned and flopped on her back. Hairstyles were the least of her problems at the moment. Number one was getting to the waggoneer's with enough time to get her oxen in their traces, and then manage to drive the wagon to Westport to meet the train coming from Independence.

Westport.

Of course.

A port to the west.

Blake chuckled a little as the name of the meeting spot suddenly made sense.

The other wagons in the waggoneer's yard were also being packed yesterday, so Blake knew she was not the only one joining the train. That meant she would not get lost if she followed the others out of the yard.

She noticed that several of the families were sleeping in their wagons tonight. Blake assumed that was because they had already left their distant homes behind.

And of course, to ensure they will be ready in the morning. Corralling children was seldom a simple task.

Should I have slept there as well?

Blake sat up in her bed. The sky was still dark but she knew that if she fell asleep now she ran a high risk of oversleeping and ruining absolutely everything.

With a sigh of resolution, she pushed back her covers and climbed out of bed and lit a lamp.

I need to take a lamp, she realized with a jolt.

And oil.

Blake combed her fingers through her short hair and they came away stained with polish under her neatly trimmed nails. She thought about trying to clean them before she realized that dirty nails actually enhanced her disguise.

She looked at her pillowcase and the brownish smudges darkening the spot where she had rested her head. One corner of her mouth curved upward.

A simple bachelor of limited means would probably not spend money on a laundress, nor would he be particularly skilled in washing his own linens. Blake pulled the pillowcase off the pillow to take it with her.

One more prop in the role I will play.

Blake washed her face, using the cold water to revive her. She dressed carefully, making certain that every item of her masculine clothing was properly put on—a task she was well familiar with after caring for her declining father for so long.

When she pulled on the over-sized boots, she was glad for the thick woolen socks she purchased. Now the boots would hopefully not fall off when she walked in them.

Blake turned slowly, examining her bedroom for any last items that she might need. Seeing nothing, she made up the bed, grabbed the lamp and pillowcase, and headed for the stairs.

She stuffed the soiled pillowcase into the already overfull pack, slung it over her shoulder and descended the stairs. Her heavy boots clomped her loud, echoing farewell down the wooden steps.

The sound was appropriately somber.

And exhilaratingly final.

After adding lamp oil to her now un-closable satchel, Blake pulled a deep breath and opened the front door. A blast of cold air hit her face as if to dissuade her from her path.

"Stop it," she said out loud, feeling foolish and glad no one was around to hear her. "I am *leaving*. You cannot stop me."

Blake stepped outside and set the pack down while she locked the front door. Then she folded the key inside a piece of paper and placed it under the woven-rush mat for Mister Fitzwilliam to retrieve.

"It is your responsibility now, sir," she whispered. Her breath made small, disappearing clouds in the chilled air. "Take good care."

Blake shouldered the pack once more and began the three-mile pre-dawn walk to the waggoneer's shop. Each step sent conflicting emotions through her frame, but fear and exhilaration felt astonishingly similar, as it turned out.

Both made her pulse surge. Both made her take frequent

deep breaths.

And both made her feel very much alive.

When she reached the wagon yard, the sky had lightened considerably, and those who had slept there were beginning to stir.

Blake climbed into her wagon and looked for places to pack the new things she brought. Then, while she waited for the oxen to arrive, she started reorganizing the trunks and crates, using the flat ones to make a pallet to sleep on.

"Mister Blake Somersby?"

Blake turned toward the voice. The waggoneer stood at the back of the wagon and lifted a lamp to peer inside. She nodded and grunted.

The man grunted back. "You do look like your sister."

"Twins," Blake rasped.

"That's what she said. I need you to sign this receipt for delivery of the wagon." The man lowered his lamp and handed Blake a document and pen.

Blake signed the document and handed the paper and pen back without speaking.

The waggoneer looked at her signature and nodded his approval. "Your oxen should be here any minute."

"Thanks."

It turned out that three more of the wagons were receiving their teams this morning as well. As the sun hid behind the surrounding buildings in preparation for her full display, the hostlers sorted out which animals belonged to whom and the men started strapping their teams in place.

Blake imitated their actions and got her two small males in place, but panicked when she could not figure out what to do next.

"Need some help?"

Blake turned and looked at the man who spoke, surprised.

"Uh, yeah. Thanks," she croaked.

The tall auburn-haired man that she heard talking at the corral yesterday set about buckling the powerful animals.

"You are a city fellow. I could tell that right away."

Blake nodded, watching the process intently.

"This goes here, now loop that rein through here…"

It took less than ten minutes for the oxen to be secured.

"There you go." The man smiled and patted one ox on the rump. "When we stop for the night, I will show you what needs to be loosed and what can stay attached."

He is part of the team?

"Thanks." Blake cleared her throat. "Again."

"No problem." He held out a hand. "Stefan Hansen."

Blake gripped his hand firmly. "B-blake Somersby. Nice to meet you."

Chapter Five

March 1, 1845

When Stefan and Leif reported for their training last week, they were both assigned to the team as hostlers—and that suited Stefan just fine. Both he and Leif received excellent tutelage in horsemanship while they grew up and he looked forward to working with the animals.

As the Kansas City residents harnessed their teams and started to move to the western edge of the city, both Stefan and Leif passed among them assuring that all the oxen were properly strapped in their traces, and that horses which were not being ridden were correctly tethered to the back of the wagons.

"Most of the men will be city born and raised," Wagon Master Buck Schultz had warned the team. "That's why they pay us to lead them. It's our job to make sure that they all reach Santa Fe safely."

Leif mounted Heder. "I am going to take the lead and make sure no one gets lost on the way to Westport. See you there."

Stefan nodded and waved as he moved to the next wagon. He glanced back at Somersby, who was now seated on his wagon and holding the reins, looking like he might puke.

While the man was of decent height—Stefan estimated just half a foot shorter than himself—he lacked musculature. And he had no idea how to harness his team of two rather small oxen.

To be fair, he had a small wagon and was traveling alone. If he had purchased two large animals, they would probably yank him right off his bench.

Stefan checked the wagon in front of him. Finding everything in order, he waved the man on. Then he returned to Somersby who seemed to be trying to get his team to move.

"Wait here," Stefan instructed. "I will lead your team out after that last family gets going."

A visibly relieved Somersby nodded.

Several minutes later, Stefan grabbed Sterk's reins and walked the stallion over to Somersby's team. "Okay. Now slap the reins—hard—and shout *step up*."

The man followed Stefan's directions, and when he barked the command Stefan pulled the closest ox forward.

The animal understood and started moving. His partner joined him immediately and the pair got the wagon rolling.

Stefan swung himself into Sterk's saddle and rode up next to Somersby. "When you need to go right, the command is *gee*. Left is *haw*. Just pull on the appropriate rein."

Somersby nodded again, his wide eyes fixed on the path in front of them.

"Stop is *whoa*, just like horses."

Somersby nodded once more, his unmoving gaze still locked in front of him.

"You will do fine," Stefan assured the nervous young man. "We will only be traveling ten to fifteen miles a day, so nothing will be rushed."

He pointed ahead. "And when you get to the end of this road, there will only be eight-hundred, sixty-nine more miles to go."

Somersby growled and shot a glance in his direction. If looks could kill a man, Stefan swore he would be sprawled dead on the ground.

"Keep following the wagon in front of you," he instructed. "I am going to check on the others, then I will be back."

He kicked Sterk's flank and the horse jumped forward into a canter.

*****

Blake watched the man go, relieved that he was gone but nervous about controlling her team. She refused to think about the fact that he had the brightest blue eyes she had ever seen and concentrated on keeping her wagon close behind the one she followed.

So many things were already new and unexpected that she was boggled—and the sun was barely over the horizon.

Gee is right, haw is left.

Step up to go, whoa to stop.

When should she feed them oats? Night or morning?

Ask the hostler.

As the wagons rolled through the streets of Kansas City, early risers watched out their windows or paused on the street. The expressions on their faces varied between skepticism and envy.

Blake understood both.

She counted seven wagons leaving from the waggoneer's shop yard, but when they made a turn at the end of the road, she saw another line of wagons coming from the south part of the city. Another two miles and yet another group was heading toward them.

"That is the group from Independence."

Blake's head swiveled to her left—she had not noticed Stefan's return to her side.

"People coming from further east start there," he explained. "How are you doing so far?"

"Fine." Blake decided that answering with single grunted

words was her safest choice.

A shadow passed across Stefan's well-formed face.

No, his face.

Just his face.

Do not think about how he looks.

"Good. Glad to hear it." Stefan cleared his throat. "We will stop here and make sure everyone is accounted for, and then we will be on our way."

"How m-many?" Blake risked asking.

Stefan shrugged. "Last I heard, there were thirty-one wagons. But some might have changed their minds, while others might have made a last dash to come along."

Again, Blake understood both reactions.

I have never been so certain and yet so ambivalent about anything in my entire life.

Stefan rode off again and Blake pulled on the reins. "Whoa!"

Like magic, the pair of oxen halted without walking into the stopped wagon in front of them. She blew a sigh of relief.

Several people were climbing down from their wagons to greet other travelers or let their children play. Blake opted instead to check the contents of her wagon to see if anything had shifted and needed to be arranged differently.

Blake was accustomed to isolation, and decided to keep to herself as much as possible so that her true gender would remain secret. Though she did wonder, if she was successful in managing the journey after the first hundred miles or so, would she really be expelled from the group and left behind if they found out she was a woman?

In Indian territory? Alone?

Blake felt the familiar constriction in her throat that those unpleasant thoughts always prompted. Visions of her mother's dead body flashed through her mind. Her heart bashed painfully against her ribs.

"Blake Somersby?"

Not trusting her voice, she nodded at the familiar man from the Westward Wagons office standing to her left.

He handed her a board with papers clipped to it. "I need your signature on the wagon train contract."

Right.

He told 'Susan' that at the Westward Wagons' office in Independence when Blake paid for the trip. She reached for the board and the man handed her a wooden pen with a steel nib. She signed her name beside an X and handed the man the contract and the pen.

The man squinted up at her as he grabbed the board. "You sure look like your sister, you know that?"

She shrugged. "T-twins."

"Huh. Yeah. I can see that." He touched the brim of his hat. "Have a good journey."

Blake touched the brim of her hat in response, feeling at that moment like she might actually succeed in this crazy plan.

*****

That feeling did not last.

The Wagon Master walked down each of the three lines of wagons and introduced himself, shaking each man's hand.

"Hello. My name is Buck Schultz. I'm the wagon master." He stuck out his hand and once again Blake gripped, squeezed, and shook her greeting as forcefully as she could.

"Blake Somersby."

"Nice to meet you Somersby. Just so you know, my word is law once we cross out of Missouri and into the Republic of Texas."

Blake nodded.

"I will not tolerate any sorts of shenanigans or flagrant disobedience," he warned. "My job is to get all of you safely to Santa Fe, and that requires strict discipline."

Blake nodded again.

"So, we understand each other."

Blake nodded a third time and touched the brim of her hat.

Schultz walked to the wagon behind hers.

Please protect me, Father God.

After what felt like at least half-an-hour the three groups of trains met at Westport. There they were ordered to form one line of twenty-nine wagons, with the Wagon Master directing which wagon was to go next.

Blake succeeded in getting her team to move after commanding them twice and she followed the wagon that preceded hers. The sun was fully up now, but softened by a hazy film of cloud cover which kept the air chilly.

At least there is not any wind.

The going was initially slow but steady, and the sparsely wooded terrain fairly flat. Blake wished she could dig her clock out of its trunk, but then realized that time did not matter now—only distance did. But she had no familiar landmarks on the prairie to judge their progress by. Clearly this journey was going to test her long-held need to be in control of her environment.

"There is nothing to do about it but relax," she scolded herself softly. "Just trust the men in charge, and do what they say."

*****

Stefan and Leif rode side-by side at the end of the train so that if any animal had problems, that wagon could simply stop and wait for the hostlers to catch up with them.

"Did you meet everyone?" Leif asked.

"No. You?"

Leif bounced a quick nod. "I did. I went down the line and introduced myself."

Stefan was angry at himself for not doing the same. "I will do that tomorrow."

"I saw you talking to that one chap who is traveling alone." Leif looked at Stefan. "What is his name?"

"Blake Somersby." Stefan paused. "There is something not quite right about him."

Leif's brow lowered. "What makes you say that?"

"He's... I don't know... Delicate." Stefan searched for better words. "He is a city fellow for sure, and does not know what he is doing yet."

Leif chuckled. "You just described almost every one of the people here."

"True." Stefan flashed a brief smile. "He's tall enough, but he does not have a strong build..."

"Tall, slender, citified, and traveling alone?" Leif glanced at the wagon they were following, reined in his mount closer to Stefan's, and lowered his voice. "Do you think he is escaping a 'forbidden' love?"

"You mean like that reporter when Pappa was first running for office?" The thought had not occurred to Stefan, but now the accusation seemed to fit. "He prefers the company of his own gender?"

Leif shrugged. "It is possible. What better escape than to run far away from conventional civilization?"

Stefan was quiet for a while, examining how he felt about that. On the one hand, he had no romantic interest in men nor befriending any man who did. The thought of being naked with another man made his skin crawl.

But on the other hand, Stefan had always nurtured a soft spot for the underdog. The victim. The one no one else would protect, be it animal or human.

"I will talk with him some more," he resolved. "To see if I can get him to tell me more about his life and why he's headed to Santa Fe."

"To turn him in?" Leif frowned. "I assume homosexuality is forbidden in Texas, just like Missouri."

"No. Not for that." Stefan was working out his thoughts as he spoke. "If he is that way, then I feel sorry for him."

Leif's lips twisted in a knowing grin. "Another one of your abandoned strays that needs protecting?"

Stefan's mind was made up. "Something like that."

*****

By the time word came down the line that the train was stopping to make camp for the night, Blake's arms had gone numb. She managed to shout *whoa* and pull back on the reins, but believed her oxen only stopped because the wagon in front of them did.

She watched the wagons in front circle back around until the twenty-nine wagons formed an enclosed space.

"Tighten the line!" one of the scouts—a Negro—shouted as he rode past the wagons. "We are making a corral for the animals' protection."

Stefan rode to her. "I promised I would show you how to un-harness your oxen."

"Yes." Blake forced her stiff legs and arms to function. "Thanks."

Stefan dismounted. "We make an enclosed space so the cattle and horses can graze overnight," he explained as he unbuckled one harness. "This also keeps them from running away or being stolen by Indians."

Blake startled. "Might we b-be attacked?"

Stefan shook his head and pulled the loosened ox forward. "It is highly unlikely. Do you have rope?"

Distracted by the terrifying prospect, Blake blinked. "Rope?"

"To hobble your beasts and keep them close to your wagon." Stefan grinned, displaying a disarming row of slightly crooked but white teeth. "So that you will not need to chase after them in the morning."

"Oh!" Blake went to the other side of the wagon where the circle of rope hung and brought it back to Stefan. "Here."

"And your feed box?" he prompted while he began tying the rope to create the adjustable hobbles. "You will want to move it to this side of the wagon tonight."

Feed them the oats at the end of the day.

That question answered, Blake went to the wagon's far

side again, unhooked the box, and carried it to the back where
the sack of oats rested just inside the opening. She used a pair
of steel scissors to cut a hole in the top of the bag and scooped
out the grain.

When she hung the feedbox on the same side as her team,
Stefan was slipping the rope onto the first ox's front ankles.
"He has room to take small steps, but he won't be running
anywhere."

"Thank you."

He was already at work on the second hobble. "I am a
hostler, so caring for the animals is my job."

Blake's stomach rumbled—she had not eaten all day,
because keeping her wagon moving required both of her hands
and all of her concentration.

Stefan noticed. "Go on and start your supper. I am almost
done."

Though her cheeks flamed with internal embarrassment,
she had barely stopped herself from asking Stefan if he wanted
to join her. It would be so nice to eat across from someone
whose conversation would be coherent, and who did not have
food dribbling down their chin.

Instead, she turned around and shuffled stiffly to the back
of her wagon. She groaned a little when she climbed in.

Her wooden food box—holding every edible morsel or
ingredient left in her father's house—was in the middle of the
wagon. Blake lifted the lid and pulled out a loaf of bread and a
round of cheese wrapped in cloth. She used her knife to slice
off a chunk of cheese, then broke the bread in half, and half
again.

She set her simple supper on what would be her bed
before scrambling to the front for her canteen of water. When
she did, she saw that both her oxen were hobbled and grazing,
the remainder of the rope was on her seat, and Stefan was
gone.

Chapter Six

The sun was down before Stefan and Leif joined the rest of the wagon train employees for their supper by the cook's wagon. The brothers were not the only green men on the trail, so conversation consisted mainly of their observations about the day, the people, the pace, and the terrain.

Leif sat first, choosing the seat next to the Negro scout who had not been present in their training.

"I am Leif Hansen." Leif held his plate in his left hand and his right hand crossed his chest to reach for the man sitting on his left.

"Tom-tom," the scout replied, shaking Leif's hand.

Stefan sat next to Leif. "And I am Stefan Hansen, his 'little' brother."

Tom-tom grinned and chuckled at the reference and shook Stefan's hand. "Pleased to meet you both."

"You weren't at training," Leif observed. "So, I guess you've done this before?"

Tom-tom nodded as he loaded a bite of stew onto his spoon. "Several times."

"Anything we should know?" Stefan asked while the scout delivered the spoonful to its target.

"Never let your guard down," Tom-tom spoke out of the side of his full mouth. "As soon as you think nothing will go wrong, it always does."

"That is good advice. Thank you."

"What is your story?" Leif asked. "How did this become your livelihood?"

Tom-tom raised one brow. "You really want to know?"

"Sure." Leif used his spoon to make an all-inclusive gesture. "What else is there to do to pass the time?"

Tom-tom shrugged and set his empty bowl on the ground before starting his narrative. "I was born in eighteen-twenty and raised as an educated slave in Missouri. When the master of the property was dying, this fancy woman—"

He paused and met Stefan and Leif's eyes. "You know what I mean by that?"

Stefan nodded. "I assume you mean whore."

"Actually, I think she was a Madame." He waved a dismissive hand. "But that's not important. Anyway, she paid for me and set me free."

Leif looked incredulous. "Why?"

Tom-tom shrugged again. "She said she knew where my parents were, but I must not try to find them."

Stefan understood immediately. "Because if you were caught you could be re-enslaved."

"Yes, sir." Tom-tom drew a deep, resolute breath and let it out slowly. "She told me to head west and stay out of the slave state of Missouri."

"How long ago did that happen?" Leif asked.

"About five years or so, when I was nineteen or twenty. And I took her advice."

Stefan was intrigued. "Have you heard from her again?"

"She does not know where I am." Tom-tom picked up his bowl. "Though she told me to write to her if anything in Missouri changed and she would tell me where my parents are."

"But nothing has changed…" Stefan said softly.

Tom-tom stood. "I have been meeting wagon trains on this

side of the border and scouting for them ever since."

Leif stood as well. "The Republic of Texas allows slavery, does it not?"

Now Stefan rose to his feet. "Yes, but look around us, Leif. The majority of this land is deserted, not like Missouri where half-a-million people live in an area less than a quarter of the size."

"More importantly..." Tom-tom grinned at the brothers. "I have an agreement with the wagon masters that they will claim ownership of me if I am challenged or threatened."

Stefan was impressed. "Has that happened?"

"Never." Tom-tom waved his bowl toward the pot over the fire. "All this talk has made me hungry again. I am going to have another bowl. Will you join me?"

March 2, 1845

The loud, jangling triangle signaled time to rise and start the day. When it shocked Blake awake, initially she was not sure where she was. She sat up, looked around her cramped and dim surroundings, before the realization of where she was slammed into her.

Every muscle in her body ached. Her mind was fuzzy from exhaustion, both from not sleeping at all the night before her departure, and from the physical exertion of driving a wagon for the entire next day.

What have I done?

Blake sank back onto her thin mattress and pulled her warm quilt to her chin. She slept in the shirt she wore yesterday—not her original plan, but she was far too tired to do more than remove her jacket, trousers and boots, and wrap herself in the quilt before resting her head on the polish-stained pillowcase.

Her belly was empty, but so was her resolve. One day into her grand plan and all she wanted to do was go back to sleep and wake up in her bedroom in Kansas City.

Tears began to roll from her eyes into her hair, and annoyingly into her ears. When she sat up to wipe them away, she took another look at her tiny home.

Every item there stared back at her angrily, as if to ask why she was giving up so soon. One day. It has only been one day.

But I can't do this.

Then curl up and die.

Blake sucked a startled breath. The challenge was as clear as if someone—or something—had spoken the words aloud. Those were her options: curl up and die, or get up, get dressed, and get back on that seat. Not much of a choice.

But it was still a choice.

Blake stood on stiff legs and folded the quilt. Then she picked up every piece of clothing off the wagon's floor and methodically put it back on, turning herself once more into Blake Somersby, city bachelor.

Too tired to try and start a cooking fire, Blake made another meal of the bread and cheese before folding back the flap of the wagon's cover, climbing to the ground, and looking for a place to use as an outhouse.

Another complication arose when she found herself following women.

Whoops!

Blake whirled around and headed in a different direction. She crouched behind a bush away from everyone, male or female, to void her bowels and bladder. Thus relieved, she headed back to her wagon. It was time to find her team and get them back in their traces.

She was trying to remove the ropes from one of them when she heard, "Let me help you."

Stefan.

Gratitude flooded her so strongly she almost forgot that he thought she was a man.

Careful.

"You slide the knots like this," he demonstrated. "See?"

Blake nodded. "Thanks."

Stefan straightened and peered at her. "Are you well?"

"T-tired." Her voice sounded raspy without her even trying to disguise it.

He gave her a knowing look. "Driving a team is more physically demanding than life in the city, but you will get used to it in time."

Blake removed the hobble from her other ox and stowed the ropes under the driver's seat where she could easily retrieve them later.

Stefan was still standing there, and that made her nervous. And that made her throat tighten and her words choppy.

What does he want?

"Did you make a fire?"

Blake shook her head.

"What did you eat?"

"B-bread and cheese." What difference did it make?

Stefan wagged his head. "That's not enough."

Blake pulled one ox into position and tried to remember how to strap him into the harness. Stefan led the other animal into position and waited until she tried to put a rein though the wrong ring before he interfered.

"No. This one."

Blake was both irritated and grateful. "I will d-do it right t-tomorrow."

"I have no doubt." He still stood there, hands on his hips, staring at her.

"What d-do you want?" she growled, angry that he made her nervous and her stutter came out.

"Have you met any of the families?"

Blake scowled and shook her head.

"You should."

"Why?" she demanded.

"Because you are a young man traveling by yourself."

A 'young' man?

Stefan's expression shifted as he pulled himself off point. "How old are you anyway?"

"How old d-do you think I-I am?" she stammered.

Stefan wagged a finger and smiled knowingly. "I have played that game myself. I will say you look to be twenty-one, and even though you are only sixteen you will agree. Am I right?"

Blake lifted one unconcerned shoulder, desperately trying to decide on an answer.

A younger age explains my lack of facial hair.

And my higher voice.

"Seven-t-teen."

Stefan narrowed his eyes. "You know you have to be eighteen to drive a wagon."

She did not.

Damn.

She must have looked frightened because Stefan leaned closer. "Your secret is my secret. But if you get sick or injured, you will need someone in the group to help you."

He quickly put up one hand, forestalling what he accurately thought she might say. "And don't think it will be me. I am limited to animal care, and the longer we are on the trail the busier I will be."

Blake stomped around him without answering and climbed into the driver's seat.

Stefan followed and put a hand on her boot as if to hold her in place. "That is why, when we stop tonight, you need to introduce yourself to whoever is parked on either side of you."

Blake nodded reluctantly. Stefan made a good point, but the closer she got to anyone, the more she ran the risk of being discovered.

"Good." He tipped his head to his left. "I need to go finish introducing myself. I will see you later."

Blake watched him walk away, her foot still tingling from his grip.

*****

After Stefan spoke to the passengers in each of the wagons he had circled back to where he started.

"Did you see the mare?" Leif asked.

Stefan nodded and poured himself a second cup of strong black coffee. "I think you are right. In spite of what they claim, she seems to be far enough gone that she will likely foal on the trail."

"I was afraid of that." Leif shook his head. "Do you think they realize the foal will have to ride in their wagon? There is no way a newborn will be able to keep up."

"What were those people thinking?" Stefan blew on his steaming coffee before he took a sip.

Leif looked at him sideways. "They were thinking that they are moving to the edge of civilization and would not leave a good brood mare behind."

Stefan froze.

Of course, that is what they were thinking. He and Leif would head back to Missouri after resting for a bit in Santa Fe, but the people in the train were not. This was their one chance to make sure they had all that they needed.

He looked at Leif. "I suppose I would have made the same choice if I was in their position."

Leif's lips quirked. "I bet you would not have packed a piano, though."

Stefan almost spit coffee. He wiped his mouth, laughing. "I saw that. Several of the wagons are way overloaded."

"Happens every time." Buck Schultz walked over and lifted the coffee pot from the fire. He poured himself a hefty serving. "We will see it along the way eventually. As the teams get more worn out, people start leaving things behind to lighten their loads."

Stefan found that surprising. "You mean they just unload a chifferobe in the middle of the prairie and leave it there?"

"Yep. Of course, some others might pick it up and then leave something of their own behind to make up for the weight." The wagon master shrugged. "Depends on how long it's been there and how bad the weather's been."

He turned to leave and spoke over his shoulder. "It's time to move. Saddle up, gentleman."

*****

At the end of the second day on the trail, Blake's physical resources were completely drained. She was again too tired to make a fire, but knew another meager meal of bread and cheese would not be enough to sustain her.

The families on either side of her wagon had fires going, and she wondered if she might be allowed to cook over one of them when they were finished.

With Stefan's admonition echoing in her ears, she climbed out of her wagon and approached the people parked behind her.

"Hello."

The woman who was bent over and stirring a cast-iron pot looked up. She smiled tiredly. "Hello."

Blake pulled off her wide-brimmed leather hat. "My name is B-blake Somersby. I was wondering if I could c-cook something over your fire when you are f-finished."

The woman's eyes traveled over Blake's frame. "You are traveling alone." It was not a question.

"Yes, ma'am." Blake took another tentative step forward, her fingers worrying the edges of the hat. "And to be honest, I'm t-too tired to build my own fire."

The woman went back to stirring whatever was in the pot. "I don't mind. What are you cooking?"

I have no idea.

"I-I have some sausage to make gravy, and I-I'll make a batch of b-biscuits, I guess." Her stomach gurgled hungrily at the idea.

"You have your own pots?"

Blake nodded. "Yes, ma'am."

The woman nodded as well and held out her free hand.

"I'm Mary. My husband is Frank. He's gone hunting before it gets too dark."

Blake closed the gap between them and shook Mary's hand. "Nice to m-meet you."

A young girl with messy pigtails and a soaked apron ran around the end of Mary's wagon. "Thomas splashed me!"

An older boy followed quickly. "She did it first!"

"Never mind!" Mary barked. "Did you both wash your face and hands?"

Brother and sister nodded.

Mary tipped her head toward Blake. "This here is Mister Somersby. He is going to borrow our fire when supper is done."

A stocky bearded man walked up as she spoke. He carried a brace of rabbits and smiled at Blake.

"Somersby? Frank Waldon."

"Blake." The men shook hands, then Blake asked, "How are you going to c-cook the rabbits?"

*****

By the end of the evening Blake had shared her meaty sausage gravy and flaky biscuits with the family of four before seasoning and roasting the fresh rabbit meat.

"Your cooking outshines anything in the state of Missouri, I swear." Frank sopped up the last bit of the gravy with a biscuit. "And with the rabbit cooked we have supper for tomorrow."

"Thank you so much!" Mary took the sleepy-looking children by their hands. "I am going to get these critters to bed. I will see you in the morning."

Frank watched his wife disappear into the wagon before he leaned close to Blake. "My wife is good at many things," he whispered. "But cooking is not one of them."

Blake wisely said nothing.

"So I was thinking—if I hunt, would you be willing to cook for us again?"

Blake heaved a sigh of relief. "I would be happy to, as long as I c-can eat as well."

Frank's evaluative gaze swept over Blake. "Not to be rude, but you are not a large man. Feeding one more mouth would not be a burden."

"In that case, sir, you have a d-deal." Blake sealed it with a handshake. "And now if you will ex-excuse me, I am going to go into my wagon and c-collapse."

Blake stood, collected her cleaned pans, and climbed the little ladder at the back of her wagon. She closed the canvas, tying it shut, and dropped to her knees.

Thank you, Lord.

The offer of meat in exchange for doing the one thing she loved most in the world was a blessing she had never considered possible.

She stood again and disrobed before washing her face and her cropped hair with plain water. When she saw how much shoe polish was on the towel, she decided to replenish the darkener in the morning.

Blake pulled off her dusty shirt and laid it over a trunk along with the trousers. Then she retrieved a clean shirt from another trunk and slipped it on over her head. If she had to wear men's shirts to sleep in, she decided she should wear a clean one.

Away from the fire's heat and shivering in the chilly night, Blake got under her down-filled comforter and top quilt. Curled on her side, it did not take long for her body heat to start soothing her aching muscles. She sighed.

I just might survive this ordeal after all.

Chapter Seven

Stefan found the odd concept of dropping and gaining items along the trail intriguing, and it occupied his thoughts for most of the day. Mostly he wondered if there could be any money made by facilitating those exchanges.

He mentioned the idea to Leif as they spread their bedrolls under the chuck wagon.

Leif looked intrigued. "Do you mean like trade posts?"

"Yes. Scattered along the trail." Stefan was thinking out loud. "Maybe a family forgot something important, or something broke, or whatever scenario fits. And another family abandoned that exact item—or maybe something similar—so they could get what they needed."

"That idea has possibilities." Leif pulled off his boots. "Could they actually trade for it? Or would they have to buy it?"

Stefan did the same and tucked his belt inside one boot. "Trade, I think. But what if every item was appraised and given a value so the trades were even?"

"And they could pay the difference if they wanted to trade up?" Leif slid inside his bedroll. "I like it."

Stefan was still sitting on his bedroll, hunching his tall

frame under the bottom of the wagon. "We could even pay the families the difference, if they brought something in and wanted something of less value."

"We?" Leif huffed a laugh. "Are you serious?"

Stefan shrugged. "I might be."

Leif was quiet for a moment, then he offered, "If it is an item people generally want, we could buy from them as well."

Stefan was getting excited by the prospect of starting a legitimate and useful business—one his father would both approve of, and be proud of.

Finally.

He snuggled into his blankets. "We could also hire young men to search the trails for abandoned furniture and retrieve it before it gets ruined."

Leif chuckled. "Thereby eliminating the free trade that happens now."

Stefan propped himself on one elbow and faced his brother.

"The very *wasteful* and *inefficient* free trade that happens now," he pointed out.

"I guess we shall see for ourselves." Leif yawned. "We can take stock of what we find on this journey and determine if this is a workable plan."

Stefan flopped onto his back, his mind racing with possibilities.

I wonder if I should buy a cart to begin with.

                                            March 11, 1845
                                            Council Grove

Eleven days after leaving Kansas City the wagon train arrived at Council Grove, the only trading post between Missouri and Santa Fe in the Mexican-claimed Republic of Texas.

Stefan walked down the line of parked wagons. "This is

the last chance for anyone of you to procure anything that you might need for yourselves and your animals."

And yet another reason to consider my idea.

"Please ask any of the men working the train if you have a need," he told each family. "We will try to help you meet it."

Stefan realized he was intentionally heading for Blake Somersby's wagon. For some reason that he could not explain, Stefan was worried about the young man from the city who was so clearly out of his element on the trail.

He did not want to pry into areas that were not his concern, but he did still wonder why the young fellow was traveling alone, and how someone so young managed to pay for the expensive journey.

Was he banished by a wealthy family wishing to hide his predilection? His way paid and wagon stocked in exchange for disappearing and not bringing shame on his family?

Up until now, he had not found a chance to ask.

One of the reasons he had not was that Somersby had befriended a family, just as Stefan suggested, and had been sharing their evening meals ever since. Apparently, the father hunted and Somersby cooked, then they all ate together.

It was actually a brilliant idea, benefiting all involved.

One evening Stefan passed by after checking on the pregnant brood mare and the father—Frank—waved him over.

He lifted a spoon. "Taste this."

Stefan accepted the dripping utensil. "What is it?"

"Best duck I ever had." Frank grinned. "Go on."

Frank was not a liar. Stefan's mouth watered with the memory. Blake Somersby was an excellent cook.

When he reached Somersby's wagon, he found the man deep in conversation with Tom-tom.

"It is called the underground railway," the Negro explained to Somersby. "There are sympathetic owners of farms and houses throughout Missouri who open their barns or cellars to escaping slaves during the days."

Understanding brightened Somersby's expression.

"Because they travel at night. In the dark," he said.

Tom-tom nodded. "Exactly."

Somersby was clearly intrigued.

So was Stefan. His father had always been against slavery, even though his lifelong friend and brother-in-law Rickard Atherton owned hundreds of slaves. In fact, those slaves worked the land Nicolas's father had leased to Rickard's father.

"May I join you?"

Somersby nodded from his perch on his wagon's ladder but did not remove his attention from Tom-tom. "How do the slaves know where to go?"

"There are maps in the quilt patterns that they use."

Stefan's jaw dropped. "There are?"

Tom-tom chuckled. "Yes. The quilts are hung outside, as if to dry. The men and women read them, if you will, and know where the next safe place is."

"That is brilliant." Somersby wagged his head slowly. "I wish I had known about this."

That piqued Stefan's interest. "Why?"

The man blinked and seemed momentarily flummoxed. "B-because my father has a large house and I-I might have been able t-to help."

"Would you have stayed behind for that?" Stefan probed. "If you had known, that is."

Stefan believed the man shuddered. "No. remaining behind in K-kansas City was not p-possible for me. I would have d-died there."

Because the sentence for homosexuality in some places is death?

"Would your father have allowed you to use the house this way?" Tom-tom asked.

A dark shadow shifted over Somersby's face wiping away any visible emotion. "I would not have g-given him the option t-to say no."

Stefan was thinking of his own father, and the escaping slaves he eventually bought and freed.

"I wonder if he would be would be amenable to the idea,"

he murmured aloud.

"My father is dead."

Stefan's thoughts moved away from Nicolas and his attention shot back to Somersby. "I am sorry."

"I am not." The young man's expression remained blank. "I am finally free."

Tom-tom nodded slowly. "And starting a new life."

Somersby's cheeks flushed. "Yes. Far, far away."

"We will leave you to the rest of your day, Somersby." Tom-tom turned to Stefan and clapped his hand on Stefan's shoulder. "I need to check my stock of ammunition and perhaps purchase a new knife. Care to come along?"

*****

Blake retreated into her wagon and waited until the men walked away. She wanted to explore the trade post for herself, but did not want to be near Stefan when she did. Too many things about that man set her on edge and she had no idea what to do about it—or if anything could be done.

The first thing she noticed about him was his striking good looks. Well over six feet tall, unruly auburn hair, those impossibly bright blue eyes...

And he was so kind and helpful to her. And it was not because she was a woman. He believed her to be a boy in his teens and had no idea she was an old maid facing thirty years of age in the not-too-distant future.

Even though she was now sharing supper duties with the Waldon family, just as he suggested, Stefan still passed their wagons and checked on her at least once a day.

I am afraid I am smitten.

That was not in any way helpful in her situation. First of all, she could never let anyone working the wagon train know that she was a woman. Secondly, if she waited and confessed her gender when they reached Santa Fe, Stefan would rightfully be angry at her deception.

And, most importantly, he and the other men were returning to Missouri, not settling like she and the families were.

No, there was nothing that could be done. Pursuing any attraction once her gender was revealed was futile.

Blake sighed resolutely. She jammed her hat over her short hair and climbed down the ladder to go exploring.

*****

Though the terrain in the last eleven days had become more prairie-like and less wooded, Council Grove had a wide grove of trees sheltering the post.

Blake walked past a sawmill, enjoying the scent of freshly-cut wood and sap. Buck Schultz was there, negotiating prices for lumber. She thought that was odd.

She stopped walking and watched the mill working, chips flying from the water-powered saw. Why would a wagon master need lumber?

"Fascinating, isn't it."

Damn.

Blake spoke to Stefan but did not look at him. "Why is he b-buying lumber?"

"Wagon repairs."

Of course.

"This is my first wagon train as well," he continued. "But when they were training us, they told us that once we pass this point trees will be scarce."

Blake looked up to see if he was joking with her. "I find that hard to believe."

"So do I. I have never seen land that was not wooded and needed to be cleared." He spread his hands in a conciliatory manner. "But they have no reason to lie to us."

"I suppose…" Blake frowned. "Did they say what they

meant b-by scarce?"

"Apparently we will travel for days without seeing a single tree." Stefan looked as skeptical as the claim.

Blake scoffed. "Were there any other fanciful t-tales?"

"Have you heard of buffalo?"

"Of course. There are b-buffalo in Missouri."

"Not like what we might encounter," Stefan qualified. "They told us that there are herds several thousand strong that roam the plains."

Blake found that alarming. Buffalo were enormous animals and one could destroy any man-made pen if provoked. What sort of damage would thousands upon thousands do?

"Will we b-be in danger?"

"They will not attack us, if that is what you mean," Stefan assured her. "But there is a phenomenon called a 'stampede' where the entire herd runs blindly. Hopefully, not in our direction."

Good Lord!

This was getting worse not better. "Why d-do they run?"

"Something has spooked them. And it seems that if a few bolt, the others follow."

Once again Blake questioned the wisdom of her choice. She assumed the trek would be grueling, and prayed nightly that they would not encounter Indians, but she had no idea about buffalo stampedes with the huge animals numbering as high as ten thousand.

The prospect was terrifying.

"The entire wagon t-train could be destroyed. The people c-could be killed!"

Stefan looked extremely uncomfortable. "I should not have told you."

She yelped, "No you should not have!" before common sense returned and corrected her.

"I am sorry. I do not mean that." She pulled off her hat and scuttled her fingers through her cropped locks. "It is b-better to be prepared."

Stefan's relief was obvious. "I am glad you think so."

Blake plopped the hat back on her head. "What are we to do if we see one of these stampedes?"

"First we pull the wagons tightly together as quickly as possible." He used his large hands to create a circle. "Then all the men stand on the wagons and shoot at the buffalo."

Blake's eyes widened. "To kill them?"

"To scare them—so they change direction," Stefan qualified. "But if we do kill any, the families can take the meat."

One thing Stefan said sent jolts of concern through her frame. "So *all* of the men are expected to shoot at the herd?"

"Yes. The noise needs to be loud enough that they veer away from the wagons." Stefan cocked his head and looked at her oddly. "Is that a problem?"

"A little one…"

"What?"

Blake offered an apologetic shrug. "I do not have a gun."

*****

Stefan stared at the young man. "You do *not* have a *gun?*"

Somersby shook his head, his lips pressed in a thin line.

"What the hell were you thinking?" he blurted. "How could you expect to survive in the west without a gun?"

Somersby's face flushed a furious red. "I d-did not th-think about it."

Stefan's jaw dropped. This fellow was far greener than he imagined. "How did you expect to hunt for food?"

"I d-did not know I-I would need to."

Clearly, if it was not for the Waldon family, Somersby would have starved on this journey. "How could you undertake this journey when you are so unprepared?"

Oh God, he is going to cry.

"I d-do not kno-know." Somersby ran an arm over his eyes, leaving a streak of damp, dusty dirt across his cheeks.

Stefan immediately regretted his stunned reaction. This poor kid was running *away* from something, that was obvious now. So either he did not have the time, or the opportunity, to get adequately organized.

"Well, I am very glad to find this out now," he said gently.

Wet brown eyes squinted up at him. "Why? Are you turning me back?"

"Turning you—no!" Stefan forced himself not to laugh. "To be honest, you would never find your way back."

More tears spilled and he wiped them away again. He was starting to look like a homeless urchin. That was saying a lot, considering the rough conditions on their long journey.

"I am glad to find this out *now* because we have not left the trading post," Stefan explained.

Somersby's brows pulled together. Apparently, he was not catching on.

Stefan leaned forward, lowering his eyes closer to Somersby's level. "I will take you inside, and help you buy a gun."

Somersby recoiled, eyes wide.

Another unsettling thought occurred. "You do have money, don't you?"

He nodded.

Thank goodness.

"Then let's go inside and see what they have."

*****

Blake lived her entire life in a city and never had need of a gun. Now she stood in the trade post with Stefan while he rambled on about cartridges and barrels and lead balls and was completely lost.

"This is an eighteen-thirty-six Hall carbine." Stefan handed her the gun with a one-shoulder shrug. "Guns with barrels longer than twenty inches are usually called rifles, but

Hall calls them carbines anyway."

Blake awkwardly lifted the gun and looked down the nearly two-foot barrel as she had seen the other men do.

Stefan manipulated the metal mechanics behind the barrel. "This is the moveable receiver. See this? It pivots and comes up for loading."

Blake nodded numbly.

"The receiver is actually a short-barreled muzzle-loading pistol," Stefan continued to explain in some completely foreign language. "To load it, you insert powder from a flask, then put the lead ball above it and push it into place."

Stefan mimed his actions for now. Blake assumed the flask and powder and ball were reserved for loading the rifle out of doors, not inside a crowded building.

"Then you push the receiver down and it locks into alignment with the barrel. See?" Stefan looked pleased.

"Then I shoot it?" she ventured.

"Not yet. It is not primed."

Another step.

Great.

"You use a percussion cap which has fulminate of mercury inside." Stefan looked giddy—he was obviously enjoying this, though she was completely lost. "When you pull the trigger the hammer strikes the cap. The fulminate of mercury explodes and ignites the powder."

Blake stared at him blankly.

"The powder explodes and pushes the ball down the barrel…"

Blake waited.

Stefan's brow furrowed in confusion. "That is the shooting part."

Blake gasped. "Oh!"

Stefan wagged his head and huffed a laugh. "This will make sense once we actually load and shoot the gun."

I certainly hope so.

"Do I b-buy it now?"

"Yes. It is the best gun they have here and worth the

money, even if the price has been doubled." Stefan shot a narrow-eyed glance at the man behind the counter.

He smiled back, clearly aware that his customers had to pay the higher prices or walk away with empty hands.

Blake sighed. "I will go g-get the money."

"And I will collect all the things you will need while we wait for you to return," Stefan stated.

Chapter Eight

So now I own a gun.
And now I need to learn how to shoot it.

Blake stood beside her wagon on the less windy side, squinting in the cloudy but glaring midday, and watched intently while Stefan's brother Leif painstakingly showed her how to load and prime her rifle.

"Stefan gets impatient sometimes," Leif explained. "So he asked me to teach you."

"Do you m-mind?" Blake asked sincerely. "I am very sorry to be so much t-trouble."

"It's no trouble." Leif smiled. "And it means Stefan has to deal with the horses that are already lame, not me."

Leif proved himself to indeed be patient. Blake fumbled with the whole system until she started thinking of the process as a recipe.

"So I open the grinder and insert the spices and the meat," she said as she opened the receiver and put the powder and lead ball in position. "Then I close it securely, so nothing leaks out."

Leif laughed. "That is the most interesting explanation I have ever heard."

Blake smiled at the man. "Then I have to light the stove. Right?"

She cocked the hammer and put the cap in place.

"Perfect!" Leif laughed again. "Are you ready to cook?"

Blake nodded nervously. "Will you shoot first?"

Leif put the stock of the rifle against his shoulder and looked down the barrel. "Point the end of the barrel at what you want to hit, then squeeze the trigger."

The loud bang of the gun made Blake yelp and slap her palms to her ears without thinking about it.

Leif lowered the gun. "It is loud, I admit."

Loud enough to scare away buffalo, I hope.

Blake lowered her hands. "My ears are ringing."

"That's common. Are you ready to try?"

"Yes," she said as confidently as she could manage.

Leif handed her the rifle. "Be careful, because the barrel of the gun is hot after you shoot."

That was something she did not expect. But it made sense considering an explosion just happened inside of it.

Blake went through her steps: grinder, spices, meat, close it, open the stove, light it.

She hefted the gun to her shoulder.

"Are you left-handed?" Leif asked.

Blake looked at him with alarm. She had been chastised all of her life for using the 'wrong' hand to do things. As a result, she was almost as good with her right hand as her left.

"Why d-does that matter?"

"It does not. But you are holding the rifle like a left-handed person would," Leif explained. "I only want to assure you are doing what is right for you."

"Oh." Relief replaced alarm. "Yes, I prefer my left hand."

"Good, then. Now, be prepared for the kick back."

Blake frowned. "K-kick back?"

"When the explosion pushes the ball down the barrel, the gun jerks backwards," he warned. "It can knock you down if you are not braced."

Blake nodded and spread her feet. "Like this?"

"Yes."

"Should I shoot?"

"Yes. Just press on the trigger until it releases the hammer."

The next thing she knew, Blake was violently thrown backwards onto her ass. She dropped the rifle and tried unsuccessfully to break her fall. Her ears rang even louder as she stared wide-eyed and stunned straight up at a clear blue sky.

Leif's face appeared in her line of vision. "Are you hurt?"

Her shoulder and her dignity were both bruised, but she was otherwise fine. "No. I am well."

Leif offered her a hand up and she scrambled to her feet, glad she was in trousers and not a dress.

When she bent down to retrieve her hat Leif asked, "Ready to do it again?"

Blake straightened and determinedly faced her fears. "I sure am."

Leif grinned. "Good for you."

Blake grinned back.

I can do this.

March 18, 1845

A week later, Blake's left shoulder still showed the yellow and green tinges of her fading bruises, but at least she felt like she could load, prime, and fire her rifle if she needed to.

Leif had been so kind and patient with her last week that she bought some eggs from a family wisely traveling with chickens and baked him a little cinnamon and brown sugar cake.

"You should open a restaurant in Santa Fe," he said with his mouth full of the confection. "You really know how to cook."

"C-cooking was the one thing I used to escape the misery

of my life," she admitted. "Nothing else was t-tolerable."

Stefan ambled up and squatted next to Leif. "What have you got there?"

"A thank you cake. From Somersby."

Stefan's eyes shifted to Blake. "Thank you for what?"

She smiled softly. "For being p-patient and k-kind when he was teaching me to shoot."

I wish it had been you.

Stop that.

Leif helped himself to another slice of cake. "You would have hated it, Stef. Took him forever to learn."

Leif winked at her, dispelling the sudden unease his words had prompted.

Stefan reached for the pan. "Give me a piece."

Leif twisted away from him, the pan gripped close to his chest. "Ask nicely, you uncivilized Nordic oaf."

Blake bit back her laugh.

"Please." Stefan tried to reach around Leif.

Leif stood and moved out of range. "Please what?"

Stefan glared up at him, but his eyes were twinkling. "Please give me a piece."

"A piece of what?" Leif taunted before stuffing the rest of the slice in his mouth.

"A piece of your hide if you don't give me a piece of that cake *right now!*" Stefan leapt toward his brother.

Blake jumped up as well and reached for the cake pan before the rest of her gift ended up lost in the dry prairie grass beneath their feet. Leif let her take it.

When she turned away, however, her boots tangled with his. She lost her balance and pitched forward toward the fire, dropping the cake pan.

Before she could scream an arm circled her waist and pulled her backwards. She was pressed against Stefan's chest and his right hand covered her left breast.

Oh NO!

Blake jerked violently forward and his hand fell away. Thank God she always bound her bosom. Tightly.

"Thanks," she croaked as she put distance between them before turning around. Then to break the awkward silence, she added, "That was c-close."

She bent over and retrieved the cake pan which thankfully landed on its bottom. She held it out in Leif's direction and did not dare to even glance at Stefan.

"You can return the pan tomorrow."

Without waiting for another word, she whirled around and hurried back to her wagon.

*****

Leif threw a back-handed fist hard against Stefan's chest.

"You really are an uncivilized Nordic oaf, you know that?"

Stefan made a face and dropped to his ass on the ground. "Sorry."

"You should be."

Stefan twisted and looked up at Leif. "He made you a cake."

Leif glared at him. "And?"

"And that is what lovers do." Stefan winced. "Is it not?"

The blood drained from Leif's face and he sank to his knees in the grass next to Stefan.

"Do you think he has developed feelings for me?"

Why that idea made Stefan jealous was not anything he wished to dwell upon. Not in the least bit.

"He said you were patient and kind. That is what a woman might say."

"Blazes!" Leif looked at Stefan. "What should I do?"

"I have no idea. I have never been friends with anyone like him before."

Stefan reached over and claimed the last slice of cake. "You want me to take the pan back for you?"

March 26, 1845

Stefan brought her the cake pan the next day, but Blake had not seen much of Leif for the past week. That was not so very unusual, but she could not help but worry that something she said or did might have offended him.

She wondered if she should ask Stefan about it, but had not yet worked up the courage.

Yesterday at the end of the day the wagon train reached the Arkansas River. Today the train was staying put, allowing the settlers to take advantage of their first significant water source since leaving Missouri.

Laundry and baths topped the list for the women chatting at supper that night. Blake walked her oxen to the river and let them drink their fill before hobbling them in the center of the wagons' enclosure. She longed to be able to get in the river herself and wondered if there was a way to do so without revealing her true identity.

Probably not.

At least she could take buckets of water into the safety of her wagon and wash herself there.

The weather had shifted over the last couple days, promising rain but not yet delivering. The ground that passed beneath the wagons waited for water, and the prairie stretched outward in all directions in a dead and undulating sea of pale golden grass.

The oxen loved it, however, and snatched huge mouthfuls as they lumbered along.

Stefan was right about one thing: there were no trees. Blake believed he and the other men were the subject of a prank when they were told that the majority of their route was treeless. Now she knew that unbelievable fact to be true.

If she ever returned to Missouri, she would have an interesting story to tell. As it was, the only person she would ever write to was her lawyer. She would not waste those words on him because he would not care.

An advantage to being on the open prairie was that the wagons were able to move side-by-side in a wide swath instead of stretching out half-a-mile in a single line. The wagons at the end of that line were no longer subjected to the windblown dust and debris kicked up by the dozens of wagons in front of them.

That dust and debris chapped and dried her checks in spite of the cream she rubbed into them after washing her face every night. Now that her back and arms had grown accustomed to reining her team, the constant wind was the most uncomfortable thing about sitting on the driver's bench for ten hours a day.

Until today.

The familiar cramps woke her this morning and she groaned. There was no way that she could avoid her cycle in the nearly twelve-week journey and she knew that. At least the timing of this onset meant she should only bleed twice before reaching the safety of Santa Fe.

Blake got out of bed before she stained her sheets and dug out the torn rags she packed for this purpose. After tying them securely in place she went ahead and dressed in her manly clothes for the day, then prepared a pot of willowbark tea to steep once a fire was started.

She planned to drink some of the bitter tea right away to ease the pain of her cramps. The remainder would be allowed to cool and be available to her for the rest of the day.

By the second day her cramping usually abated. Hopefully this cycle would follow that pattern, because tomorrow she would be back in the driver's seat. It was going to be hard enough to find opportunities to go inside her wagon to change her soiled rags while on the move, without having to deal with the cramping pain.

Blake quietly went out into the predawn morning and found a sheltered spot to empty her bowels and bladder, squatting and squeezing her belly for as long as she could tolerate it before retying the rags.

She watched the overcast sky as she did, fascinated by the tendrils of lightning which skittered through the clouds in the north and west. There was no audible thunder so the storm was forty or fifty miles away at least.

As the sky gradually lightened, she was disappointed not to see evidence that rain was falling from those clouds.

Maybe tomorrow.

Blake noticed movement in the camp so she quickly reassembled her woman's rags and men's garments then stood to rejoin the settlers.

Chapter Nine

Stefan watched the sky to the northwest. He had not ever been any place where the sky was so widely visible. The vast expanse engulfed him and made him feel very small.

"They were right about no trees, which means we can see forever," he said to Leif. "That lightning has to be miles away."

"Fifty miles if it's a foot," Leif agreed. "And dry lightning to boot. No rain so far."

Stefan sniffed the wind, smelling nothing but dry grass and dust and manure. Because of the danger of fire in this dry and windy terrain, the families were restricted to building small, shared fires in a circular area dug out by the hostlers and mechanics each evening.

The men on the train were charged with carrying buckets of water from the Arkansas River, whose bank lay on the south side of the trail and defined their westward path. The buckets were placed around the fire circle, both to stop any flames that tried to escape and to thoroughly quench the fires when the cooking was done.

When Stefan understood that the treeless prairie was real, he also understood how quickly fire would spread over the unimpeded expanse of dry fuel, consuming anything—or anyone—in its path.

He looked toward the families sharing breakfast fires in the circle and searched for Somersby. Ever since he pulled the youth back from falling to the fire, he had not been able to shake the feeling of that slender body pressed against his.

Blazes I need a woman.

He snorted.

No chance of that here.

Leif looked at him. "What are you snorting about?"

Stefan startled. "I was just hoping it would rain. I am disgusted that it does not look hopeful."

*****

Washing her clothes in the river was a lot harder than washing in a tub at home. Believing Blake to be a young man, a couple of the women offered to help her. At first she declined, saying she needed to learn how to do this herself.

But after breaking a sweat and having to sit down because the effort made her cramps so much worse, she accepted the help.

"You know," a ruddy-cheeked mother of four said as she washed Blake's trousers. "Most men see this sort of thing as beneath them."

Blake nodded and continued washing her stack of socks.

"So I say, good for you, sir." The woman handed Blake the cuffs of her pants. "Now hold this."

The woman stepped back and began twisting the waist end of the cotton and linen trousers. Water streamed from the fabric as the pair twisted the garment as tightly as they could.

"Now go back to your wagon and flatten these with your hands before you hang them up." She handed Blake the twisted pants. "You will look less like a dried-up prune that way."

"Thank you," Blake said, sincerely meaning it.

"Glad to help." The woman's gaze moved toward the circle of wagons. "I think I will get my boys down here. They might as well learn to do for themselves, too."

Blake snickered. "Just do not t-tell them that I suggested it. I d-do not wish to make enemies with my own gender."

"Do not have a care." The woman grinned widely and her eyes twinkled. "Anyway, I would be proud to have a son like you."

Blake felt her cheeks heating. She found the compliment deeply satisfying—if this woman was proud of what she accomplished as a young man, that spoke volumes about what she was actually accomplishing as a grown woman.

"Thanks again." Blake gathered her wet clothes and headed back to her wagon.

I need to change my rags.

*****

She was too late. Before hanging her clean, wet clothes to dry, Blake removed the trousers she was wearing and scrubbed the new blood stain from the crotch. Then she got out the wool trousers to wear since both pairs of the lighter-weight trousers were now wet.

Blake tied one end of a rope to the driver's seat and the other end to a pole that was strapped to the side of her wagon. She stretched the rope from the side of the wagon facing outside the enclosure and dug the end of the pole in at an angle away from the wagon. Here the clothes would catch the wind more easily and dry more quickly, and their flapping would not scare the animals. Plus, the dust the animals stirred up and smoke from the cooking fires would not dirty the garments before they were worn.

Blake stepped back from her clothesline with a sense of triumph. She could now drive a wagon with a pair of oxen for ten hours a day. She could load and fire a rifle with gradually increasing accuracy. She could do her laundry in a river.

And best of all, she was cooking every evening. Not just for the Waldons either.

Frank and Mary had apparently been telling other families about Blake's culinary skills and by ones and twos some of the women had come to watch her. Blake was happy to teach the women the most effective use of spices, or how to boil tough meat before frying it, or how to bake biscuits and cakes in the flames.

Just like her, the majority of the women heading west had never lived rough before, and their knowledge of cooking did not necessarily transfer from a stove to a fire.

Nor from butchered beef to freshly shot rabbit.

Blake helped them as best she could and they repaid her with genuine friendship, including her in their conversations as they shared the cooking fires. In spite of all the challenges she still faced, Blake had never in her life been more content.

March 27, 1845

Stefan thought he was dreaming that the ground was trembling until Buck Schultz bellowed, "STAMPEDE!"

He sat up so quickly that he hit his head on the floor of the chuck wagon.

Leif was scrambling out of his bedroll. "Shit!"

Stefan did the same and yanked his boots on. The faint rumble of hooves was growing louder. He grabbed his rifle and pouch and crawled out from under the wagon.

"Which direction?" he shouted.

"Northwest!" Tom-tom shouted back as he ran past Stefan and Leif. "Hurry!"

There was no time to move the wagons closer together. Stefan and Leif followed the Negro scout to the northwest side of the enclosure and climbed up the side of one of the wagons there.

Buck was rousing and ordering the family out of that particular wagon, plus two others which the men were climbing on top of.

"Go to the other side!" he barked. "Take shelter!"

In the pink dusk of sunrise Stefan saw a wide cloud of dust billowing into the sky.

"How far away, do you think?" he asked Leif.

"Not sure. It's hard to measure out here." He stared at the growing dust cloud. "Five miles?"

The stampeding animals were still out of sight beyond one the innumerable swells of the endless prairie landscape.

"C-can I have a hand?"

Stefan turned towards Somersby's voice. He leaned down and grabbed the youth's hand.

"Come on!"

Somersby clambered up the side of the wagon until he reached Stefan's side. "Thanks."

"Load and prime," Stefan ordered. "And get lots more ammunition ready. We have to keep shooting."

Somersby nodded and set to work. Stefan noticed his fingers were shaking, but the young man quickly loaded his rifle without spilling or dropping anything.

"Good," Stefan complimented as he made a pile of scraps of fabric with gunpowder and another pile of caps. "Put yours here. We can share."

"Here they come!" Tom-tom shouted.

The overwhelming sight of thousands of buffalo topping the swell and spilling down its near side in an ever-widening surge of bellowing brown stopped Stefan's breath.

"When do we shoot?" Leif hollered.

"When they are close enough to hear us!" Buck hollered back.

Stefan shouldered his rifle and aimed into the herd.

The terrifying realization that these massive animals could, by their sheer numbers, completely decimate the wagons, the draft animals, and all the men women and children who owned them set his blood to fizzling.

God save us.

*****

Blake aimed her rifle at the swiftly approaching herd and wondered how it would feel to die.

She could never imagine such a terrifying scene as the one that appeared before her now. Thousands upon thousands of enormous wild beasts were charging toward the gathered wagons, seemingly out of their minds with fear.

What spooked them?

She could not help but worry that whatever it was might be headed toward the wagon train as well.

If we survive this assault, we might discover that answer.

"FIRE!"

Blake squeezed the trigger of her rifle. The explosion of sound around her made her ears ring, and the kickback from her gun re-bruised her shoulder.

But she did not fall.

Without hesitation she stuffed the gunpowder and a ball into her rifle, added the cap, then aimed and shot again. She did not wait to see if the gunshots were having any affect on the herd, but repeated the process over and over again.

Explosion after explosion filled her awareness, and the knowledge that she was still atop an intact wagon was the only thing that she allowed herself to think about.

Do not stop.

Divert the herd.

Save the people.

"Somersby!"

Blake shoved another ball and pouch of gunpowder into the scorching barrel of her rifle.

"Somersby!"

Drop the cap into place.

"Blake!"

Stefan's voice.

Blake paused and lifted her eyes, watering constantly from the sting of smoke and dust.

Stefan's bloodshot eyes met hers. "You can stop."

"What?"

His hand rested on her arm. "You do not need to reload."

Blake turned disbelieving eyes to the scene around them.

The ground was torn up and trampled and the dead grass flattened into it. The herd had split around them, with the majority heading to the east of the wagons. Several bellowing buffalo had been felled, and a few of the men from the train were heading toward them with their own guns.

Blake had no idea how much time passed, but the sun had cleared the horizon and now lit the gruesome landscape.

Stefan said something, but she did not understand him. The ringing in her ears was so loud that she could barely hear anything.

She turned back to look at him. "What?"

Stefan tried to smile, but he was obviously as shaken as she was. "You did well. Good job."

"You t-too."

Leif motioned for them to climb down. Blake's arms trembled with overuse and she could not feel her legs.

I do not think I can.

Somehow a ladder appeared. She only had to slide down a few feet to the top rung.

"Follow me," Stefan instructed her.

Leif stayed up top. "Give me your hands."

Blake swung her rifle around to her back and grabbed Leif's hands. She laid on her stomach and stretched down the canvas cover until Stefan guided her boots to the top rung of the ladder.

"Step down."

Blake did as she was told, forced to trust that the men who held on to her would keep her safe.

Leif let go of her hands.

She grasped the top of the ladder.

When she reached the bottom, her legs would not hold her and she collapsed to the ground.

*****

It was only Somersby's weakness that kept Stefan upright. He had never been so truly terrified in his entire and admittedly unconventional adult life.

Even though he was warned, mere words could not adequately describe the assault on his senses that the stampede inflicted: the staggering sight of the huge and dangerous brown swarm pulsing, growing, and streaming all around them.

The choking scents of dust, dirt, and male bovine musk, and the unpleasant tang they left in his mouth when he breathed.

The deafening sounds of gunshots and the deep screams of the animals.

The thundering of hooves.

The ground literally shook so violently under the combined weight of the frightened and confused beasts that the wagons wavered. Stefan's own body quivered in the aftermath.

He reached down to help Somersby regained his feet, hoping that he did not topple over in the process.

"That was something, huh?" Stefan tried to sound casual but he heard the tremble in his tone.

Somersby nodded mutely and accepted Stefan's hand. He stood, albeit unsteadily.

Stefan watched Leif descend the ladder. "I hope no one got hurt."

Somersby nodded again, but still didn't speak.

Stefan peered into his reddened eyes. "What are you thinking about?"

He hesitated. "M-my c-clothes."

"Your clothes?" That was odd. "What about them?"

"L-laundry."

It took Stefan a moment to figure out what the man was talking about. "You washed your clothes yesterday and they were drying outside the circle."

Somersby nodded a third time.

Stefan realized of a sudden that the youth was anxious. "You stutter when you are nervous," he observed. "Have you always?"

Somersby gasped. His eyes went round as plates and his cheeks flamed red.

"I am sorry—I do not mean to upset you further," Stefan hastened to explain. "I only just now realized it."

"N-not your c-concern!" he barked.

Stefan tried again to apologize, but all he addressed was Somersby's furiously departing backside.

*****

How dare he?

Even as Blake wiped streaming tears from her eyes, she knew that the question, as embarrassing as it was, was an honest one. Ever since her mother was killed and the humiliating stutter began, she had been asked the same question countless times.

Her father was brutal about it, demanding that she stop that 'ridiculous affectation' because she sounded 'feeble-minded.' Eager to please her one remaining parent, she tried desperately—but her fraught efforts only made her stammer harder.

If I could control it, I would!

Blake wiped more tears away and walked around her wagon to discover what damage had been inflicted on her clothes.

The line was down and some of the clothes were trampled. She examined each piece as she retrieved it, assessing the needed repairs. One shirt was destroyed. Three socks were missing. The trousers were still wearable, thank goodness.

And everything needed to be washed again.

Blake sighed and went inside her wagon to change her rags, hoping the wool trousers were not stained. There was no time once the alarm was sounded for her to do more than pull on her pants and boots before grabbing her rifle and running to the task.

Unfortunately, they were stained.

Blake donned her fourth and final pair of trousers and added the newly soiled pants to the pile before heading to the breakfast fires.

I hope we stay here another day so I can do my laundry again.

*****

"We'll stay another day so we can butcher a few of the buffalo," Leif told the people gathered around the breakfast fires. "Are any of your animals hurt?"

A few of the men nodded and raised their hands, including the family with the pregnant mare.

"My gelding was outside of the circle," one man spoke up. "He's hurt bad."

Leif walked toward him with purpose. "Let's go now."

Thankfully, there was no sign of Stefan. Blake made a quick meal of boiled oats with a little sugar before heading to the river with her bundle.

She was disheartened to see that the buffalo herd apparently crossed the river—or at least tried to—and their attempt had stirred up the mud. She decided not to worry about the shirts for now, but the trousers were a necessity.

If they get browner, it will not matter.

Blake took off her boots and socks and rolled up the legs of her wool pants. She waded into the river as far as she could while keeping both her footing and her pants dry.

Mostly dry.

She bent over and rinsed the three pair of trousers to remove the caked-on mud, then applied a bar of lye soap to the blood stains. She scrubbed the fabric against itself until the stains were as close to gone as she could manage to get them under these conditions. Then she carried the sopping garments back to the shore.

No one else had ventured to the river yet, so after putting her socks and boots back on she gathered her wet bundle and headed back to her wagon.

Chapter Ten

Stefan lifted his chin and sniffed.

He looked at the man who owned the ox with the cracked hoof. "Do you smell smoke?"

The man mimicked his action then nodded. "Is that not from the cooking fires?"

"I hope so." He lowered the animal's injured foot. "I can bind his hoof with a salve and he might recover if it does not fester. But he cannot be in the harness."

"Damn." The man hawked and spat on the ground. "What good is he now? Just a mouth to feed for nothing."

"You could let him forage for food while you wait to see if he will recover," Stefan suggested. "There may be hope."

The man snorted. "Nah. Leave him be."

Stefan touched the brim of his hat and walked away. When he heard the gunshot from the other side of the wagon he was not surprised.

He sniffed again. The scent of this smoke was definitely different from the camp cooking fires. And it was coming toward him on the wind.

Shit.

Stefan broke into a run.

Buck Schultz stood on top of the chuck wagon with binocular telescopes pressed to his eyes. When Stefan rounded the wagon to get an unobstructed view of the northern horizon, he saw what Buck was looking at.

Smoke rising from a wide swath in the distance.

"That's what spooked the buffalo," Buck growled. "Prairie fire. Probably started by the lightning."

Buck lowered the implement. "The wind is blowing this way, men. That means the fire is headed toward us."

He climbed down from the top of the wagon. "Get everyone up and moving *right now*. We need to cross the river before it catches us."

The mechanics and scouts trotted in opposite directions around the circle of wagons to instruct the settlers to move, and move quickly.

Stefan searched for Leif, and found him bent over, examining an open gash on the leg of a gray gelding.

"You smell smoke?" he called out as he approached.

"Yeah." Leif did not cease his examination. "Why?"

Stefan stopped beside the men. "That is not the cooking fires."

Leif straightened, his expression alarmed. "Prairie fire?"

Stefan nodded. "Probably started by lightning. That is what spooked the buffalo."

The horse owner paled. "What will we do?"

"We cross the river," Stefan stated. "And we do it now."

*****

Blake harnessed her oxen with shaking fingers. The smoke she smelled when she was hanging up her clothes was stronger now. Tom-tom told her about the lightning and the fire.

"Get across the river, Somersby. Do not dawdle."

"Y-yes sir."

All around her she heard panicked voices calling for children and the cacophony of jangling harnesses, lowing oxen, and neighing horses—all resulting from the scent of doom carried towards them on the wind.

Blake climbed into her driver's seat and shouted, "Step up!" She slapped the reins on the oxen's backs to punctuate the command.

As the beasts leaned into their traces and started the wagon moving, Blake looked to see where the wagons were crossing.

Tom-tom and the other scout were gesturing for the wagons to follow them. Blake did.

About a quarter mile upriver was a shallow run of rapids. "This is your best bet!" Tom-tom hollered. "But be careful! Let your animals find their own footing!"

The first wagon driver urged his oxen forward. When they balked, he handed the reins to his son and jumped down to lead the front pair of his team. Once they got moving through the knee-deep water, two more wagons entered the river side-by-side.

So far, so good.

Blake disappeared into her wagon and removed her only pair of dry trousers. If she had to go in the river as well, she wanted something dry to put on when she got out.

She flinched as she pulled the wet woolen trousers over her legs. As cold as they were wet, she knew that wet wool still held warmth, while wet cotton or linen did not.

Before returning to the driver's seat, she hung the dry pants from the top of the center stave in the wagon.

As the line in front of her grew shorter, the sunlight grew dimmer, shrouded by a thickening, smoky haze. Blake drove her team around the waiting wagons to a spot slightly farther upstream. The water was calmer there and she could see the bottom of the shallow river.

Stefan rode up to her on a beautiful dark gray stallion with black points. "Do not go in there, Somersby."

Blake frowned. "Why not? I can see the bottom. It's

shallow here."

"It's shallow with sediment, stopped by the rapids. The same way wind is stopped and snow drifts form," Stefan warned. "Your team will sink into it. If you go in, you won't get them or your wagon out."

Blake turned her team back toward the rapids, glad for the warning but embarrassed she did not realize the danger for herself.

But how could she know?

I have never done anything like this before.

Stefan led the way back and made a turn at the upper end of the rough, rushing water.

He pointed to his right. "Go here."

Blake obeyed and urged her team forward, but they balked just as the first team to cross did. Blake made a disgusted sound and resolutely imitated the first man's actions.

Blake yelped when she jumped into the river. The water swirling around her knees was freezing.

She had solid footing, though. She grabbed the closest ox's harness and pulled. "Come on. Let's get out of here."

She tugged and shouted, "Step up! Step up!"

Her little team started to move. Remembering the admonition to let the beasts find their own footing, Blake walked slowly through the frigid water that splashed around rocks and soaked her to the waist.

She was shivering uncontrollably and could not feel her feet when she reached the far side, a hundred yards distant.

But she was safe.

Blake clenched her jaw to keep her teeth from chattering and drove her wagon up from the river's edge to join the dozen wagons which had safely made the crossing thus far. She ducked behind her wagon's protective flaps and pulled off her sopping wet trousers.

She retrieved the woolen pants which she hung out of the water's way and pulled them on, glad for their warmth. She also changed her menstrual rags while she had the chance, and swapped dry socks and shoes for her waterlogged boots.

I wonder how long it will take them to dry.

She had finally stopped shivering but her toes were still numb.

Blake tied back the flaps of her wagon again to check on the other wagons' progress. What she saw from the slight rise gripped her chest with panic.

Flames.

Closing in on the waiting wagons not yet in the water.

Hurry up!

Get in the river!

She wanted to shout a warning but the tightness in her throat told her she would not be able to get any words out smoothly.

She watched as Stefan and Leif rode their mounts into the river repeatedly, pulling the reins of reluctant teams of oxen who were panicking at the ash-laden smoke blowing around them.

Horses neighed and pulled at their tethers, until Tom-tom shouted at the boys riding in the various wagons to untie the horses and ride them across.

The only thing slowing the progress of the fire was that the grass was trampled into the churned-up soil when the buffalo changed direction, avoiding the guns and the gathered wagons.

It was slowed, but not stopped.

Half a dozen wagons remained when one of the canvas canopies began to smoke.

Blake gasped, and her hand covered her mouth.

Not the Waldons.

*****

Stephan wanted to punch the man with the piano for being stupid enough to pack such a ridiculous item in the first place.

"You have to move—now!" he shouted.

"I am trying!" he shouted back.

Stefan reined Sterk around and saw smoke coming from the Waldon's canopy.

"Fire!" he shouted and kicked Sterk in their direction. "Do you have a bucket?"

Mary Waldon pushed the canopy out of the way and threw a bucket at Stefan who caught it.

"Keep moving!" he bellowed. He jumped from the saddle and hurried to fill the bucket. He turned around and faced Frank doing the same.

Who is driving the wagon?

Stefan looked up and saw Mary at the reins, urging the team forward. He shook off his surprise and splashed the bucket's load of water on the canopy as the first pair of the team stepped into the water.

Frank threw his bucket of water on the canopy as well but it still smoked. Both men repeated their actions while Mary resolutely drove the quartet of oxen into the river.

Stefan grabbed Sterk's reins and vaulted into the saddle. The stallion remained in place like he was trained to do, but with Stefan back in the saddle he pranced nervously and shook his head, eager to get away from the encroaching flames.

Stefan followed the Waldon's wagon into the river, leaving the remaining five wagons—including the piano guy—to the care of other members of the wagon train's staff.

Somersby was closer to the Waldons than any other family on the journey so Stefan was determined to see them to safety.

Unfortunately, the fire had other plans.

The smoking section of canvas burst into flames.

Frank was walking in the water so he filled a bucket and handed it to Stefan. Stefan tried to douse the flames from his elevated position while Frank refilled the second empty bucket which Stefan still had possession of.

Six cycles later the fire was quenched, though the hole it left in the wagon's cover was sizeable.

"And our bedding is soaked," Mary said sadly when they

reached the far side and assessed the damage.

"At least we still have bedding," Frank countered.

"It could have been much worse," Stefan added.

He held Sterk's reins tightly as the stallion snorted and watched with white-rimmed eyes as the fire teased the opposite bank of the river. Ash rained over the group and smoke stung Stefan's nostrils.

Somersby hurried over, his face a mask of worry. "Are you-you well? What a-about the children?"

"We are all fine," Mary answered stalwartly. "A few repairs and a day of sunshine and we shall be right as rain."

A loud, discordantly melodic crash pulled their attention to the river. The last wagon to cross moved forward, leaving the crooked corpse of a piano jutting from the rapids while water rushed around the new obstacle in a sinister hug.

"Good riddance," Stefan muttered. "Who carries a piano on a nearly nine-hundred-mile wagon train?"

Somersby looked up at him, his expression earnest. "I saw you helping Frank p-out out the fire. Thank you."

The youth's sincere gratitude warmed Stefan's chest. "I was glad to help. I know they are your friends."

Somersby's expression shifted. "You helped them because of me?"

Blazes.

How do I get out of this?

"No. I—I helped them because it is part of my job," he deflected.

Somersby's eyes widened and his cheeks flushed.

"Of c-course." He turned an awkward smile to Mary. "I am g-glad you are safe."

Once again, he quickly walked away before Stefan could apologize. Stefan's shoulders slumped.

Damn.

He needed to figure Somersby out before the youth drove him completely out of his mind.

*****

Blake was drying her boots and trousers next to three fires where she was roasting large chunks of fresh buffalo meat. She rubbed them with a blend of spices before setting the spits in place and the resultant aroma was very satisfying.

Stefan approached. He sat on one end of the bench that Blake was sitting on. She slid to the opposite end.

"Can we talk?" he asked quietly.

Blake's gaze skittered in all directions to ascertain who might be listening. Seeing that the nearby families were occupied with reorganizing the contents of their wagons and hanging things to dry, she turned her attention back to Stefan.

"I suppose we c-can. If you can manage to b-be civil."

"*I*—" Stefan shut his mouth before he said anything else.

Blake was surprised that she dared to challenge him. She doubted that many people ever did.

It was probably good for him, then.

Stefan took off his hat and combed his fingers through his wavy auburn hair. "I am sorry that I mentioned the stutter."

So that is where we are starting.

Blake nodded her acceptance of the apology, but said nothing.

"You are right," he continued. "It is not my concern."

Stefan looked so sincerely remorseful that Blake took pity on him. She heaved a steadying sigh and prepared to enter an uncomfortable conversation.

"No, it is not. B-but… the answer is no. I d-did not always stutter."

"When did it start?" Stefan smacked himself in the forehead. "Agh! Again, I am sorry. I cannot seem to remember my own words today."

Blake chuckled in spite of herself. The man was darned charming when he was not trying to be.

"I cannot think you want to hear my sad t-tale today. It has been a long d-day already."

Stefan did not reply.

Blake stood and went to each fire to turn the spit and adjust the cast-iron pans which were propped underneath to catch any juices from the lean meat.

When she sat back down, Stefan was still quiet for a minute before he said, "In truth, I do want to know."

"Curious?" Blake poked.

Stefan's brow puckered. "Only because I want to understand you better."

Now Blake was quiet, pondering the risks of allowing him to know her more deeply.

After Santa Fe I will never see him again, so what does it matter?

"I saw my mother m-murdered—b-by Indians—when I was five."

Stefan's only visible reaction were his briefly widened eyes. "I am so sorry."

Blake shuddered. "It was t-truly t-terrifying for me, as you can imagine."

"How…" Stefan stopped and pressed his lips together.

"We were traveling from Saint Louis to K-kansas City when we were attacked by rogue g-group of Sauk. They were angry about b-being moved out of Missouri."

Blake stared into the fire, hoping to burn away the memories going through her mind like a grotesque stage play. "My mother t-tried to fight them—to keep them from g-getting ahold of me, my father always said later—when one of them sliced her-her throat."

Blake drew a ragged breath, forcing air into a chest that had tightened uncomfortably. "Her b-blood spurted everywhere. It was an impossible, p-pulsing fountain of red. It ruined my favorite—"

Blake gasped.

I almost said dress.

Be careful!

"My favorite t-toy. A s-stuffed horse with real hair." That was also true.

If he noticed her falter, Stefan did not show it. "That would indeed be truly terrifying for anyone, no matter their age."

Blake nodded, not trusting her voice.

"And that is when you started to stutter?" he asked softly.

She nodded and risked looking into his eyes. "Only when I am nervous or uncomfortable. As you p-pointed out."

Stefan held her gaze for a moment, then cleared his throat and looked into the fire. "I *did* help the Waldons because they are your friends."

Blake's spirits rose dramatically. She turned and smiled at the fire. "Thank you, again."

"I do not know why I said otherwise."

"It d-does not matter."

Stefan sighed and ran his fingers through his hair again. "Anyway, I apologize for that, too."

"Forgiven."

He held his right hand to the side. "Friends?"

Blake gave it a firm shake. "Yes. Friends."

Chapter Eleven

March 29, 1845

After a day of respite, the wagon train was on the move again. Stefan sat in the saddle and watched the wagons roll slowly along the river on the unburned side of the prairie. Seeing how many miles it took them to finally put the blackened ground behind them was sobering.

Thank You for saving us.

Stefan spent the night of the stampede and fire wrestling with his feelings about Somersby. He really liked the youth. Not in a physical way, of course, but in a protective sort of way. Whenever the somber young man deigned to smile, it made Stefan's mood lift.

Poor kid has had it real rough.

Stefan finally came to the conclusion that he should just be Somersby's friend, and not concern himself that his friendship might be misconstrued as anything else. If that ever happened, he would deal with it then.

So yesterday Stefan paid closer attention, watching how Somersby spent the day and with whom. Stefan saw that he spent his time either alone, or with the handful of women on the train. He gave lots of cooking advice and talked about their children.

Stefan found that confusing.

Was he spending time with the women because he actually liked women and hoped for a romantic connection with one of their daughters?

Or, was he with the women because he thought as they did about things. Including men.

Stefan scratched his chin, reaching through a month's growth of beard. That was another thing.

On the trail, most of the men gave up shaving and sprouted facial hair. Some beards were sparse and patchy while others would make a hibernating bear proud. But Somersby's face was smooth as a baby's.

Is his preference for men the reason *he does not have a beard?*

Was it possible that could happen?

Stefan shook his head, completely flummoxed about what to think.

All I know is that he makes the best biscuits I have ever had.

And in the end, that was reason enough to befriend the singular young man.

Stefan nudged Sterk into motion and rode up alongside Somersby's wagon.

*****

Blake turned her head toward the sound of horse hooves. Seeing Stefan approach always made her stomach quiver, and not in an entirely unpleasant way.

When he reached her side, she pointed at the sky. "Are we going to get rained on?"

Stefan tipped his head back and considered the low, heavy-bottomed clouds. "I would not be surprised."

Blake grunted like the men did. "My clothes are not

completely dry as yet."

"What have you done with them?"

Interesting question since Stefan seemed to wear the same thing every day. Is that because he had to do his own laundry?

Blake tossed a thumb over her shoulder. "I strung a rope through the wagon to hang them on. I have the flaps open to let the breeze go through."

Stefan rode around to the back of the wagon and Blake twisted in the driver's seat to see what he was doing. He seemed to be examining the contents inside.

Thank goodness I tossed my used rags in the river last night.

Bloody rags would guarantee questions, no matter how they became soiled.

"What are you doing?" Blake demanded.

"You are very neat," came the reply.

Blake scoffed. "Cleanliness is next to godliness, is that not what they say?"

Stefan's laugh reached her through the hanging laundry. He kicked his mount and came up on her other side. "You seemed to have packed lightly, compared to the others."

That sounded like a compliment.

"I am starting a new life in Santa Fe. And a restaurant, I hope." *There. I said it out loud.* "I will buy what I need when I get there."

Stefan's brow furrowed. "That will require money."

Blake rolled her eyes. Of *course* it would. Did he think her a fool?

"I have a little bit." She shrugged. "Enough to start."

Stefan rode alongside her for a while, examining the sky and not meeting her eyes. Blake sensed he wanted to ask her something, but did not wish to encourage his probing into her past any more than he was already wont to.

She decided to head him off. "So, you never married?"

Stefan's head jerked back in her direction. "What?"

"Married," she repeated.

"No, I was not married. Am not."

He looked uncomfortable.

"And your brother?" she pressed.

He shook his head. "No."

Blake found that confusing. A man as good-looking and capable as Stefan Hansen must have had women falling all over him back in— "Where are you from?"

He seemed relieved at the apparent change of subject. "Cheltenham. Ten miles southwest of Saint Louis."

"Are there no women in Cheltenham?"

Stefan's jaw went momentarily slack. "Of course there are women in Cheltenham, *and* in Saint Louis where we spent most of our time."

"You and Leif."

"Yes."

Blake decided to lay out her hand. "I do not understand how two educated, eligible bachelors have survived until the age of thirty-and-something without being ensnared into marriage. I mean, it is not as if either of you is in any way hard on the eyes."

Stefan appeared stricken. "I cannot say I am particularly good looking."

Blake huffed a laugh. "Leif is lean and muscular, with kind eyes and a warm smile. You are well over six feet in height, you have thick hair, and very blue eyes."

Stefan was clearly growing more uncomfortable by the minute. "That may be true, but it's not important."

"It *is* important to someone looking for a potential mate," she countered. "And you know that men are the same way. The pretty girls always get the marriage proposals."

A huge raindrop hit Blake's hat. And then another. Then three more.

Stefan looked up. "It's going to come down hard."

"Will we stop?" She honestly did not know how rain would affect the wagon train's progress.

He shook his head and peered forward. "Not unless the ground washes out from under us." He returned his gaze to hers. "I have enjoyed our conversation, but I must get back to work."

He kicked Sterk's sides and cantered off leaving a very bemused Blake to ponder why a man such as Stefan was so uninterested in marriage.

And why his brother chose to remain single as well.

March 31, 1845

For two full days the skies opened up and drenched the dry prairie with more rain than she could handle. Low spots filled with water creating sudden ponds which the wagons had to maneuver around. The Arkansas River swelled, breeching her banks and sending tendrils in all directions. There was not a dry spot for miles in the treeless expanse.

And because they were now on the opposite side of the river from the Santa Fe Trail, Buck Schultz needed to keep the river in sight until they reached the spot where the trail made the crossing.

Stefan was exhausted. With the ground as soggy as it was, none of the hostlers, scouts, or mechanics could sleep under the chuck and supply wagons. That meant the men crawled inside those wagons and found whatever level space they could to lie on and try to rest.

"I never expected to wish to sleep on the ground again," he muttered to Leif as the men plodded along on their wet horses. He snugged the collar of his leather coat closer to his neck. Rain had already run down the inside of his shirt so the effort was basically ineffective.

"It cannot keep up much longer." Leif sounded more hopeful than he looked. "And there should not be any dust for days afterwards."

Stefan twisted in his saddle to look back at Somersby. The man sat dejectedly in his driver's seat staring at nothing. Stefan decided to mention the question the youth asked him a couple of days ago.

He turned his attention back to Leif. "Why aren't we married?"

Leif looked horrified. "To each other?"

Stefan yanked off his soggy hat and hit his brother with it. "Are you daft?"

Leif knocked the hat aside. "Then phrase your questions better, idiot!"

Stefan growled and tried again. "Why have neither one of us ever courted a woman and asked her to become a wife?"

"Are you seriously asking this question?" Leif looked at Stefan like he was the daft one.

"Yes. Well, no. But..." Stefan shrugged, sending another cold rivulet of water down his shirt. "Perhaps I am."

Leif chuckled. "The whoring for one. A man does not seek a single woman when he enjoys many women."

Stefan knew that was true. Whenever the urges grew strong he simply went to one of Aunt Rosie's establishments for the night.

"And, if we are honest, we have never had a steady income of our own." Leif looked embarrassed by that. "Sure, one day we'll inherit something—you more than me, obviously. But while we have played at different occupations, we have never stuck with one long enough to make a go of it."

That was true.

"What do you think of the trade posts along the trail?" Stefan asked. "I want your honest opinion."

Leif expression turned pensive. "We saw evidence that people do dump their things when that German guy hove his piano into the river."

Stefan waved a finger in the air. "And before that we passed two crates of books and a box of broken pottery."

Leif brows lifted. "We did?"

"Yeah. It was when the wagons were spread out. I was still following the trail's tracks."

"Oh."

The brothers rode without talking for a couple minutes, then Leif said, "I think the idea has merit. I really do."

"But?" Stefan prodded.

"But—the key will be trading things people actually need, not just the possessions they give up."

Stefan agreed. "Food, for certain. Grain. Dried buffalo meat would be easy to stock."

"Hatchets. Rope." Leif scratched his lightly bearded chin and looked around them. "Lumber for sure."

Stefan snorted a laugh. "That piano was made from wood. And piano wires are strong. We can salvage supplies from what people abandon."

"Good thinking." Leif shot him a sideways glance. "What will this cost to set up?"

Good question.

"We only need a single room cabin at each location to begin with. The proprietor can bed down in the rafters." Stefan looked at Leif for confirmation. "Twenty foot square?"

Leif nodded. "Figure five or six hundred dollars to build. We get the wood cut in Kansas City and assemble the cabins on site."

Stefan snapped his fingers and grinned. "We will use sod for the roofs. Like in Norway. There is an endless supply, after all."

"How close together should the posts be?" Leif asked. "It took us eleven days to reach Council Grove."

"That was about one hundred and forty miles from Independence—one-sixth of the total miles." Stefan did the computations in his head. "So if we place one every one-hundred and forty miles, that means four posts."

Leif smiled. "I like it."

"So do I. And we will have the entire journey covered with only four posts." Stephan felt relieved and excited, like he had a realistic plan and a solid purpose for the first time in his adult life. "If we say a thousand dollars per post, plus a thousand in travel and salary costs, I think we could do this."

Leif chuckled. "All we need are investors."

Stefan winked at his brother. "That will be the easy part."

April 1, 1845

Apparently, the sun decided that the settlers had suffered enough and decided to push the clouds away. One month after starting this fraught adventure, Blake awoke to a morning with no rain and no bleeding.

She felt reborn.

Though her boots were still damp, her clothes were finally dry after hanging in her wagon for three days. She was able to wear the cotton and linen trousers again and change into a clean shirt and dry socks.

And there was no mud.

Because the wagon train was forced to cross the river early to escape the prairie fire, they were traveling over virgin grass instead of the worn tracks from previous wagon trains. The journey was turning out to be quite tolerable.

Late this morning the settlers reached the point where the trail crossed the Arkansas River and rejoined that path. That meant they were almost half of the way to Santa Fe.

It also meant that the discards which Blake had heard about were starting to litter the trail.

As he usually did now, Stefan rode up to her wagon once the train was moving.

"Look at what's being dumped!" he exclaimed. "Such a waste."

Blake agreed. "I guess some people have a hard time deciding what is a necessity and what is not."

Stefan flashed a conspiratorial grin. "Have I told you about my idea for setting up actual trading posts along the Santa Fe Trail?"

Blake was intrigued by his puckish expression. "No, you have not. What do you mean by 'actual' trading posts?"

As Stefan outlined his plan, Blake became excited. It was both clever and sensible.

"Setting up four stations seems manageable enough," she observed. "And I could even see little communities growing up around them."

"Huh. I had not considered that." Stefan nodded pensively. "You could be right."

Communities that could perhaps support a little café?

"How nice it would be for the families if they could purchase a reasonably priced meal there that they did not have to cook," Blake mused.

Stefan's attention focused on her. He was obviously considering that idea. "I am not sure there would be enough business."

Blake was not going to give up the idea too quickly. "How many wagon trains travel in a year?"

Stefan's brows pulled together. "I actually do not know. I suppose that is important information, though. I will ask Buck."

Blake watched him ride off on that beautiful stallion of his and wondered what other twists might arise. The thought that she could own more than one café was intriguing. And exciting.

Stefan was beaming when he returned. "Two hundred and fifty wagons last year!"

Blake was gobsmacked. "There are twenty-nine in this train. If the average train is thirty wagons that makes at least eight trains traveling a year."

"One after the other." Stefan squinted in thought as his gaze met hers. "That also makes a thousand times a wagon would stop at one of my trading posts."

And if each wagon carried four people, the possible number of meals served would be four thousand.

Blake almost told Stefan that she would invest on the spot, but something held her back. She had only known him a month after all, and under false pretenses at that.

Aside from the fact that he may want to kill her when he found out she was actually a woman, he might also balk at taking on a female as a business partner.

There would be plenty of time to make the offer once they reached Santa Fe. Biding her time for now was definitely the sensible plan.

"That is an impressive number. And certainly, an intriguing idea," she said noncommittally as she turned her attention to the path in front of her. "I think you should continue to work on it."

Chapter Twelve

Stefan rode off in search of Leif, the new numbers bouncing through his thoughts. He had not considered how much business the posts would require to be profitable, but with settlers streaming west by the hundreds he was sure there would be a way to succeed.

He found Leif at the front of the line riding on the side of the trail and leading the family with the pregnant mare who wanted to stop and graze at very short intervals.

"They will be at the back of the line when we gather at the end of the day," Leif said. "But they can start at the beginning again tomorrow and do the same thing."

Stefan thought that was a good plan. "How close is she?"

"A week? Two at the most, I reckon."

"Have you noticed all of the dumped belongings along the trail?" Stefan could hardly contain himself. "And did you know that last year there were two-hundred and fifty wagons that traveled along the Santa Fe?"

Leif's surprised reaction was gratifying. "Is that true?"

Stefan grinned. "Yep. Buck Schultz told me himself."

"With four posts, that means almost a thousand wagon stops!" Leif slapped his thigh. "We will be rich!"

"Well, at the least we should be able to make a solid go of it."

Stefan noticed a pile of sodden material ahead, tucked under a low granite outcropping off to the side of the trail ahead. "Speaking of discarded things, why would anyone throw away fabric? It is not heavy and generally useful."

Leif shrugged. "I have no idea what people are thinking."

But when the pair got closer, Stefan's gut twisted.

The heap of material had hair.

Long, black, tangled hair.

Stefan leapt from his saddle. "Leif—it is a body."

He knelt beside the crumpled and filthy form. His knees sunk into the still-damp ground, and his pulse thrummed in his ears. Stefan stretched his hand over the still figure and hesitated, hoping for some sign of life. There was none. He gently turned the body toward him.

The woman exhaled a faint moan.

"It's a woman, Leif!" Stefan called over his shoulder. "And she's alive!"

His gaze skimmed the woman's mud-smeared face. Dark brows arched over blackened eyes and her nose appeared to be broken. Her lips were blue with cold.

She was dressed in the costume of the Indians Stefan was familiar with in Missouri, so he guessed she might be Sauk or Fox. She mumbled something Stefan could not understand.

Leif leaned over his shoulder and spoke to the woman.

Stefan looked at him. "What did you say?"

"I asked for her name." Leif repeated the question, adding more words.

"Che—chenoh—ah."

"We need to take her to the medical wagon." Stefan wiggled his arms under her body and hugged her to his chest as he stood.

She moaned again and her brow knit in pain.

Stefan could not mount Sterk with the woman in his arms. "I will carry her. Will you lead Sterk?"

"Yes." Leif grabbed the stallion's reins and mounted

Heder. "I will ride ahead and tell them you are coming."

"Thanks."

Stefan strode past the wagon Leif had been leading. Five pairs of curious but concerned eyes watched his progress. He understood what they might be thinking.

Rescuing a Fox or Sauk Indian squaw was risky business. The woman was alone and battered for a reason. Either she was banished and under punishment, or she had run away.

If she ran away, the tribe would probably want her back.

And I cannot think that she will want to go.

Stefan decided to worry about that if the woman survived. For now, he moved as quickly and smoothly as he could, not wanting to accidentally misplace a broken bone and cause the woman more harm.

She moaned again and squirmed weakly.

"Shhh." Stefan said quietly. "Be still. I will not hurt you."

He was almost at the medical wagon when her eyes fluttered open and met his. What he saw made him stop still in shock.

Her eyes were blue.

Pale blue.

"You are not Indian," he said aloud.

Her brief response was raw and rough. "Help…"

*****

Stefan and Leif rode alongside the wagon while the doctor examined the mystery woman.

"She must have been abducted at some point," Leif posited. "She is dressed like an Indian and speaks Sauk—or Fox—but if her eyes are as pale as you say, then she is at least half white."

"At least," Stefan agreed. "I hope she is able to tell us where she came from."

The flap of the medical wagon opened and the doctor

waived the men inside. "I hope you speak Indian."

"I do. Stef, you wait outside." Leif dismounted and tied Heder to the back of the wagon, then climbed inside.

Stefan wanted to be inside the wagon out of curiosity, but realized that probably was not a good idea. Between Leif and the doctor, he would only be in the way.

Stefan was about to give in to his curiosity and climb inside the wagon anyway when Leif reappeared.

"Thank you. I will be back with food." Leif jumped down from the moving wagon and untied his gelding. Once he was back in the saddle, he told Stefan what he learned.

"She used the fire and the storm to escape from a tribe of Fox Indians. Apparently, she was taken at the age of fourteen and forced into marriage with the chief's nephew."

"How old is she now?" Stefan asked.

"She is not sure. She asked what year this is and when I told her she looked confused and said she must be twenty-five."

"So she speaks English?" Stefan continued. "She seemed to understand me when I said I would not hurt her. And she asked for help in English."

"I think so." Leif's expression was uncertain. "She mixed her languages when she was talking to me, but I believe that was the result of her recent experiences and injuries."

"The fire was five days ago." Stefan frowned. "Has she been without food or shelter for that long?"

"Yes." Leif swallowed thickly. "She found the wagon trail and was following it, hoping to find help. But the doctor said one more day out in the prairie would have been her last."

Stefan sucked a breath. "Thank God we found her."

"Exactly." Leif. drew a deep breath. "Doc says she can stay in the medical wagon for a day or two, but because she is only badly bruised and weak from hunger. She cannot stay longer than that."

"Then what do we do with her?"

Leif wagged his head slowly. "All I know is, she is never *ever* going back."

April 4, 1845

Stefan and Leif managed to find enough materials to coble together a cart for Chenoa, as she was called by the Fox, to ride in until she was strong enough to walk.

With the illicit help of the train's mechanics, staves were added and canvas stretched over them to provide protection from the sun, and would probably be effective in a gentle rain as well.

"Not like the storm we just had," Leif said as he fashioned a harness for Heder to pull the cart. "But if the weather turns again, perhaps one of the families will take her in for a day."

For some reason, Stefan thought of Blake—but that made no sense. The young man could not host a female in his wagon even if he had no physical interest in her gender.

Besides that, Stefan had not yet told the youth about their fugitive. With Blake's traumatic history of watching a Sauk man slice his mother's throat, Stefan thought it best to remain silent until Leif figured out what to do with the woman.

Even though Stefan initially found her, Leif had definitely taken over the care of Chenoa. And while that made sense because he could communicate with her more easily than anyone else, Stefan knew his brother well enough to recognize that it had swiftly become far more than that.

Leif was smitten.

Probably because of his own upbringing in Norway as the bastard orphan of a nobleman who never acknowledged him. Leif struggled to survive by working in the royal stables until Stefan—or more accurately, Nicolas—happened into his life.

Leif knew what it was like to be an outcast. One who needed to find a way to survive until he could somehow be rescued from the depths to stand in the light of acceptance.

Chenoa had the wherewithal to escape.

Now Leif wrapped her with safety and acceptance.

Stefan helped Leif with the harness adjustments until the cart was secure.

"You help Heder grow accustomed to that contraption,

and I am going to warn Blake that we have a Fox refugee traveling with us now."

"She is a white woman," Leif cautioned.

"I know." Stefan flashed an apologetic smile. "And I will remind him of that fact."

*****

Stefan squatted beside the cooking fire where Somersby was adding spices to a simmering supper pot. "Have you heard anything about the fugitive Leif and I came across?"

"Fugitive?" The young man straightened and looked at him with a puzzled expression. "Fugitive from what?"

"She was taken by Indians, probably ten years ago." Stefan watched Somersby's reaction carefully. "She used the fire and then the storm as a chance to escape. We found her unconscious by the trail three days ago."

Somersby's gaze darted around the dark featureless prairie. "Are there Indians here now?"

Stefan stayed low, hoping that would encourage Somersby to relax his stance. "Not close by, we do not think. She had been walking for days."

The youth's eyes met his. "Where is she?"

"She has been riding in the medical wagon, but Leif has constructed a cart for her. Heder will pull it until she is strong enough to walk again."

Somersby reached for a narrow wooden paddle and stirred the stew.

"Which Indians?" he asked with his eyes fixed determinedly on the steaming pot.

"Fox."

Somersby nodded. "They are joined with the Sauk."

"They are," Stefan admitted.

Somersby sniffed and ran a sleeve across his cheek.

Stefan kept his voice low. "How do you feel?"

The young man faced him, his eyes red and brimming. "I c-cannot imagine how s-scared she was, the poor thing."

Stefan did not expect that. "Her connection with the Sauk does not upset you?"

His brow furrowed and his expression was disbelieving. "Why would it? She survived. And now she is safe."

April 6, 1845

Two days later Stefan and Leif brought the woman to meet Blake. She was dressed in a mishmash of Fox leathers, a settler's blouse, and a jacket. Blake was not certain how she would react when she saw the Indian trappings, but the moment she looked into the woman's pale blue eyes, any trepidation she might have felt evaporated.

"Come and sit." Blake gestured toward the little bench she sat on when she cooked. "Will you share our supper?"

The woman nodded and sat on the bench.

Blake went back to filleting the fish Frank caught in the river. Biscuits were already baking in the fire. "What is your name?"

"The Fox called me Chenoa," she said hesitantly—it was clear she was readjusting to her first language. "But I used to be called Dorcas."

Blake glanced at Leif, wondering what he called her before she asked Chenoa the obvious question. "Which do you prefer?"

She did not answer right away. Her gaze dropped to the grass. Blake looked to Leif again.

"I told her Chenoa was a beautiful name," he offered.

"It means dove," she whispered, her attention still on the ground.

"It is a beautiful name," Blake said softly. "But does it hurt you?"

The woman's gaze jumped to Blake's. "You understand."

Blake turned her regard to Stefan and Leif. She got the sense that the presence of the men was preventing the woman from speaking freely.

"Don't you two have anything you need to be doing?" she asked the brothers.

A startled glance passed between the men.

"We were going to check on the mare again," Stefan replied.

"Do you mind if we go do that, and then return?" Leif asked his charge.

Blake easily saw his sincere concern for the woman's comfort and well-being. She wondered if he was developing feelings for her that went beyond merely protecting her.

She is beautiful.

"I am fine." She offered Leif a small smile. "You go."

She watched the brothers walk away then turned back to Blake. "I never liked Dorcas."

"But Chenoa reminds you of the Fox."

"Yes."

Blake continued preparing the fish to keep the woman—and herself—calm. "Why did you escape?"

"I was fourteen when they took me. I was given to the chief's nephew to be a wife. He had many more years than I."

"You must have been terrified." Blake wondered if the brothers had told the woman about her own experience.

The woman nodded. "I knew nothing of men. And he was not patient."

"He raped you." It was not a question.

Her voice was barely above a whisper. "Every time."

Blake was shocked. "For ten years?"

"I only now know how long."

Blake could not imagine such a hopeless existence. "Did you bear children?"

And if so, did she leave them behind?

"No. And that was bad of me." The woman wiped her eyes. "And with every moon, my husband was more angry."

"He beat you." Again, it was not a question.

She nodded. "When the fire came, I hid in the river. I think if I die, I do not care. I must get away. When it passed me, I got out of the river and walked to find the trail."

"How many days did you walk?"

"I saw the sun rise three times. Then I do not remember anything."

Blake rolled the fish fillets in flour and dropped them into the pan of oil heating over the fire. For the next few minutes the satisfying sizzle of the fish was the only sound.

Then Blake said, "A Sauk killed my mother when I was five. I watched him slit her throat."

The other woman sighed shakily. "You are lucky you were too young to bed."

Blake startled. Shock fizzed through her veins. Before that moment she had never considered the attack from that perspective.

But this poor woman was right. She *was* lucky. Something inside her flipped and she suddenly felt free.

Then the reality of the woman's words sunk in.

Too young to bed.

Blake turned rounded eyes on her companion. "What?"

Chenoa leaned closer. "How do they not see you are woman?"

Chapter Thirteen

Stefan and Leif examined the pregnant mare.

"I would say any day now," Stefan stated.

"And I would agree." Leif looked at the husband of the family. "You do know that the foal will not be able walk all day with the mare."

He exchanged a startled look with his wife. "We had not considered that."

"Well, consider it now." Stefan rolled down his sleeve after he rinsed off his arm.

Leif mimicked his brother's actions. "Find us when she starts to labor. And I do mean starts."

"Yes." The man nodded, still looking stunned. "We will."

The brothers headed back to Blake's fire.

"Do you think they are getting along?" Leif sounded anxious.

"I do," Stefan replied. "They both had terrible experiences with Indians, so Somersby can understand some of Chenoa's trials."

Leif looked sideways at him. "But talking to a man?"

Stefan huffed. "Sort of a man, anyway. And he is young and fairly sensitive. I think Chenoa will find him empathetic."

Leif sighed. "I suppose that is what counts."

As the men approached, Chenoa leaned back as though she had just whispered a secret in Somersby's ear.

"The fish smells wonderful!" Stefan's belly rumbled.

"There is enough for the two of you," Somersby answered the question Stefan did not ask. "Frank and his son had a very successful day."

Stefan sat on the grass. "Are there biscuits?"

Somersby laughed gruffly. "Yes. There are biscuits."

Leif sat on the bench next to Chenoa. "Did you have a good talk?"

She nodded. "Yes. He understands me."

Somersby stopped turning over the fish in the large pan and looked at the woman. "I still do not know what to call you."

Leif looked confused. "Not Chenoa?"

"Chenoa was what her Fox husband named her," he explained patiently. "But the man was not kind to her."

Stefan shot a startled gaze at Leif. "We did not know that."

"However," Somersby continued. "She does not like her given name, Dorcas."

Stefan covered his mouth and scrubbed away his smile.

No one could like that name.

Somersby went back to flipping the fish and spoke to Chenoa. "I would like to give my opinion, if I could."

She nodded.

"Dorcas is a Bible name, even though it is not a very pretty one," he began. "Chenoa means dove, and in the Bible the dove represents the Holy Spirit when it comes over Jesus."

Chenoa nodded slowly. "Yes. I do remember that story now."

Stefan listened, entranced by Somersby's words.

"The Holy Spirit is called the Comforter, is he not?" Somersby looked at the trio for confirmation.

"Uh, yes," Stefan blurted.

He remembered hearing that a very long time ago in the

little Lutheran church in Cheltenham.

"So we should think of the name Chenoa as the moment when the Holy Spirit came over you." Somersby's voice was so soothing and his words so transforming that Stefan barely breathed. "He came to comfort you when you were sad, and to protect your salvation in the midst of your trials."

Chenoa burst into tears.

"Oh! Please do not cry." Leif looped an arm around her shoulders and hugged her to his side. "We can call you Dorcas. It is fine.

"Noooo," she wailed.

Somersby dropped to his knees in front of the crying woman. "I am so sorry. I did not mean to upset you."

"No!" She sniffed and wiped her nose. "You did not!"

Stefan frowned. "I am confused."

Chenoa waved her hands and shook her head. "No! Blake gives me a new way to think about my name!"

Somersby leaned back on his heels, clearly relieved. "So…"

She flashed him a watery smile. "So now Chenoa has a new meaning. I will think of this and be glad."

Somersby's gaze dropped, then rose again to meet Chenoa's eyes. "Just like you gave me a new way to think about what happened to me."

She did?

Stefan's curiosity was uncontrollable. "What did she say?"

"It is personal. I prefer not to say." Somersby looked at Stefan over his shoulder. "At least, not tonight."

With the subject abruptly closed, Srefan rose to his feet. "Who is hungry?"

*****

Blake climbed onto her mattress and pulled the blankets to her chin. She needed to take a few minutes in the quiet darkness to think about everything that transpired this evening.

Chenoa's story was horrific, and her mistreatment by her Fox husband inexcusable. But she was not surprised that Chenoa had not said anything about it to Leif or Stefan.

Rape was humiliating. Especially in the marriage bed.

Blake also understood reaching that moment when she would rather die than continue one more day, so the risk of hiding and then running became insignificant.

That is exactly what I did.

Blake ached for the day she could leave Kansas City behind her and create an entirely new life for herself—one that she could enjoy, no matter how hard she had to work to get it. In that light, the risk of packing up everything and traveling to an unknown land became insignificant as well.

But above all else was the moment Chenoa said she was lucky she was too young to bed that caused a shift inside her. One that rocked the foundation of who she was. It was so startling that at first Blake did not realize that Chenoa saw through her disguise.

How do they not see you are woman?

Stefan and Leif walked into earshot immediately after Chenoa uttered those words. Blake turned her focus to the fish and tried not to allow her surging panic to show. She had no way of knowing whether the stranger she just met would reveal her secret or keep it safe.

Only when Chenoa answered Leif's question with '*he* understands me' could Blake begin to relax.

Though she did say that Chenoa's husband was not kind, Blake kept the woman's personal shame a secret. In return, she would keep Blake's gender a secret. Their silent agreement was solidified.

Blake's secret would be revealed after she reached Santa Fe, but she did not know if Chenoa would ever reveal hers. That was of no consequence. For now, the two women were bonded by their individual situations and the tacit agreement that they would watch out for each other.

April 9, 1845

Stefan stood behind the mare and wondered if he should reach inside and try to grab the foal's forefeet. She had not been laboring long, but the wagon train was moving past them and he did not want to fall too far behind.

Do it.

"Hold her steady," he instructed her owner as he rolled up his sleeves.

The man nodded.

Stefan slid his right arm into the birth canal and immediately encountered the still-soft hooves of the baby. He slid his hand up the leg to be sure the foal was coming forelegs first.

It was, and that was good news.

But the nose of the little horse was still inside the uterus. Until that came through, Stefan could not pull.

He blew a frustrated sigh.

Hurry up, mama.

Push your baby out.

He waited with his arm in place through three more contractions before he felt the muzzle extrude into his palm.

"The nose is coming," he told the man holding the mare's head. "I can start pulling when she contracts."

The fellow nodded nervously but he looked confused.

Stefan waited for the mare's next contraction and wondered if the man had any idea about how babies managed to get outside their mother.

He has three children. He ought to know.

On the other hand, Stefan knew plenty of men who bolted from their home with their wife's first contraction and did not return—usually quite well lubricated—until everyone involved in the process was washed, dressed, and swaddled.

The fact that his own father participated in the birth of his sister was a frequently commented upon anomaly. As was the fact that Aunt Rosie, who was still a working woman and not yet a brothel owner, was present.

My family is certainly unique.

In so many ways.

Stefan felt the next contraction begin so he grabbed the two little hooves in his hand and pulled.

Come on mama.

Help me.

The baby moved several inches, but when Stefan checked the head was not yet clear.

He pulled a little harder with the next contraction and the head came into the canal.

The rest was relatively easy. Three more contractions and Stefan pulled the little filly from the mare and let her fall to the grass-covered ground.

The man let go of the mare. She swung her head around and set to work cleaning her baby, stimulating both the infant's circulation and breathing with the ministrations of her rough tongue.

The man stood beside Stefan while he washed and dried his arm. "The miracle of birth, eh?"

"Yep."

"It is a girl."

Stefan nodded. "Sure is."

He handed the man his towel. "We will get her standing and let her nurse for a few minutes. When the afterbirth is expelled, we need to catch up with the wagons."

The man frowned at him. "How fast can the little one walk?"

Stefan shrugged and rolled his sleeves down. "It does not matter."

"Why not?"

Grinning, Stefan slapped his shoulder. "Because you are carrying her."

*****

An hour and a half later Stephan caught up to the wagons as they were forming the circled enclosure for the animals. He led the mare toward the man's family with her owner stumbling along behind him carrying the newborn filly.

Blake hobbled her oxen then hurried over to see the baby.

"She is so small," Blake marveled. "And I have never seen anything so adorable."

Leif had taken charge of the little girl and was encouraging her to nurse. Chenoa hovered nearby. When she saw Blake, she moved to her side.

"I see so many horses born," she said softly. "Always cute."

As the man's family clustered around the newest member, Stephan reminded them that they needed to make arrangements for the filly to ride.

"She is too young to be able to keep up," he warned. "Unless you want to carry her."

"No!" The man was sweating with the effort and breathing heavily. He pointed at their oldest son. "You will have to move out of the wagon."

The young man's brow lowered. "Why me?"

"Because I cannot move your sisters out, that is why."

The boy's tone shifted from blustery to whiny. "Where am I supposed to go?"

The father looked around the small circle of observers. He pointed at Blake. "He is alone in his wagon. Stay with him."

"No!" Stefan and Leif chorused.

Their unexpected denial, barked in tandem, halted conversation.

Blake stared at the brothers in shock. Had they figured out she was a woman? Or had Chenoa told them?

No matter what, Blake obviously needed to come up with a good reason for not allowing the strapping nineteen-year-old young man to share her wagon. And quickly.

"Why not?" the father asked. "He is the perfect choice."

Stefan had the oddest expression on his face. "His wagon is too small."

"That's true," Leif confirmed. "And two men cannot share that narrow bed."

Blake was very grateful for their concern, but...

Why are they doing this?

"I can sleep on the floor," the boy replied. "I do in our wagon anyway."

"Then it is settled." The father waved at his son. "Junior, get your things."

Stefan and Leif exchanged frantic looks which made absolutely no sense unless they knew the truth. But Blake could not risk them revealing her secret any more than she could share her tiny space with the young man.

"I will take the horse!" she blurted.

Eight pair of eyes rested on her.

"Great idea!" Stephan clasped his hands looking inordinately relieved. "The filly can ride in Somersby's wagon. It is the perfect solution. That is settled then."

"It is not the perfect solution," Chenoa said softly.

Blake turned her regard to the woman.

What is going on?

"Why not?" she challenged.

"Because lifting the baby in and out will be hard."

"She is right about that," Leif admitted. "And if her legs get tangled in the process she could fall and break one."

The man nodded. "I agree. Junior. Pack up."

"I-I d-don't think—" Blake stammered

"The horse will have my cart," Chenoa interrupted, her voice firm. "I am well enough to walk."

Leif face was a mask of concern. "Are you certain?"

"Yes." She touched his arm. "I must move out of the medical wagon now."

"We need to find you a place to sleep, then," Leif stated. "You cannot join the men under the wagons."

"No, I cannot." Chenoa turned her face to Blake. "If he does not mind, I can stay in Blake's wagon."

Her words were met with another stunned silence.

Blake stared at her. "W-with me?"

"That is not proper!" the man's wife exclaimed.

Chenoa moved her pale-eyed regard to the woman. "I lived with the Fox. Men and women sleep in the same houses all the time. It is only sleep, nothing more."

Blake found her voice. "I-I am amenable t-to this."

Stefan clapped his hands together again and addressed the family. "And *now* it is settled. The cart will be connected to the back of your wagon and the filly will ride next to her mother."

"You will need to stop every couple of hours for her to nurse," Leif added. "And you must continue to start each day at the head of the line, so you are not left too far behind by the end of the day."

"Follow the wagon wheel tracks if you lose sight." Stefan clapped the man on the shoulder. "And we will ride back to collect you if need be."

The man nodded, looking a little stunned, and Blake got the impression he was disappointed that he could not foist his son off onto someone else.

I would bet he has a healthy appetite.

Speaking of which, "I need to start supper."

Blake turned around and headed back to her wagon.

And tonight, I will ask Chenoa if she told Leif or Stefan the truth.

*****

"No, I did not." Chenoa kept her voice low. "I also was surprised by their words."

The mattress and blankets from the cart were now on the floor of Blake's wagon. Blake lay on her back on her pallet, confused by some of what had transpired.

"Then why were they both so adamant that that boy should not share my wagon?"

Chenoa sighed in the dark. "It is possible they are not as

blind as we think."

Blake tried to recall her interactions with Stefan and examine them with that idea in mind.

I suppose that could be true.

"If that is so, then I need to thank them for letting me stay on the train."

Chenoa was quiet for a few minutes and Blake thought she had fallen asleep.

"They are good men," she suddenly whispered from the floor.

"Yes, they are," Blake whispered back.

"Especially Leif. He is so kind."

Blake realized she had been thinking that Stefan was the standout. Not that it mattered, but at least she would not have to watch Chenoa grow close to the younger of the brothers.

"Leif is a very special man," she opined. "Has he told you about his life?"

"Yes." Chenoa sighed again. "We have things in common."

"He has more patience than Stefan does. Leif was the one who taught me to shoot a rifle."

Chenoa shifted on the floor. "Why are you here?"

The truth? "My life was miserable, and the memories intolerable."

"Will you tell me about this?"

Blake unexpectedly welcomed the chance to talk about her life to someone who would understand her, and not judge her. The startling opportunity lifted yet another shroud from her view of her past.

She turned on her side and faced Chenoa. "I decided to leave Kansas City about four years ago..."

Chapter Fourteen

April 17, 1845

A week had passed since the filly was born, and the accommodations made both for the horse and Chenoa were proving to be quite satisfactory.

Of course, there were still sideways glances and curious stares with the refugee woman bedding down with the single youth, but the fact that Chenoa spent nearly all of her waking hours at Leif's side seemed to confirm that nothing untoward was happening between the pair sleeping in Somersby's little wagon.

And as Leif now focused his attention on Chenoa, Stefan found himself at odds. Leif had been his companion since he was seven years old, and to have his adoptive brother now interested—truly interested—in a woman was a jarring shift.

Though there were a few mothers on the train who clearly hoped their daughters might snag Stefan for a husband, he managed to keep a safe distance. He was not opposed to marriage, and he expected to marry in the not-too-distant future, because he assumed that would please his father.

Just not yet.

Thus abandoned, Stefan usually made his way to the

safety of Somersby's fire, unabashedly hoping to sample whatever the man cooked up that night. He now took time along the route to hunt for some meat to bring to that table—duck or rabbit being the most common. When the train moved parallel to a river or stream, Frank Waldon and his son successfully fished.

Tonight, for some reason he could not put his finger on, Stefan was restless. The full moon rising over the eastern horizon, and looking impossibly large and close, was probably the cause. A fiddle was being played somewhere in the camp, so clearly he was not the only one who found the idea of bedding down unappealing.

With relief, he spotted Somersby sitting cross-legged on the ground, leaning against one of his wagon's wheels. He sauntered up, trying to act like that was not where he was intentionally headed in the first place.

"Hey," he greeted.

Somersby—who looked even younger without his hat—smiled up at him. "Hello."

"Do you mind if I join you?"

"I would welcome the c-company." Somersby dragged his fingers through his short, shaggy hair as Stefan lowered himself to the ground. "It seems m-many of us are restless tonight."

Stefan leaned back against the same wheel as the boy. "It is the full moon, I think. So much light."

"I suppose." Somersby considered the large, pocked orb. "Is it brighter out here than in the city?"

"No. I believe we have simply become accustomed to the dark."

Somersby faced him again. "Will you t-tell me something?"

"That depends," Stefan hedged. "What do you wish to know?"

He tilted his head and fixed his eyes on Stefan's. "Why have t-two mature, educated and c-capable men, who must have other resources judging by the quality of their mounts and t-tack, chosen to work a lowly wagon train?"

Stefan stared into the youth's eyes, wondering how candid to be—but he had no real reason to hide anything. Only his stubborn pride held him back.

I am not my father.

Stefan pulled a deep breath. "When your father cuts off his financial support and changes his will until you 'make something of yourself' then you do what you need to do."

"Ah. You d-do come from money." Somersby shrugged. "That explains the horses."

Stephan flashed a wry smile. "My father and my mother are horse trainers. And breeders."

"Is that how they made their fortune?"

The questions felt genuine, not probing, so he answered it. "They do not have a true fortune. But my father is a very good manager of their estate."

Somersby grinned. "He is a c-country gentleman, then."

"Among other things."

That clearly piqued the young man's curiosity. "What other things, if you do not m-mind my asking."

Stefan hesitated, wondering if he should reveal the truth. He decided to give a vague general answer. "Politics."

Somersby blinked. "Wait—not—your last name is Hansen."

Stefan winced and did not respond.

The youth straightened and stared at him. "Is your father Senator Nicolas Hansen?"

Stefan clicked his tongue against his teeth. "I see you know of him."

"Know of him?" Somersby looked giddy. "I attended one of his speeches in K-kansas City! I would have voted for him if I c-could!"

"If you—oh, of course." Stefan nodded. "You are too young to vote."

"Uh—yes. Of c-course that is the reason." He leaned back against the wagon wheel. "I had no idea."

"Could we please keep it that way?" Stefan asked. "I

would prefer no one knows."

"Certainly." Somersby peered at him. "But why?"

Stefan felt his face heating in the cool night. "My father is right. I have not brought honor to our name up until now. To be honest, that is rather embarrassing."

"B-but you will. Once you build the t-trading posts."

Somersby sounded so certain that Stefan believed him. "Yes, I believe I will."

Somersby shifted so he was sitting on his heels, facing Stefan.

He crossed his heart. "Even though my secret is much b-bigger than yours, I will k-keep yours just as you have k-kept mine. Thank you, Stefan."

So he is homosexual.

Just as we suspected.

He smiled softly into the youth's earnest eyes. "I appreciate that, Blake. I really do."

For a brief moment neither one of them moved.

Then slowly—incredibly—Somersby leaned toward Stefan. His eyes fell from Stefan's eyes to his lips.

He is going to kiss me!

Stefan opened his mouth to object just as Somersby's lips hit his.

With a startled roar he shoved the youth away with enough force to knock him flat on his back.

"What are you doing?" he bellowed and scrambled to his feet. "Why would you—NO!"

A wild-eyed Somersby scrambled to his feet. He shoved his way past Stefan, vaulted over the wagon's tongue, and ran into the open prairie.

Stefan swiped the back of his hand across his tingling lips and swore. Somersby was going to get himself lost.

Damn it.

I have to go after him.

*****

Blake ran blindly, not caring what happened to her. She tried to kiss Stefan and he was horrified. Obviously, he did *not* know she was a woman disguised as a man, and she could only wonder what secret he thought he was keeping on her behalf.

It does not matter.

Nothing matters.

If it was possible to die of embarrassment and humiliation, Blake figured she had less than two minutes of life left in her.

Sobs wracked her chest and she could not breathe. She staggered stiff-legged to a stop and bent over, hands on her knees and scooping gasps of cool grass-scented air.

Only then did she hear footsteps behind her.

Indians.

Please kill me.

"Somersby?"

Stefan Hansen.

Why oh why could it not be bloodthirsty savages that had chased her down?

"G-go away," she croaked.

"No." The footsteps came closer. "You will get lost."

"I do not c-care."

Stefan reached her. "Look at me."

"No."

Stefan grabbed her arm presumably to keep her from bolting again. "Your secret is still safe. I will not tell anyone. I just…"

She snapped upright and glared into his blue eyes—colorless in the bright moonlight.

"Just what?" she demanded through her tears.

He looked extremely uncomfortable. "I—I prefer women."

Blake's jaw dropped in shock.

He does not know after all!

"I should not have knocked you over," he continued hesitantly. "I am very sorry about that."

Blake's tears turned to hysterical laughter as the absurdity of the situation slammed into her.

"Stop that!" Stefan grabbed her other arm now and held her in front of him. He shook her. "Calm down—now!"

In her experience, no one *ever* calmed down when those words were shouted at them.

She wagged her head and wiped her nose on her sleeve. "Is that my secret, Stefan? That I p-prefer men?"

Stefan looked lost. "Do you *not* prefer men?"

"Of course I do!" she cried. "But not for the reason you think!"

Blake twisted around so that the moon shone full on her face. "Look at me, Stefan. *Really* look at me."

His stunned grip on her arms loosened.

She grabbed his hands and pressed them against her bound bosom so each palm cupped a flattened mound. "What do you feel, Stefan?"

"SHIT!"

He yanked his hands away like they were burned. "All blazes be damned to hell!"

Blake stepped backward in case Stefan's anger grew physical. She did not imagine he would hit a woman, now that he knew, but she had already been knocked back once tonight.

Stefan stepped forward and grabbed her chin. He tilted her face into the moonlight and stared at her. "How the hell—"

"It's the only w-way I c-could escape," she managed.

Stefan let go of her chin. He whirled around and stomped in a tight circle, his huge hands jammed on his hips.

Her tears returned and flooded her cheeks. "Please don't be angry."

Stefan glared at her over his shoulder. "Who knows?"

"O-only Ch-Chenoa." Blake's breath came in spasms and made it even harder to talk than her stutter did. "She s-saw it r-right away."

"Leif?"

Blake shook her head.

Stefan seemed to be reclaiming his senses. "Why did you think I knew?"

Blake sniffed wetly and once again wiped her nose on her sleeve. "B-because you d-didn't want that b-boy to sleep in m-my wagon, b-but you let Chenoa."

Stefan spread his hands and walked forward. "Because Leif and I believed you to be homosexual." His tone indicated that was the only and obvious reason.

Blake's jaw dropped. She had no idea how to respond to that startling statement.

That particular idea had never occurred to her. Not even once.

As the realization of all the weight that such a serious accusation encompassed hit her, she grew increasingly horrified.

What has Stefan thought of me?

The wide-eyed pair stared silently at each other while the night breeze set the grasses around them to waving, until they stood in an undulating silver sea under the cloudless sky.

Blake finally found her words. "Which would you rather I b-be—a woman or-or a homosexual man?"

He threw his arms wide. "Neither!"

"Well, it is too late, sir!" She sniffed again and angrily crossed her arms over her chest. "But do not w-worry. Once we reach Santa Fe in t-two weeks you never need s-see me again."

That thought stabbed her heart in dangerous ways and made her tears flow harder.

"In the m-meantime, I will c-continue to d-dress and act as I have." She lifted her chin with a confidence she wished she owned even a small fraction of. "And—I will not t-tell anyone that your f-father is a Missouri State Senator."

She turned back in the direction of the wagons and left him standing alone on the prairie.

*****

What the hell just happened?

Stefan walked slowly behind Somersby—*Blake*—going just far enough to see him—*her*—safely enter the circle of the wagons before his knees gave out and he sat down hard on the grass-covered ground.

Blake Somersby was a woman.

Not a seventeen-year-old youth with an attraction to his own gender.

"How did I not see that?" he murmured.

Leif did not see it, and neither had the Waldons—nor any other settlers on the train, apparently. That was some sort of comfort.

But Stefan felt that he had been made an enormous fool of, nonetheless.

His concern for the youth, which led him to spend time with Somersby and assure his safety and comfort, was based entirely on lies.

Damn the man.

Woman.

Stefan grunted and flopped onto his back. He stared up at the few stars which shone brightly enough not to be washed out by the full moon's light.

Men under the age of eighteen were not allowed to drive wagons, but Stefan was willing to ignore that fact because Somersby was doing a decent job.

But keeping silent about a woman under the age of eighteen was asking too much.

Was she under eighteen?

Blake tried to imagine her face. He accepted her word that she was seventeen because of her lack of facial hair and the higher tone of her voice. But thinking about her under a different situation meant she could be older.

Then only one rule is broken.

The one which specifically forbids women from driving in

the wagon train on their own.

And he already admitted she was doing a decent job, though from a legal standpoint Buck could still abandon her to fend for herself the rest of the way.

With only a fortnight to go, Stefan knew he would never reveal her secret and risk her being left behind.

He also knew that he had to tell Leif. The brothers had never kept secrets from each other, and with Leif's interest in Chenoa growing daily, this was information that his brother needed to know.

And—Chenoa was the first one to figure it out, after all.

I need to find out how old Blake is.

With a resolute sigh, Stefan climbed to his feet and strode toward the wagons wagging his head in disbelief.

Chapter Fifteen

Someone pounded their fist on the side of Blake's wagon. She turned startled eyes to Chenoa, to whom she just related the evening's upsetting events.

"What if I am being taken off the train?" she whispered.

Chenoa grabbed her hand. "Then I stay with you. We travel to Santa Fe together."

Blake nodded gratefully and squeezed the other woman's hand.

The pounding repeated.

"Somersby!"

That was Stefan's voice.

Blake climbed to the back of her wagon and untied the flap. She pulled it aside and looked down at him, but said nothing.

He did not look pleased. "Will you please come out and speak with me?"

She really did not have a choice. "Only if you k-keep your voice d-down," she chastised.

He nodded.

Blake climbed down the ladder until she stood on the ground looking up at him. Only half-a-foot taller than her five-feet nine-inches, it was not a strain.

"What?"

Stefan gripped her arm. "On the outside."

Blake let him lead her to the side of the wagon away from the enclosure. Then they sat on the ground and leaned against the wheel, in the same manner in which their conversation took place earlier.

"I need the truth. All of the truth. And nothing but," he growled. "Do you understand me?"

Blake nodded. He deserved that. "Yes."

"How old are you?"

She flinched a little. "I am an old maid of eight and t-twenty years, almost twenty-nine, so I am far beyond the legal age to d-drive this wagon."

Stefan was obviously relieved about that part. "And you disguised yourself as a man to meet that particular requirement?"

"In part, yes," she admitted. "But also for my p-personal safety. If the single men on this t-train found out I was a single woman, who knows what I m-might suffer at theirs hands? There is no help for me out here."

He clenched his jaw, rippling the muscles in his cheeks, but he seemed to accept her answer.

"But why do this in the first place?" he probed. "Why not start your café in the safety of the state of Missouri?"

Blake shuddered. "I hate Missouri. There nothing good for me there."

Stefan relaxed a little. "Tell me the whole story."

After a shuddering sigh, she did.

She told him how her father always blamed her for her mother's death, his descent into senility and increasing verbal brutality, and how after ten years of being shackled to that existence, she decided to leave Kansas City forever.

"I started p-preparing for my escape months ago when I knew for certain my father was near d-dying," she explained. "I altered my father's c-clothes and—"

Blake stopped. She almost blurted her arrangements for

the money she inherited. As much as she liked Stefan, it was probably wise to keep that information to herself.

"And I t-took what he had at the house, plus all the money I saved. That was enough for me to m-make this journey and have a little fund to get me s-started in Santa Fe."

Stefan's expression was unreadable. But his anger seemed to have passed.

"Do you blame me?" she asked softly, hoping she had won him to her side.

The shake of his head was almost indiscernible. "No."

That was encouraging. "And you understand why I have d-done what I have d-done, then?"

Stefan's brows pulled together. "I only wish you had been honest with me from the start."

*****

Blake laid a hand on his arm, her palm warm and comforting through the fabric of his shirt. "Surely you understand why I c-could not."

He did, of course. But why he wished she would have was becoming clear to him in the light of tonight's discovery.

If I want her to be honest, then I must be honest, too.

He cleared his throat before he spoke. "I must admit, there was a part of me that was attracted to you."

Somersby's—*Blake's*—eyes rounded. "But you thought I was a man."

Stefan snorted. "So you can see my dilemma."

Her eyes narrowed. "Did it begin when you kept me from falling into the fire?"

That question floored Stefan.

How did she know?

"I believe so." He held his arms out in the same way he had cradled her. "I felt something physical when I held you against me. And, truth be told, I was not at all happy about it."

"I imagine not." Her tone was apologetic. "Your right hand was on my-my breast, and I was t-terrified you would figure me out at that moment."

"I should have known." Stefan considered his hand, remembering the feel of her. "But I was not thinking that anything like that was possible."

She smiled a little and gazed up at the moon. As Stefan examined her features in its light, he wondered how he had been so blind.

"But that was the night that Leif and I concluded you were a man who preferred men," he continued. "Because you baked a cake for Leif."

Blake looked startled. "I never thought of that. I mean, that baking a cake to thank someone is a decidedly female thing to do. But I suppose it is…"

The pair sat quietly for several minutes before Blake asked, "What now?"

Stefan looked at her. "As you said, you will continue as you have been until we reach Santa Fe."

"And you will continue to t-treat me like a man?" she pressed.

Something in Stefan clenched. He wondered if he would be able to do so.

"I must tell Leif," he deflected. "If I know and Chenoa knows, but neither of us tells him, he will be fighting mad when he does find out."

Blake drew a deep breath and let it out slowly before she agreed. "That does make sense. And t-truthfully, I would not blame him."

Stefan leaned closer and took a chance. "Should we try that kiss again?"

Blake's eyes moved to his lips. She licked hers before catching her lower lip in her teeth.

"In spite of my impulsive actions earlier," she said finally. "I d-do not think that would be wise."

Stefan tried to hide his disappointment. "Yes. You are probably right."

"At least…" Her eyes moved back up to his. "Until I am returned to being a woman. Then we shall see."

We shall see?

Stefan was not accustomed to women turning down his advances. He might need to covertly woo her for the rest of the journey to assure her capitulation.

"Until Santa Fe, then."

"Until Santa Fe." She regarded him with an earnest expression then. "And I am still quite interested in the t-trading posts, if you will accept a woman as a p-partner."

So stunned by the suggestion, all Stefan could think of to say was, "We shall see."

*****

Leif stared at Stefan like he had grown an extra head. "Blake Somersby is a woman."

"Yes."

"Are you *sure?*"

Stefan spread his hands. "Ask Chenoa."

Leif smacked his own forehead. "We kept that boy out of her wagon, afraid he—*she?* Might make advances on him."

"Yep."

"And put a woman in there instead, believing that 'he' would not."

"And we were correct on one count, as it turns out." Stefan huffed a chuckle. "But rather than make advances on the boy, she knew she would be found out."

Leif frowned. "When did Chenoa discover the truth?"

"It would seem that she saw it right away." Stefan shrugged. "She asked Blake how *we* did not see it."

"So that is why she moved into Somersby's wagon without any objection."

"Yep." Stefan crawled under the chuck wagon and unrolled his bed.

Leif copied his actions.

"What now?" he asked once the men had laid out their bedrolls.

Stefan removed his boots and climbed into his bedroll. "Blake will continue as she has until we reach the safety of Santa Fe. Then she will return to wearing her feminine attire."

"That is not what I am asking about." Leif propped himself on one elbow. "I mean you and her."

Stefan's heart thumped painfully. "What do you mean?"

"To be honest, Stef, I was getting worried about your interest in the boy," Leif admitted. "You cared more about Somersby's well-being than you have cared about any woman for as long as I have known you."

While that was actually true, Stefan did not think it was so obvious.

"That bothered me as well, to be honest." Stefan scratched his scalp and combed his hair with his fingers. "I could not understand it, and I tried to believe it was simply out of worry over a defenseless creature."

"I sincerely doubt she is defenseless." Leif lay on his back. "Did you kiss her, now that you know?"

He knows me well.

"I tried. I mean, she did try to kiss me first."

"And?"

Stefan forced himself to sound nonchalant. "She declined. She said she wanted to wait until Santa Fe and the end of her charade, then we shall see."

"We shall see?" Leif laughed. "Since when does Stefan Hansen get turned down?"

"It has happened before," he grumbled.

"When you were a schoolboy," Leif observed. "Not since."

"She did not say no," Stefan countered. "She said wait."

Leif chuckled. "I look forward to seeing what happens next."

"This *is* interesting…" Stefan settled on his back and clasped his hands over his chest. "She still wants to be our partner in the trading posts, in any case."

"Really?" Leif sounded surprised. "What did you tell her?"

Stefan smiled in the dark. "I said we shall see."

Leif guffawed.

April 18, 1845

The next morning dawned cloudy and dark, the clear skies and full moon of the night before having fled the prairie. Blake was finishing breakfast with Chenoa and the Waldons when Stefan rode up on his stallion.

Blake tried not to smile too brightly.

Magnificent man, magnificent steed.

Stefan was not smiling at all. "The scouts spotted a small group of Indians heading our way. We need to stay where we are and fortify the wagons. Men, get your guns."

Blake saw Stefan's gaze flick to her when he said *men* and she startled.

I have to get my rifle.

When he rode on to the next fire, she turned to Chenoa. "Will you c-clean up?"

"Yes. You go." The woman looked scared and that did not help Blake's already set-on-edge nerves.

"What is wrong?" she asked.

"I will not go back," Chenoa said softly. "I will die first."

Blake gasped. "D-do you think they are looking for you?"

"It may be so."

Does Stefan realize that?

Blake turned around and strode to her wagon, mentally reviewing the steps to load and prime her gun.

*****

"They are looking for Chenoa, I'd wager. She told me they might do so when we first found her," Leif said matter-of-factly. "But she escaped over three weeks ago and we both hoped they decided not to."

Stefan checked his supply of caps. "This might be a different tribe," he offered hopefully.

"How many were in the party?"

"Four, I think."

Leif looked relieved. "If it is the husband, then only three friends have come. He does not have the support of the entire tribe."

Stefan considered his brother. "Do you think they know he was so rough on her?"

Leif gave him a knowing look. "They know he had two wives before her, and that neither one of them bore him children, nor survived his abuse."

Stefan rubbed his eyes and swallowed thickly as he considered what that poor woman has been through. "That suggests that, if this is him, he is acting on his own."

"Yes. That is what I—and Chenoa—believe."

Stefan looped the rifle's strap over his shoulder and grabbed the pouch of ammunition. "Let's go."

Leif's actions mirrored Stefan's. "What about Somersby?"

Stefan shot him a grim glance. "I told *him* to get his gun."

*****

Unlike when they were scaring off the buffalo, this time the men took cover under the wagons and sat behind the wheels. They would shoot between the spokes if it became necessary.

"In the meantime," Stefan told Blake. "We hope the sight of dozens of rifles pointed in their direction will dissuade them from attacking us."

Every man in the train was sitting under his own wagon,

along with his sons if he had them, and protecting his own property. Because Stefan and Leif did not have a wagon, they crouched under Blake's

Chenoa remained hidden in the wagon above them.

Leif had not said anything obvious to Blake, but he did offer his hand when she climbed down from her wagon, and helped her prepare little packets of gunpowder without prompting.

"You did well before, remember?" he asked gently. "You can do this again."

"Thank you," she murmured.

He smiled at her. "Make me proud."

The camp was quiet, save for the lowing of the oxen and the snorting of the horses in the protective center of the gathered wagons. The little filly nursed happily and pranced around her grazing mother when her belly was full.

But under the wagon, Blake smelled her own nervous sweat as she waited for the small band of Indians to appear, and their purpose to be confirmed.

The sweat of her palms released the metallic scent from the barrel of her rifle and mingled with the gunpowder in the heavy and unmoving air under the wagon.

I hope it rains.

The constant dust and flecks of grass or seed stirred up by the wagons covered everyone and everything in the train. Blake longed to reach Santa Fe and finally take a real bath.

When they traveled along the Cimarron River the other women were free to bathe, but Blake could not take that chance. She had to make do with a bucket and towels in the privacy of her wagon.

Voices to the right pulled her attention. The sight of the approaching Indians sent shards of panic throughout her frame.

"Steady on," Stefan murmured.

Steady on.

Blake shifted her position and aimed her rifle at the men on horseback. "What are they saying?"

"He says his woman was…" Leif was clearly concentrating. "Lost from him. In the prairie fire."

"That confirms that he is looking for Chenoa."

Leif nodded. "He wants to search the wagons."

Blake looked at him. "The wagon master will not allow that, surely."

"He might have to," Stefan said grimly. "If he does not, he risks creating a situation. And we do not know for certain that he lacks the support of his tribe."

Buck Shultz's jaw was thrust forward as he continued to try and dissuade the men, but Blake knew in her gut how this was going to turn out. And when the wagon master pointed in her wagon's direction, that course was confirmed.

Without hesitating, Blake grabbed a packet of gunpowder and a cap. She was only going to get one shot.

Then she scurried out from under her wagon into the protected enclosure.

"Blake!" Leif's loud whisper was rough. "Come back."

She did not respond. Instead, she climbed into the back of her wagon.

She heard Stefan swearing beneath her, but the men held their locations.

Chenoa was not hiding like she promised, but was sitting on Blake's bed. She had Blake's sharpest butchering knife gripped in her hand.

"I will kill him." Her voice held no emotion.

"And I will help you." Blake set about loading the gunpowder and setting the cap in place. "And if we miss with knife and shot, Stefan and Leif will back us up."

Blake sat on the bed behind Chenoa and waited.

When the back flap of her wagon was thrown aside, Chenoa rose to her feet and set her stance. Blake lifted the rifle to her shoulder and looked down its barrel.

The shocked features on the angry Indian's face when he saw the pair of armed women would have been comical if the situation was not so deadly.

Then his expression turned lethal and he barked jagged

words at Chenoa.

She answered in their language and spat on the floor of the wagon. Blake's finger was tense against her trigger. Neither woman moved.

With a roar of fury, the man launched himself into the small confined space.

Blake pulled the trigger. The explosion hurt her ears and her eyes watered from the pain of the kickback against her shoulder.

She lowered the gun, her arms shaking and her heart bashing painfully against her ribs.

An empty-handed Chenoa stood over her husband. Blake's butchering knife protruded from his chest and there was a bleeding hole in his torso about six inches lower.

Which wound was deadlier was hard to say, but bloody bubbles frothed from his lips as his eyes rolled wildly in their sockets. Chenoa spat in the man's face and kicked him in the groin.

He was already too weak to react beyond exhaling a long, low moan.

The sound of a fight erupted outside. When shots were fired, Blake dropped to the floor of the wagon and pulled Chenoa down next to her.

Chapter Sixteen

Stefan was furious when Blake crawled out from under the wagon and he reached out to stop her, but she was too quick. He and Leif stayed in place while he swore profusely.

The brothers scrambled out and flanked the man's three companions. As the shouted argument began inside the wagon, other men from the train joined the brothers, guns at the ready. When the man in the wagon was met with Blake's shot, his friends turned their wide-eyed attention on the settlers.

Miraculously, two of the Indians put up their hands and stepped back. Only one of the group attacked. In a matter of moments he crumpled to the ground, mortally wounded by multiple shots from the settlers. One settler stepped up and methodically sliced his throat to end him mercifully.

"He deserved this," one of the two remaining Indians stated. "The woman stays with you now."

Then they turned around and loped away from the train.

Once they were a hundred yards away, Stefan and Leif scrambled inside Blake's wagon. What happened was immediately clear.

The dead Indian was sprawled on his back with a butcher

knife stuck high in his chest and a hole blown through his lower ribs.

Blake and Chenoa huddled together on the floor at the front of the wagon.

"I-is it o-over?" Blake stammered.

"Yes," Stefan answered.

Leif scrambled over the body to reach Chenoa. "Are you hurt?"

"No." Her gaze fell to the dead man. "I am good for the first time, in a very long time."

Stefan motioned for a couple of men to join him and they pulled the dead Indian out of the wagon.

Leif followed the body out and helped Chenoa climb down the ladder to the ground. "Did you know these men?"

"Yes." She seemed unconcerned.

"Do you think they acted on their chief's orders?" Stefan pressed.

"No. That one," she pointed to the dead man, "was banished and lived as outlaw."

Buck Schultz walked up. "And the other two said you will stay with us and left peaceably. That is all I need to know. Let's bury these two bodies quickly and get on our way."

As the gathered men headed for their wagons and shovels, Stefan looked back at Blake's wagon.

Blake stood in the opening, her face pale and her jaw set. Stefan approached her, wishing he could hold her in his arms.

"Are you all right?" he asked.

Her somber gaze met his. "Yes."

"You did well."

She nodded. "I need to wash the blood away before we move on. Would you please fetch me a bucket of water?"

Then she disappeared inside the wagon without another word.

*****

After Stefan delivered the bucket of wash water to Blake, he went from wagon to wagon to check on the families and their livestock. Leif stayed with Chenoa to coordinate the Indian burials under her supervision.

Stefan smiled when he saw the week-and-a-half-old filly, tail wagging like a dog and visibly stronger. He told her owner that she could walk part of the day now, but to keep an eye on her and be sure to cart her when she grew tired.

The man looked relieved. "Yes, sir."

All of the oxen were much leaner than when they began the journey, laden under loads which had grown lighter along the way—both in used supplies and discarded furnishings.

And one piano.

When he got around to Blake's wagon, he was surprised to see her still scrubbing the wooden floor of her wagon.

"We are about to move on," Stefan told her. "Are you finished?"

"Almost." She answered without looking up.

Stefan frowned and went to get her team. He removed the hobbles from each ox and walked them to the wagon.

The sound of the scrub brush had not abated.

Stefan harnessed the animals in place and gave each a drink of water, then went to the back of the wagon again.

"Somersby," he said sternly. "It is time to go."

When she did not acknowledge him, he climbed into the wagon and squatted down to grab her hands and still their frantic actions. "Blake. Stop."

She looked up at him. "I am almost finished."

"No." He took the brush out of her hand and dropped it in the bucket. "You are finished. The blood is gone."

*****

Blake watched Stefan stand up. He lifted the bucket by its handle and dumped the red-tinged water out of the back of her wagon.

He set it down and faced her again. "I harnessed your team. You are ready to go."

"Thank you." Blake stood to face him. "I k-killed a man."

Stefan did not look entirely convinced. "It is more likely that Chenoa's blade did the trick, so if you are worried about mortal sins—"

"I shot him with the intention of k-killing him," she declared. "It is the s-same thing."

Stefan's contrite expression proved he knew his New Testament verses as well as she. "It was self defense. Even so, pray for forgiveness with a sincere heart and you will be forgiven."

"There is the problem." Blake's fists clenched. "I wanted him dead."

Stefan's eyes narrowed. "I can understand that."

"I needed to k-kill my mother's murderer." Stefan opened his mouth but Blake waved away the coming objection. "I know it was not the same man. Obviously."

Stefan's expression eased and he nodded. "But he represented the man who took your mother's life."

"Yes. And he needed to d-die." Blake was surprised at how satisfied she was. This was a side of her personality which she had never experienced before, and it was more than a little disturbing.

She looked into Stefan's bright blue eyes. "Have you ever killed a man?"

"No," he admitted. "Though I was accused of murdering a working woman at one point and thrown into jail."

Blake resolved to return to *that* story at some point, but for now she asked, "Has Leif?"

Stefan shook his head.

"I would doubt that Chenoa has before this, though living with the Fox I c-cannot be certain." Blake sighed. "I will talk to her about it."

Stefan shrugged. "I wish I could be of more help."

Blake heard the sounds of wagons around hers jangling

into motion.

"It *is* time to go."

Stefan turned and headed for the ladder. He spoke to her again before he climbed down. "I will find Leif and Chenoa and bring her to you. Go ahead and join the train."

Blake nodded and went forward to the driver's seat. She sat on the bench and lifted the reins.

"Step up!" she shouted and slapped the reins on the oxen's backs.

As the animals leaned into their traces and eventually settled into their steady plodding gait, Blake considered her reaction to the Indian dying in her wagon. Getting every drop of his blood out of the wood was imperative, because doing so completely eradicated the man's existence.

Her determination in this could not be swayed.

She wondered if she would feel anything about today other than a sense of satisfaction, and then realized with a shuddering jolt that on this journey she had been unexpectedly set free from each of the shackles of her childhood experience.

First was the realization was that, because she was too young to wed or bed, she was not taken captive by the Indian who sliced her mother's throat.

Thank you, Father.

And today she was given the equally unexpected chance to exact revenge. Not only that, but if what Stefan said was true, she did not have the man's death on her accounting.

The blast from her rifle was not what killed him.

Please forgive me, Father. I did intend to kill him.

And thank you for sparing me that guilt.

Blake wondered if she would still stutter when she became upset about a situation. She still stuttered after Chenoa reminding her that she was lucky to be too young to be taken, but today's events had a much stronger impact on her.

But after more than two decades, was the impediment so ingrained in her that she would experience it for the rest of her life?

I will have to wait and see.

April 23, 1845

Five days later, Blake had her answer when she once more saw blood on the floor of her wagon. Panic surged through her frame, along with the ridiculous memory of Shakespeare's Lady Macbeth trying to wash away blood that was not actually there.

"I am sorry!" Chenoa climbed into the wagon. "I had to go ask women for rags. I will wash the floor."

She stood in front of Blake. "I cannot ask from you because you are a man."

Her cycle.

Of course.

Blake's core ached when she awoke and she knew her cycle was close as well. She drew a deep breath and tried to sound calmer than she felt.

"I must admit, my first thought was the ghost of your dead husband."

"I feared that." Chenoa removed her leather leggings. Her undergarment was soaked.

Blake turned away and reached into a crate for a cast iron pot with a heavy lid. "I use this pot until I can dispose of my rags. You can put your soiled rags and scanties in here until you can wash them."

Chenoa accepted the pot. "Thank you."

She untied her undergarment and dropped it in the pot, replacing the lid.

Blake rubbed her lower back. "My cycle is about to start as well. At least with you here I do not need to worry about raising suspicion when I dispose of my rags."

Chenoa smiled a little. "Women who live together usually have their moons together."

That was interesting. "I have never lived with a woman."

"I did with the Fox. We were always on top of each other." Chenoa tied the clean rags in place. "Do you dispose of the rags because a man cannot wash them?"

"Yes."

"Do you want me to wash them?" Chenoa's offer was sincere, but the thought of her hands in Blake's blood made Blake uncomfortable.

"No, I have plenty more packed with my women's clothes. But thank you."

Chenoa shrugged. "Blood is common with the Fox. Hunting, cooking, women."

"It is not common in Kansas City." *Thank goodness.* "I suppose we will see about Santa Fe."

Chenoa donned her leathers pensively. "I will need white men's clothes when we are there."

A new thought occurred to Blake. "How will you live? And where?"

The woman looked suddenly sad. "Leif wants to marry me. But I cannot."

That was surprising, and Blake wondered if Stefan knew. "Why on earth not?"

"I—" Chenoa's pale blue eyes filled with tears. "I am not good for a wife. Not now."

"Do you mean because of your husband?" Blake asked gently.

"Yes."

Blake wondered if the damage he had done was physical as well as emotional.

Probably both.

"I plan to open a café in Santa Fe," Blake stated, keeping her tone light. "You can help me with that if you want, and share my rooms until you can find your own."

Chenoa looked like an enormous weight had been lifted from her slender shoulders. "Thank you, Blake. I accept."

Blake was also relieved by the impromptu plan. Now she had an ally—someone who could share the workload, and provide companionship in the process.

"Then it is settled." Blake climbed into the driver's seat. "How many days until we reach Santa Fe, do you think?"

*****

By nightfall Blake's cramps painfully constricted her core and she brewed enough willowbark tea for both her and Chenoa to last the entire next day.

Chenoa offered to drive the wagon but Blake did not see how she could explain away the bachelor taking a nap while the woman was made to drive the team.

"I will be fine in a day," she told Chenoa. "And I did it alone a month ago."

As she expected, Stefan came to the shared fire just before supper was started—but he came with a trio of grouse tied together by their feet.

Mary Waldon set to cleaning them while Blake made biscuit dough and put it to bake in the fire.

"How far are we from Santa Fe?" she asked Stefan.

"Less than a hundred miles." He used a cleaver to butcher the cleaned birds. "Seven or eight days, I would guess, depending on the terrain."

Blake's spirit soared. Just one more week and she would drive into her new home and her new life.

"That is good news."

Stefan looked askance at her. "You look pale."

Blake shook her head. "I am fine."

"Are you sure?"

Blake looked over at Mary Waldon who was cleaning the last bird to see if she was listening. "I am tired. Nothing more. I, uh…" *Think.* "I sometimes have dreams about the dead Indians."

The tender look Stefan gave her should have betrayed her secret if anyone was paying attention.

"Excuse me. I left something in my wagon."

Stefan's cleaver paused in mid-chop. "Do you need help?"

"No."

Blake strode away from the fire circle and climbed into her wagon, wondering what she could collect from there that would verify her excuse.

Stefan followed.

"You should not have done that," Blake growled.

"I only wanted to assure myself that you were well," he growled back. "What do you need?"

Blake answered without thinking. "A pot large enough for the grouse."

"How about this one?" Stefan lifted the covered cast-iron pot from the wagon's floor.

"No!" Blake yelped but Stefan lifted the lid anyway.

His eyes rounded in shock and he slammed the lid back on the pot.

Blake was furious. "You deserved that! Why would you not leave me be?"

He looked stricken. "Who is dying?"

"What? No one is dying you ignorant Nordic oaf!" Blake borrowed Leif's satisfying insult.

"Then where did these bloody rags..." His voice trailed off as he reached an understanding. "Oh."

Blake grabbed the pot from his hands and set it back on the floor. The stark embarrassment replacing her anger was stultifying. "Please get out."

"I have a mother," he offered weakly. "And a sister."

Blake glared at him. "Then you should have known better."

When Stefan did not move, Blake stomped her foot and pointed at the back of the wagon. "Get. Out."

"But I—"

"NOW!"

Stefan scrambled down the ladder.

Blake sat on her bed holding her flushed face in her cool hands. Not only had she suffered the humiliation of trying to kiss Stefan when he thought she was a man, he just held the bloody proof of her female state in his hands.

I can never face him again.

Chapter Seventeen

May 1, 1845
Santa Fe

Late in the afternoon, twenty-nine dusty and battered wagons drove into Santa Fe from the south, past the two-hundred-year-old San Miguel Mission. They crossed a shallow wash and gathered on the opposite side, south of the main square.

"You can stay here in your wagons while you get settled," Buck Schultz instructed them. "But you cannot drive the wagons through town. Understood?"

Blake understood that she needed to find an inn with a bathtub.

"The hostlers can take any livestock you wish to sell to the stockyards," Buck continued. "In addition to selling your wagons if you no longer have need of them."

He turned and pointed toward the north. "The main square is a quarter mile in that direction. The land agents' offices can be found in the Palace of the Governors on the north side of the square. Any questions?"

Blake had so many questions, that she had no idea where to start. "What is the date today?"

"May the first. Any other questions?"

Blake sucked at breath.

It is official.

I am twenty-nine as of three days ago.

She turned to Chenoa. "I am going to find an inn with comfortable beds and take a long, hot bath. Would you like to join me?"

The woman frowned. "And leave your things unguarded? That is not wise."

Blake looked around at the men and families with whom she shared the last two months. "I can pay someone to watch my things…"

Perhaps she should stay in the wagon until she found more permanent lodging and could move her things inside.

Resigned to another day of filth and men's clothes, Blake deflated. "Then I suppose I will go see the land agents tomorrow."

Chenoa shrugged. "Why not today?"

Why not indeed.

"Will you watch the wagon while I do?" Blake moved boxes and dug into the case where she hid her money.

"Of course."

Blake straightened her trousers and quickly donned her cleanest shirt. She combed her shaggy hair before plopping the wide-brimmed hat on her head.

"Wish me luck!"

*****

Stefan and Leif spent the hours before sunset walking teams of oxen to the stockyards and carrying back payment for the settlers.

"This is far less than I paid for them," one man complained.

"Do you want me to bring them back?" Stefan asked.

The man scowled. "No. I cannot feed them."

"Then be happy," Stefan replied. "Because they do not make very good eating."

He wondered where Blake was. He had not seen her since arriving in Santa Fe. And to be honest, her attitude toward him had cooled a bit since the day he found the bloody rags in her wagon. Apologizing only seemed to antagonize her, so Stefan ended up leaving her alone.

When he and Leif reached Blake's wagon at sunset, only Chenoa waited inside.

"Blake went to the land agents' offices," she told the brothers. "She wants a small house where she can have a café."

"Already?" *She is not wasting any time.* "Should she not be back by now?"

As if conjured by his thought, Blake rounded the end of the wagon. "Oh! Hello."

Stefan touched the brim of his hat. "Any luck?"

Blake nodded. "I looked at three houses and p-paid the first month's rent on one of them."

"That was fast," Stefan cautioned. "Are you sure you are not being too hasty?"

Blake huffed a chuckle. "Not according to the land agent. He said every available building will be rented before noon tomorrow."

Stefan was increasingly encouraged to consider Blake as a business partner—clearly she had a good mind for it. "When can you move in?"

"Tonight, if I had the strength. But tomorrow will have to do." She pulled off her hat and straightened her cropped hair with her fingers. "In the meantime, I wish to enjoy a meal that I d-do not have to cook over a fire. Would anyone like to join me?"

*****

It was obvious that Santa Fe was a much less strict town

than Kansas City, and that the permanent residents were accustomed to influxes of tired and bedraggled settlers every couple of weeks in the spring and summer—many of which were continuing on even further in their quest for new homes.

As a result, even though Blake could barely tolerate her current unkempt state for one more day, no one seemed the least bit concerned when the shabbily dressed quartet asked to be seated in the dining room of a hotel one block off the center square.

"I will go talk to the clerk and procure two rooms for the night," Leif said to Stefan once their supper was ordered. "We do not have a wagon full of supplies we need to protect."

Stefan looked pleased. "I want to shave and take a bath so badly I can taste the soap. Order me one for later while you are at it?"

Leif chuckled. "I will order that for *each* of our rooms."

Blake tried not to shudder at the reality of going yet another day in her state of diminished cleanliness.

"I look forward to moving into a house tomorrow and taking my own bath," she said to Chenoa. "I think I shall be up by first light to b-begin moving in."

"What will you do with your oxen?" Stefan asked.

Blake had thought about that, but decided that selling the animals immediately might prove to be something that she would regret. "I will probably sell them, once I know I am not moving again."

"And the wagon? Will you sell it to those settlers continuing on?"

Blake felt her face warming. She had come up with a rather unusual idea during the endless hours she sat on that small wagon's uncomfortable bench while driving here, and now she looked to Chenoa for support.

"I thought about using it as private sleeping quarters to rent out." She shifted her gaze to Stefan to try and discern his reaction. "Or perhaps to let incoming settlers know that they are welcome to eat at my cafe once they arrive in town."

"I like both ideas," Chenoa offered. "Do not sell it. At

least not yet."

"I do have enough money to live on for a while, not like the men who need to get their investment back in order to support their families." Blake shrugged when Stefan said nothing. "I can afford to wait a b-bit."

Leif returned with the keys to two rooms, interrupting the discussion. He grinned as he handed one to Stefan.

"They are small rooms on the third floor, but we will both have our baths."

Leif reclaimed his seat at the table and addressed Stefan. "The clerk mentioned that we should all check the post office for mail."

"Who would be sending us a letter here?" Stefan shook his head. "And how could it arrive before we did?"

Leif wagged his head "I have no idea." Then he smiled. "What kind of wine did you order?"

May 2, 1895

Stefan and Leif graciously offered to help unload Blake's wagon the next morning. When they appeared with the rising sun, freshly shaved and bathed, the pair left Blake momentarily speechless.

I forgot how good-looking Leif is.

She slid a glance to Chenoa. The woman looked stunned.

"I never see your face," she said softly. She reached up a hand and stroked Leif's smooth cheek. "You have hidden your beauty."

Leif took her hand and kissed it. Blake had never seen a man look at a woman with so much love.

Perhaps there is hope for them.

If Leif looked handsome, Stefan challenged the very sunrise to outshine him.

Without two months of untrimmed beard hiding his features, his strong jaw and slightly crooked white teeth were again visible. His impossibly blue eyes glinted in the sunlight, framed by a web of thin creases that were formed by laughter. His wavy auburn hair turned copper in the morning light, and though he attempted to tie it back, unruly strands broke loose in the morning breeze and danced around his head.

Damn.

I too am smitten.

Blake keenly felt the weight of her man clothes, her short, shoe-polish-smeared hair, and the general filthiness of her current state.

"You put me to shame with your finery," she said to him. "I hope your labors this morning d-do not soil your clothes too badly."

"There is a laundress at the hotel." Stefan looked unconcerned as he grabbed the closest ox's harness. "So where is this house?"

The furnished house Blake had secured was on Shelby Street, one block south of the center square. She walked alongside Stefan as he led her team through the quiet streets. Leif and Chenoa walked behind the wagon.

"He loves her," Blake said quietly so the couple in back would not hear.

"I am afraid he does," Stefan confirmed. "He wants to marry her."

Blake wondered how much she should reveal. She settled on, "She is terrified, you understand. Her husband was cruel."

"My brother is nothing if he is not patient." Stefan smiled down at her. "And he is persistent. He learned that from my father."

"But…" Blake paused to try and state her question clearly. "Leif is not p-planning to live in Santa Fe—is he?"

"No. I expect he will want her to return to Missouri with us when we begin to set up our trading posts."

"Has he told her that?"

Obviously Stefan had not considered that. "I honestly do not know."

"Would it be dangerous?" Blake pressed. "For her to

travel b-back through Fox lands?"

Stefan shook his head. "I do not believe so. Not since her husband was killed and no one else came looking for her."

Blake was still not convinced. "Do you truly believe there will be no repercussions from that?"

"Think about it, Blake." Stefan counted his points with the fingers with his free hand. "The tribe would have to know where those men were headed and why. And *if* they met up with the wagon train. And if she was even *with* the wagons when they did, before there was any concern."

"And then they would have to find the exact spot in the prairie where the men were buried, and then d-dig them up to ascertain their identity." Blake was definitely feeling better about the prospect.

"Do not forget that one was an outcast," Stefan added. "I do not believe her husband acted with any bit of the tribe's blessing."

That made sense.

Blake pointed. "That is the house."

The square building was solidly constructed of plastered adobe with a log-and-tile roof topping the second story.

Stefan stopped the wagon in front of the house. "Shall we take a look inside before we begin?"

Blake walked through the front yard of the house. She climbed the two steps to a wood-planked and covered front porch, and stopped at the heavy, dark-stained wooden front door. She unlocked it with the large bronze key the land agent had given her after she paid the first month's rent and his commission.

This is my own home.

Mine.

Blake drew a steadying breath, pushed the door open, and stepped inside. Stefan, Leif, and Chenoa followed in a line behind her.

The furnished bottom floor had a sitting area and a dining area with a large oak table and ten chairs. An enclosed kitchen with an iron stove and rounded brick fireplace extended off the back. The water pump was just outside of that.

The second floor had two spacious sleeping rooms with separate dressing areas, each furnished with a framed bed and mattress, side table, and a tall wardrobe.

Every room in the house had at least one large, shuttered glass window cased in oak, with deep sills attesting to the thickness of the plastered adobe walls.

"It does not require too much work," Stefan commented. "A fresh coat of paint would brighten the rooms."

Blake agreed. "And a thorough scrubbing of the floors."

Chenoa stood in one of the bedrooms. "I have not slept on a real mattress for so long, I wonder if I will find it comfortable."

"Shall we begin unloading?" Leif asked.

*****

Blake told the men in which rooms to put each crate and box while she and Chenoa carried in the softer furnishings. Blake was eager to begin unpacking, but first things needed to remain first.

"I need to wash the floors before we d-do anything else in here," she stated once the wagon was unloaded. She turned to Stefan. "What do I do with the oxen?"

"Would you like me to take them to the stockyard to be boarded?" he offered.

Blake was relieved that he did so. "Yes. Please. How much money do you need?"

"Nothing today." He grinned. "But if you do not pay by the end of the week, the oxen become theirs to sell, or butcher for their hides."

Blake chuckled. "That sounds fair."

"We can pull the wagon into the yard, if you would like," Leif offered. "I do not think you will want it in the street."

Blake and Chenoa went outside with the brothers. Once

the team was unharnessed, Blake directed the placement of the wagon in front of her house until the angle suited her.

"I can hang a sign from each side once I am settled and can b-begin serving food." She walked around the wagon. "Can the tongue be removed?"

"With the right tools," Leif answered.

Blake nodded. "That can wait then."

Stefan led the team away from the house. Leif carried buckets of water inside. Chenoa opened all the windows so the breeze would dry the scrubbed floors. Blake dug out a large bar of lye soap and two scrub brushes.

She handed one to Chenoa. "And so, it begins."

*****

The women worked until sunset, stopping for a brief lunch comprised of leftover biscuits and cold roasted duck. They washed the meal down with water from the pump, which proved to be clear and cold.

Obviously at odds for the moment, and with nothing to occupy their time until they were paid, Stefan and Leif returned in the afternoon to help. They brought Tom-tom along for good measure.

The scout offered to clean the stove and fireplace, an offer which Blake accepted gladly. She assigned Stefan and Leif the heavy task of carrying all the rugs out of doors and beating the dust out of them.

As the sun lowered behind the town's surrounding red rock formations—like nothing Blake could ever imagine existing before this journey—the five friends sat at the dining room's table to assess their day's labors.

"I could never have accomplished this without all of you helping," Blake said. "And to thank you, I will cook a b-banquet to test out my new kitchen."

Stefan brightened. "When?"

Blake laughed at his eagerness. "Not today. And probably not tomorrow since I need to find the food markets and see what sort of variety there is. Hopefully the d-day after that."

"Well, we need to eat tonight." Stefan stood. "I can go to that shop on the corner and bring back food. Will that do?"

Blake stood as well. "That is a grand idea, Stefan. And while you do that, perhaps Tom-tom would b-be willing to start fires in the stove and fireplace?"

"Certainly, ma'am." The Negro smiled. "Especially if that gets me supper!"

Stefan shot the man a wide-eyed look. "You know Blake is a woman?"

Tom-tom laughed. "I am neither as blind or stupid as some." Then he addressed Blake. "I will get right to it, Miss.

Blake turned to Leif, barely able to keep from laughing as well. "Will you please fill the cauldrons with water and p-put them to heat?"

Leif nodded, looking amused. "Yes. Of course

Chenoa smiled at her. "Shall I help you rinse out the bathing tub?"

"First dinner, then a b-bath, and then sleeping on clean sheets and a real mattress." Blake sighed happily. "We are going to have such a lovely evening, are we not?"

Chapter Eighteen

May 3, 1845

Stefan offered to escort Blake through the streets of Santa Fe the next morning while she shopped for fresh foodstuffs. He selfishly hoped for her to find butchered beef, because of all the things he missed during their travels, a good steak topped the list. It made his mouth water just to think of it.

He walked the few blocks from his hotel to her house well after the sun was up, waiting until the shops and farmers began their business day.

Santa Fe was a bit of a surprise to him. He knew the city was well established, but had no idea it was almost two-hundred-and-fifty years old. Spanish was the main language spoken in the Republic of Texas because the land was originally claimed by Mexico, though settlers from the east had brought a fair amount of English with them.

Stefan thought he heard his father say something about the United States wanting to annex the republic, and was surprised to hear that the annexation was completed between the time the wagon train left Missouri, and their arrival in Santa Fe.

The beauty of the surrounding landscape was unexpected. Red sandstone backed by soaring rugged mountains was as different as could be from the expanse of featureless prairie which they traveled through to get here.

And nothing at all like the tree-covered hills of Missouri.

Stefan walked past the little wagon in the yard to Blake's front door and used the brass knocker to summon her. But the person who opened the door was a complete stranger.

"Oh! I—Blake?" he stammered. "Is that you?"

She laughed and turned in a circle while Stefan stood rooted, gobsmacked to his core.

The woman in front of him was absolutely stunning.

Her short hair curled softly around her face and was now the color of the sunrise—orange with streaks of copper and yellow. Her brown eyes, freed from the shadow of the wide-brimmed leather hat, seemed to have doubled in size. For the first time he noticed the thick eyelashes which framed them.

"I cannot believe it..." he breathed.

Her pink lips curved in an engaging smile. "How do I look?"

Stefan stepped back to get a full view of her dress. It was a simple style, the green cotton fabric tailored to her frame and devoid of the copious flounces which were popular back home.

"You are perfect." Stefan was still stunned. "How did I believe you were a man?"

"The p-power of suggestion, I suppose." Blake turned around and walked inside to a small table where she picked up her reticule and spoke over her shoulder. "You had no reason to think I was anything else, did you?"

She returned to the front door. "Shall we go?"

*****

Blake was thrilled with Stefan's reaction. The look on his face when he realized it was she who stood in front of him could not be bought at any price.

Finally able to take a real bath, wash the shoe polish from her hair, and don her favorite nightdress before climbing onto a real mattress covered with her own clean sheets, Blake experienced a euphoric glimpse of Heaven.

And the fact that she did so in her very own home was far more satisfying than she could ever imagine.

Blake pulled the front door shut behind her and looped her arm through Stefan's.

"What are you thinking?" she asked as they walked toward the busy city square.

He stared at her. "I am thinking this beautiful creature cannot be the same person who drove *his* own wagon nearly nine hundred miles, learned to shoot a rifle, and then shot a man when it became necessary."

She met his gaze. "But I am that person."

"But you started the journey as an unmarried, citified woman! It defies belief."

Blake stopped walking and faced him. "Women are far stronger than most men b-believe. We bear children and raise families—often alone—and conduct b-businesses when we are allowed to."

"I know, but—"

"Obviously I have never borne a child myself…" Blake determinedly tamped down that ugly disappointment. "But it seems to me as if doing so was the man's job, the human race would have d-died out with Adam."

Stefan wagged his head. "I have met many women in my life, mind you. But you are the first one to rival my mother in determination."

Blake blushed at the words which she took as a deeply gratifying compliment. Perhaps she might start acting more warmly toward Stefan again, now that her embarrassment over the bloody rags had faded, and she was freed from her fear of her disguise being discovered.

For now, she simply replied, "Thank you."

*****

Stefan thought Blake was akin to a child in a sweetshop as she moved happily from vendor to shop to stall.

"They have spices here that I have never heard of." She sniffed a container that made her eyes water and handed it back to the proprietor. "That one needs moderation. I will take half an ounce."

Stefan already carried an array of vegetables in a canvas sack, along with *masa*—corn flour—and potatoes. When Blake finished adding to her already impressive stock of spices, Stefan ventured to bring up his own preference.

"Might we find a butcher?"

Blake looked up at him from under the straw hat that she bought first thing this morning. "That will be my last stop. Why do you ask?"

"To be honest, the one thing I missed most of all these last months is beef."

Blake smiled sweetly, making his heartbeat stutter. "I make the best roast b-beef in Kansas City."

That sounded almost good enough to dissuade him from his original purpose. "I have no doubt about that."

Her eyes twinkled. "But?"

"But... my mouth is watering for a steak," he admitted.

Blake laughed. "Coated with pepper and garlic, perhaps? Cooked on an iron grid over a hot fire until the outside is seared, but the center is still p-pink?"

Stefan groaned good-naturedly. "You are torturing me, woman!"

Blake leaned forward and rested her hand against his chest. Looking down into her smiling eyes made the rest of the square fade from view. Her attitude seemed to be softening.

I wonder if she would let me kiss her yet.

"Find me a butcher and I will make you a steak tonight."

"I love you!" he blurted, then quickly added, "And tomorrow for the feast?"

Blake blinked. "The—the roast b-beef, of course."

Stefan forced a smile, wondering why he said such an outrageous thing. "Perfect."

*****

He loves me?

Blake held Stefan's arm as they followed the directions to a recommended butcher's shop.

More like his stomach loves me, as the saying goes.

She determinedly addressed a new subject rather than ponder a relationship that was doomed before it started. "How long do you and Leif expect to be in Santa Fe?"

Stefan looked relieved. "We have to wait until we are paid, of course, before we head back. That will be at the end of our twelve weeks of guaranteed employment, which is three weeks from now."

"And when you retrace your path, you will d-decide where to put the trading posts?"

Stefan nodded. "We will talk to the land agents here before we leave, and ask about buying or leasing an acre or two at each location for us to build on."

Blake's mind was whirling with the possibilities and battling against what she thought she should do. "I believe it should take you less time to return, b-because you will be less encumbered."

"We agree. We expect we could cover twenty miles a day, not twelve."

Blake did the cipher in her head. "You might make it back in just over six weeks, then."

Stefan stopped in front of the butcher's shop. "That is what we hope to do. Shall we go in?"

*****

Blake bought enough steak for Stefan and Leif, assuming the brothers always came as a matched set, and ordered a beef roast for the next night that would easily feed five.

While the roast marinated overnight, Blake tended tonight's steaks over the fireplace flame. Chenoa boiled and salted the potatoes, topping them with luxurious fresh butter. Then she pan-fried the green beans and pulled the biscuits out of the oven.

Blake smiled her satisfaction. Chenoa would be a good and capable partner in the café. For as long as she stayed in Santa Fe, at any rate.

Stefan's words that Leif was *nothing if not patient* and *he is persistent* left Blake with the impression that Leif might actually overcome Chenoa's objections to entering into another marriage. But if the men planned to leave after they were paid that only gave Leif three weeks to undo a full decade of fear, pain, and mistrust.

I do not see that happening.

The other thing she did not see happening was her turning right around and heading back to Missouri with Stefan. But that was exactly the idea niggling at the edges of her thoughts.

If she wanted to be a partner in the trading posts, she would have no choice but to go back with him. First, to assure that she agreed with the placement of the posts. And secondly, to collect the necessary funds from her accounts to pay her portion of the business venture.

Blake had not let Stefan know that she had any significant resources at her disposal, and she still believed that was the wisest path. If he only believed she wanted to find a way to offer freshly cooked meals, then he would not interfere with her while she evaluated his overall plans.

But how could she leave so soon after finally getting started with her new life? The one she anticipated and worked toward through literally years of misery?

The idea of doing so was crushing.

Blake pulled the steaks from the flames and called to the waiting men, "Five minutes and dinner is served!"

*****

Stefan sat at the big dining room table, his leg bouncing with anticipation. The scent of the seasoned steaks sizzling over the kitchen fire was driving him mad. He knew he was a man of big appetites, like his father, but until today he did not realize how those appetites guided many of his choices.

Sex, for example.

Stefan had not lain with a woman since the terrible night in Saint Charles six months ago when someone drugged him and charged him with murder. Since his first experience at nineteen, this length of celibacy was a record for him.

Surprisingly, he had not missed it as much as he thought he would. Probably because the strain of the day-to-day journey, and the rough conditions under which he lived, did not evoke thoughts of a soft bed and an even softer body beneath him.

Blake carried a platter into the room, interrupting his musings. "Hungry?"

Chenoa had already set the potatoes and beans on the table, and now she followed Blake into the dining room with a basket of freshly baked biscuits.

When she set them down, Stefan frowned. "Why are they yellow?"

"They are made with corn flour." Blake set the steaks between Stefan and Leif. "Be sure to leave us ladies a scrap or two."

Chenoa set a dish of butter and a little cream pitcher full of honey on the table. "Eat the biscuits with honey."

When the women claimed their seats, Leif said grace before Stefan cut open one of the seared steaks.

Perfectly pink inside with juices pooling on the platter.

He waited until all four of them had a proportionate amount of steak on their plates before he took his first bite.

He closed his eyes as the flavors filled his mouth. He hummed his pleasure and then smiled at Blake.

This is Heaven.

Chapter Nineteen

May 15, 1845

Two weeks after their own arrival, Stefan watched the wagons from the next train roll into town and stop after crossing the wash.

"Did we look that bad when we arrived?" he asked Leif.

"I hope not," his brother replied.

"How many wagons are there?"

Leif counted in whispers. "I come up with thirty-four. Or five."

"They made good time, then." Stefan slapped Leif's back. "Let's help let them get settled. We can talk to the wagon master later."

As had become their habit, the brothers walked to Blake's house to share supper with her, Chenoa, and sometimes Tom-tom. In exchange for her experimenting on them with new ingredients from the markets, and feeding them every evening, Stefan and Leif provided the meat.

Today Stefan was surprising Blake with four laying hens.

"I will build a coop tomorrow," he told Leif as he carried the chickens in a straw cage. "For tonight they can stay in the wagon.

"Did you not think of buying a rooster?" Leif asked. "She might want to raise some chickens for eating."

"I thought of it. But the one the man had looked sickly." He elbowed Leif. "Every woman deserves a healthy cock."

Leif rolled his eyes at the terrible pun. "I see you are back to your old self."

Was he?

Stefan's mood sobered. "I am not actually. I have not thought of visiting the brothels here even once."

"No?" Leif looked sideways at him. "Why not?"

Stefan drew a deep breath. "I am afraid I might be afflicted with the same ailment as you, though I am not as far gone."

Leif stopped walking.

Stefan turned back to face him.

His brother was beaming. "I knew it!"

"What?"

"Blake."

Stefan felt his face flush. "I think I fell for her before I knew the truth." He wagged a finger at Leif. "And if you ever repeat that to anyone, I will rip out your stones and force you to eat them. Raw."

"Stefan Hansen *smitten?*" Leif threw back his head and laughed. "I was beginning to think I would never see that day!"

"Come on." Stefan turned back to their path. "My stomach is growling."

Leif was instantly at his side. "Have you told her?"

Only by accident.

"No."

"Are you going to?"

Now Stefan stopped. "What is the point? We are leaving as soon as our twelve weeks of employment ends—which is next week, in case you lost count."

"We could stay longer…" Leif dangled the carrot.

"And do what? Abandon our plan?" Stefan shook his head angrily. "No. I need to prove to Pappa that I am worthy of the estate. I cannot do that if I am sitting way out here in Texas."

He resumed walking.

Leif matched his pace. "Stef?"

"What?"

"I want to ask Chenoa to return to Cheltenham with me."

Stefan stopped once again.

Will we ever *make it to supper?*

"Do you truly believe she will change her mind?" Stefan asked, hopeful that Leif was not deepening the hole he was diligently digging.

"About marrying me? I honestly do not know." Leif blew a frustrated sigh. "But if I leave here without her, there is absolutely no chance of that ever happening."

True.

Leif looked uncomfortable. "Would you mind her coming along? Be honest."

Stefan knew he could never be so selfish as to deny Leif his first real, though precarious, chance at happiness. "If she agrees, we will work it out."

A smile split Leif's face. "Yes?"

"Yes." Whether Chenoa would agree was highly doubtful, but there was no point in mentioning that at this time. "Now, can we please keep walking? I am starving!"

*****

Blake could hardly contain her excitement when Stefan presented her with the chickens.

"I intended to b-buy some after I had time to build a coop!" She peered inside the straw cage. "They are beautiful Stefan, thank you!"

He beamed at her. "The man said they are good layers.

Her excitement dimmed. "Um… where should I…"

"I thought they could stay in the wagon tonight," Stefan suggested. "Tomorrow I will build you a coop."

Blake felt a familiar and uncomfortable tug in her chest. She was capable of fashioning a coop on her own and did not need a man to do it for her.

Be independent.

Not rude.

She smiled up at Stefan. "Because the gift was your idea, I will accept the continued effort."

Stefan looked quite pleased with her reaction. "Shall I put them in the wagon now?"

Blake did not want to have to scrub chicken shit off the wagon floor, but because her yard was not fenced there was no other way to keep the birds from wandering off during the night.

Or being eaten by coyotes.

"That would be fine." Another thought occurred. "Have they b-been fed?"

Stefan grinned and pulled a packet of corn from inside his shirt. "This will keep them happy until you can procure more feed."

That extra bit of thoughtfulness warmed Blake's heart.

I could kiss him.

And that reaction shifted her mood immediately.

"I need to go b-back to the kitchen," she said abruptly and left Stefan, Leif, and Tom-tom quizzically watching her go.

Chenoa followed her and picked up a long spoon.

"What is wrong?" she asked while she stirred the gravy for the pot roast.

Blake found herself annoyingly close to tears. "I have to remind myself that they will b-be gone soon."

Chenoa said nothing, her eyes fixed on the pot.

Blake pulled the roast from the oven and looked at her friend. "Is something amiss?"

Chenoa shook her head.

Blake set the pan on top of the stove and put her hand on Chenoa's shoulder.

"Tell me?" she asked gently.

Chenoa hesitated, then turned watery eyes to Blake. "You

know that Leif wants to marry me."

"I do."

"But he is leaving too soon."

Understanding flooded Blake. "You cannot agree yet."

She wiped the unshed tears from her eyes. "And there is no more time."

Though Blake hated the thought of losing her companion she asked, "Would you go with him anyway?"

Chenoa huffed. "And travel alone with two men for two months?"

Relieved, Blake had to agree. "While they b-both seem to be men of good character, I can see there could be risks."

"Besides that, he has not asked me to go." Chenoa turned her attention back to the gravy. "It is hopeless, I think."

For both of us.

"We are strong women, Chenoa," Blake said firmly while she basted the roast. "We will find our way."

They finished the rest of the meal preparation in silence.

*****

"What are your plans?" Blake asked Tom-tom once the customary quintet was seated around the table. "Will you remain a scout for Westward Wagons?"

The Negro nodded. "As long as I stay out of Missouri and work for them in Texas, I should be safe."

Blake thought the answer was obvious, but she asked anyway. "How will you get back to Kansas City?"

He smiled at her like she was simple. "Horseback."

"The journey is much swifter, is it not?" Stefan asked.

"It is," Tom-tom confirmed. "About six weeks without the wagons."

"That is good to hear, because we will go back as well." Stefan handed Leif the platter of beef before his grin moved to each of his tablemates. "And we have news to share."

Leif looked like a puppy waiting for his bone. "Go on!"

"We finally received word from the land agent." Stefan paused, his blue eyes twinkling. "We now have permission to purchase one acre of land at each of our designated stops along the Santa Fe Trail."

Blake's jaw dropped. "You do?"

"We do!" Leif blurted.

Blake's glance bounced to Chenoa and back. "So you *are* going to open the four trading p-posts?"

"We are," Stefan confirmed. "As soon as we can secure our investors."

Blake stared at Stefan, considering what to say. She told him she was interested when they first discussed the idea. And now she had full confidence in the scheme—and in him. Would he balk at taking a female as an equal business partner once she made that possibility a reality?

She should speak to him privately in case he did. That way their ensuing argument would not be public.

"Where will you find your investors?" Tom-tom asked.

Stefan drew a deep breath. "We will probably begin with our uncle in Cheltenham."

Tom-tom froze, the fork halfway to his mouth and dripping gravy. "Cheltenham? Missouri?"

Leif nodded. "That is where we are from."

Tom-tom set the fork down slowly, the bite uneaten. "Do you remember what I told you about my life?"

"That a madame paid for you and set you free?" Stefan asked.

"And then told you to head west and stay out of the slave state of Missouri," Leif added.

"Yes, but... She also said she knew where my parents were, but I must not try to find them until it was safe to do so." Tom-tom looked shaken. "She said my parents were in Cheltenham."

Stefan stared hard at the Negro. "Do you know your parents' names?"

"My father had a French name." Tom-tom's brow

furrowed and his gaze darted over the tabletop as he pulled the information from his memory. "It was Jaqriel, I think. But he was called Jack."

"Your mother is Sarah," Leif sounded as stunned as he looked.

Tom-tom's eyes rounded. "Yes. Do you know of them?"

Stefan and Leif exchanged shocked looks, and then Stefan returned his attention to Tom-tom. "It seems that we have quite a story to tell you."

*****

"My father encountered two escaping slaves—a man and his pregnant wife—raiding his chicken coop when I was about six," Stefan began. "He was not married to my stepmother Sydney yet, but she insisted that they give the couple two chickens and a blanket before they sent them on their way."

Tom-tom frowned. "How do you know it was them?"

"Because I met your father when I was twelve and living under Nicolas's roof," Leif jumped in. "He was working with a stone mason Nicolas hired, and Nicolas remembered him as the escaping slave."

"Was he still a slave?" Tom-tom asked.

"He was," Leif confirmed. "But Nicolas bought him from the mason."

Stefan leaned forward. "He did not give the man a choice, mind you. He intended to free your father."

Tom-tom's gaze moved from brother to brother. "Where was my mother?"

"Well, that is where Aunt Rosie comes into the story." Stefan shifted his regard to Blake who sat silently, listening to the story unfold with wide eyes. "She is not truly our aunt."

Leif chuffed an embarrassed laugh. "She was actually Nicolas's fancy lady at one time."

Blake's eyebrows shot upward into the fringe of red hair

that curled over her forehead. "*What?*"

"But her friendship with our family is deeply treasured," Stefan assured her. "So when Jack told my father that Sarah was sold to a brothel, Rosie went looking for her."

Tom-tom pointed a finger at Stefan. "She is the woman who found me and bought me!"

Stefan nodded. "I am sure of it."

"After Rosie found Sarah, Nicolas went to Saint Charles and bought her from the brothel," Leif continued.

Tom-tom looked stricken. "Was she—working?"

"Only as a maid!" Stefan assured him.

"And once again, Nicolas would not take no for an answer." Leif smiled at Tom-tom. "He bought Sarah and brought her back to the estate, intending to free her as well."

Tom-tom blinked. "Where was I?"

Stefan looked at Leif. "I assume the same place where you were when Rosie found you five years ago."

Tom-tom seemed to be pondering that statement. "Are my parents free?"

"Yes. But—" Leif looked at Stefan to continue.

Stefan faced Tom-tom. "But they live under my father's protection. He pays them a salary and they live on the estate."

"Jack is the farming foreman," Leif explained. "Sarah was our sister's nanny."

"And mine," Stefan admitted. "I was only eight when she came to us."

Tom-tom looked like he might cry. "My mother was your nanny."

"So it seems." Stefan could hardly believe it himself.

Tom-tom pounded a fist on the table. "That settles it."

"Settles what?" Blake asked.

He looked at her, his expression blissfully determined. "I will travel to Cheltenham as well."

He lifted his glass in a toast. "And I will finally meet my parents."

The next day Blake watched Stefan build her chickens a coop and put up a fence made of meshed metal and wooden stakes to keep them in her back yard.

She was biding her time, looking for a chance to talk to him about his trading post business. She did not want to start an argument before he finished the job. And to ensure his affable mood she made him a lunch of a cold roast beef sandwich on freshly baked bread with a corn-and-pepper relish on the side.

"That was an incredible story about Tom-tom's parents," she said as Stefan popped the last bite of the sandwich into his mouth.

"I could not believe it," he said with his mouth full. "What were the chances?"

Blake handed him a cup of cold water from her pump. "If you had not mentioned you were from Cheltenham, none of that would have been d-discovered."

Stefan emptied the cup and handed it back to her. "The world is indeed small."

"And you p-plan to approach your uncle about investing in the trading posts?" she broached the subject on her mind.

Stefan untied his hair and combed his fingers through the waves. Blake watched the auburn curves slide through his long fingers and wished she could touch them herself.

"Yes," he said. "I believe he will see the wisdom of the venture."

Blake refilled the water cup. "What about your father?"

Stefan shook his head. "I will not ask him."

That made sense. If his father expected Stefan to make his own way, then asking him for money would be counter to that expectation.

"How many investors are you looking for?" she probed.

"That depends." He downed the second cup of water and handed it to Blake. "We figured we need five thousand dollars all together."

Blake accepted the empty cup. "Would you like more water?"

Stefan rubbed his hands together. "No thank you."

Blake set the cup and plate aside and sat down to face Stefan. "How much of that are you p-putting in?"

Stefan frowned a little while he re-tied his hair. "Why are you asking me this?"

Tread carefully.

"I have a little money," she offered. "And I am still thinking about offering cooked meals for the travelers."

With his unruly hair now corralled, Stefan's hands fell to his lap. "Are you saying that you want to invest?"

"Yes. I might."

Stefan smiled. "That is very sweet, Blake. But it is not necessary."

This was proving harder than she expected but in a completely different way. "Are you saying you will not *let* me invest?"

"Well, no. Not exactly…" Stefan shifted in his seat. "But I do not want you to put yourself in an uncomfortable position financially."

"Let me worry about myself," she warned. "I am not a child."

Chapter Twenty

No, you are most definitely not.

Stefan considered the beautiful and headstrong woman across from him. Perhaps he should give her a chance.

"How much would you want to put in?"

She folded her arms over her chest. "That d-depends."

"On what?"

"On how much *you* are putting in."

There was nothing for him to do but tell her. "Leif and I each will be paid six hundred dollars next week. Together we will put in a thousand."

Blake's brows pulled together. "How will you retain control with such a small p-percentage?"

The question startled Stefan—was it not obvious? "We will be doing all the work."

"But if someone invested four thousand dollars, then they would own eighty percent of the b-business and are entitled to eighty percent of the p-profits," she stated. "Is that not correct?"

It was.

And it riled him.

"How would you do it, then?" he challenged.

Blake recoiled a little at his stern tone. "Well... what if you b-borrowed the money?"

"From a bank?" Stefan scoffed. "No one would loan it to us!"

"No," she said carefully. "From your investors."

Sudden understanding flashed through Stefan's mind. "You mean instead of giving them ownership of the business, pay them back at an attractive rate of interest."

"Exactly." She shrugged. "As additional incentive, you could also offer a small percentage of the b-business once the loans were repaid."

"Like ten percent of the profits."

"Or five or fifteen—depending on how much cash they put up to b-begin with." She wagged a warning finger in his direction. "Just make sure you and Leif keep at least fifty-one percent for yourself."

Now Stefan crossed his arms and contemplated his next move. "How did you learn this?"

She gave him a mildly irritated look. "Who do you think managed my father's affairs when he no longer could?"

Stefan always assumed she lived off whatever monies her father had saved during his lifetime, and then spent what remained on her cross-country move to Santa Fe. It never occurred to him that she needed to learn how to handle their day-to-day funds during the decade she cared for the declining man.

"If I said you could invest," he said cautiously. "What would you do?"

Blake's shoulders slumped and she looked suddenly sad.

Even though he had no idea why she reacted thus, Stefan felt an almost irresistible urge to wrap her in his arms and spend the rest of his life making sure she was never sad again.

Her expression was somber. "I would want to go b-back to Kansas City along the trail with you."

*****

There they were. The words had actually come out of her mouth and could no longer be denied. But their impact on her mood was devastating.

Stefan unfolded his arms and leaned forward, his expression disbelieving. "You would abandon your café?"

"No. Not at all." Blake clasped her hands together and twisted her fingers. "I would come back to Santa Fe as soon as I could."

"Then why make the journey?" he pressed. "You have only been here two weeks."

I know.

It sounded crazy even to her. But she could not let the opportunity—or Stefan—disappear from her life without a fight.

"The remainder of my money is in a b-bank in Kansas City," she explained, hoping she did not reveal too much. "But that is not the only reason."

Stefan seemed to accept the first statement without question. "What is the second reason?"

Blake steeled herself for the masculine reaction she expected. "I want to see the locations for myself before I put money toward them.

"Do you not trust me?" he demanded.

"Of course I do—or I would never wish to be p-part of the scheme." Now she leaned forward as well. "But I want to ensure that the locations p-provide women the things that they need."

Stefan scowled. "What sort of things?"

"A clean water source, for a start. And protection from the wind and dust."

And whatever else I think of along the way.

Stefan flopped back in his chair. "Water goes without saying."

Blake wagged her head. "In business, nothing goes without saying."

Stefan was quiet for a minute before he said, "I will need to speak with Leif."

"Of course."

He peered at her. "Do you not worry about traveling alone with three men?"

Blake hoped that if she was allowed to go, then Chenoa would choose to come along as well. And while she could mention that possibility to Stefan as a bargaining point, she did not. Partly because she was not sure if Leif even wanted Chenoa to accompany him without her accepting his proposal first.

But mostly because she was still struggling with the decision to turn around and head back to Kansas City. Only thinking about doing so exhausted her.

She looked into Stefan's eyes and threw the question back at him. "Should I worry about traveling alone with the three men in question?"

"No." His demeanor softened. "You would be completely safe on all counts."

Blake stood up and reclaimed the dirtied dish and cup. "Let me know after you have talked to Leif."

*****

Stefan watched Blake walk back inside the kitchen door.

I will need to talk to Leif soon.

He hurried to finish the fencing and then retrieved the four chickens from their temporary housing in Blake's wagon. After releasing them into the fenced yard, he ducked into the kitchen. Chenoa was there, mixing chopped greens in a bowl.

Blake was apparently elsewhere.

"I have finished the coop and the fence and moved the chickens," he told her. After deciding not to ask about Blake, he said, "I will see you later, then."

"Thank you," she murmured.

Stefan hurried to the hotel hoping to find Leif. When he was not in his room, Stefan tried the stable where Sterk and

Heder were being boarded. Leif was there, grooming the horses and feeding them their extra helping of oats to restore the sturdy animals after the long trek here, and prepare them for the return journey.

Stefan ran his hand over Sterk's back and down his solid flank. "Will they be sound enough to make the journey back?"

"I think so." Leif poured another scoop of oats into the feeding trough. "They are both strong animals."

Stefan lifted Sterk's hooves one at a time and examined his shoes. "I think it would be wise to have them re-shoed before we set off."

"I thought the same thing." Leif leaned around Heder's chest to look at Stefan. "That is why I engaged the farrier for tomorrow."

Stefan smiled. "You are one step ahead of me. And I mean that in the literal sense."

He lowered the stallion's hoof and walked around him to where Leif stood. "Have you asked Chenoa to come with us yet?"

Leif sobered. "Yes. She said no."

"I am sorry." Stefan gave Leif's shoulder a conciliatory pat. "Did she say why?"

"No." Leif sighed. "And I could not pry the reason out of her."

Stefan risked asking, "What will you do?"

"I will still go back with you now, because I must if we are going to start a business," his brother stated. "And then I will return to Santa Fe while the fourth post is built. If she is still here, I will stay and run the operation from this end."

That made Stefan's part clear. He would run the business from Missouri. He wondered if he could do so from Cheltenham, or if that meant he would have to live in Kansas City.

Blake would never join me there.

Was that an obstacle they could not overcome? The possibility disturbed him more than he would have expected.

Stefan pulled a steadying breath and broached the subject

which drove him to search out Leif in the first place. "Blake wants to invest."

Leif looked at him in surprise. "She does?"

"Yes. And she has an idea that might have merit." Stefan explained the concept of providing hot meals—at a reasonable price—for the disheveled settlers when they reached the posts.

"She also says there needs to be an adequate water source and protection from wind and dust." Stefan tilted his head. "What do you think?"

"Her ideas present solid possibilities. Of course, that means planting trees." Leif rubbed his forehead in thought. "Does she expect to cook the meals?"

"No. She would hire cooks to live at the posts and prepare meals according to her instructions."

"And she would oversee this?" Leif queried. "Because while you and I are familiar with the livestock and the wagons, we do not know anything about cooking—beyond spitting a rabbit over a fire."

"I assume she would." Stefan smiled crookedly. "Let me assure you she seems to have a very good mind for business.

After he explained Blake's idea of the investors loaning them funds and only holding small percentages once they were paid back, Leif put up both of his hands.

"The woman is an absolute genius. I gladly welcome her involvement." He dropped his hands. "Even if she only has a pittance to add, that advice right there will save our hides."

"I agree." Stephan smiled. "We will tell her at supper."

*****

Blake received the news with unsurprisingly mixed emotions. "Thank you for trusting me."

Because she got what she asked for, she must now prepare to leave the only place where she was truly happy in her entire life. And she had been here less than a month.

But I will come back. Soon.

"When will we leave?"

"We?" Chenoa stared at her. "What are you talking about?"

Blake faced Chenoa and spoke slowly, willing her friend to understand the ramifications of her words. "I am investing in Stefan and Leif's quartet of trading p-posts."

Chenoa's gaze jumped to the brothers for confirmation and then back to hers. "I still do not understand. Why are you leaving?"

"Blake came up with the idea of selling hot meals to the families when they arrive at the posts," Stefan explained. "So she is traveling back to Kansas City with us to help pick the exact locations."

"And to withdraw my investment funds from the b-bank once I am there," Blake added. "That means I will be traveling with Stefan, Leif, and Tom-tom."

Chenoa's somber pale eyes met Blake's. "You have made this decision?"

"Only today. Yes."

"And you are sure of this?" Chenoa pressed. "You will not change your mind?"

"I will not." Blake gestured toward the brothers. "If I p-plan to give these men my money at the end of the journey, then I must see exactly what I am risking first."

In more ways than one, I suspect.

Chenoa waved an incredulous hand around the dining room. "But what about this house? And your café?"

Blake leaned forward and crossed her arms on the table. "I am coming back before winter, Chenoa. This is my new home. That will not change. I will p-pay the rent on this house before I leave, and you may stay here while I am gone."

Blake could practically see the wheels turning in Chenoa's mind. "You are going to Kansas City, and then coming right back to Santa Fe."

"Yes."

"As am I," Leif stated, surprising Blake with that news. "I

will return to Santa Fe while the fourth post is built, and manage the business from this end."

Chenoa nodded pensively. After a minute of silence, she turned to Leif and gave him a nervous smile.

"You and I need more time before I can do what you have asked of me. Because you must go now, but will return to Santa Fe, then I will go with you as well."

*****

Stefan did not react to Blake's strong assertion that she was returning to her new home in Santa Fe before winter, but her insistence that her decision *will not change* was at odds with how he hoped his future with her might turn.

When supper was finished and the dishes cleared away, Stefan asked Blake to walk outside with him and check on her chickens.

She looked skeptical, but agreed nonetheless.

The four chickens were tucked inside the little coop with their beaks buried under their wings. Stefan and Blake's presence caused a momentary disruption and a round of scolding clucks, but they soon settled back down.

"Thank you for this, Stefan." Blake slipped her hand into his and squeezed it. "This is probably the nicest gift I have ever been given."

Stefan doubted that was true. "Surely as a child you were doted on."

"Before my mother was killed, I remember having a d-doll with a porcelain head." Blake sighed. "But somehow it was broken soon after."

Stefan felt the sorrow in her tone. "Do you think your father broke it?"

"I never wanted to b-believe he would do anything like that." Blake cleared her throat and Stefan wondered if the painful memory would prompt tears.

"But when I got older and understood that he b-blamed me for her murder," she continued. "I could see no other explanation."

"I am so sorry, Blake," he said softly.

She looked into his eyes. "What about you? What was the best gift you ever received?"

Stefan was about to name his stallion, Sterk, before the truth smacked him into his senses. Now he was the one in danger of crying.

"It was my mother, Sydney."

"The woman your father married when you were six?"

Stefan nodded. "I cannot wait for you to meet her. She is the most capable and loving woman I have ever known."

Blake tilted her head, her expression confused. "How would I meet her? She is in Washington with your father, is she not?"

Did it again.

It was time for him to speak openly and stop dancing around his burgeoning feelings. "I must confess, I find myself hoping that we might have a future together."

Blake opened her mouth to speak but Stefan decided to act before she could object. He put his knuckle under her chin and tilted her face upward. Her wide eyes stared into his, neither encouraging him nor objecting.

When his lips landed on hers, his eyes closed and he concentrated on the sensation of her lips yielding to hers.

Because they did.

Stefan was not sure if Blake had ever kissed a man before, but he had kissed enough women to be very good at it. With the nature of his relationship with Blake on the line, he abandoned all restraint.

Chapter Twenty-One

Blake could barely breathe. And a pleasant tickling tingle grew low in her belly.

What is happening?

With her eyes closing of their own volition, Blake experienced the first romantic kiss of her almost twenty-nine-year existence. She surrendered herself to the intoxicating sensations, both watching herself from the outside, and delving deep into the visceral responses roused by a big, beautiful man whose mouth pulled hers into his.

When Stefan released her, she could barely stand.

"Was that acceptable?" he murmured.

Blake forced her gaze to focus on his. "More than... But why did you do that?"

"Because I find myself smitten by you, Blake Somersby," Stefan admitted. "You are an intriguing woman and I do not think I ever want to be away from you."

Blake leaned away from him, disturbed by the ramifications of his words. "Do you p-plan to live in Santa Fe, then?"

His brow flickered. "No, but—"

"Then we can have no future." That prospect pushed a

dagger through her heart and she struggled to take a deep enough breath.

"Will you not give me a chance to change your mind?" Stefan asked.

Blake felt like she was signing her own death warrant but the truth was the truth. "Stefan, I do not plan to marry anyone. If that was what you were thinking."

"But why not?" he asked. "What stops you?"

"The law, I am afraid."

Stefan was clearly confused. "What law?"

Blake hesitated. How could she answer without giving her situation away?

She chose her words carefully. "The law that says whatever a woman b-brings into a marriage b-belongs to her husband, and no longer to her."

Stefan's shoulders slumped in relief. "Blake. I would never claim your pots and pans, your beloved spices, or anything else you carried away from Kansas City. I promise you."

If you only knew.

"The law is the law, Stefan. Unless there is a way around it, I will not marry."

Stefan took a gentle hold of her hands. "How do you feel about me? Honestly?"

Blake risked being truthful, thinking a broken heart at this point might make her future life simpler and easier to navigate.

"I might be falling in love with you."

Stefan looked relieved. "And I might be falling in love with you."

Blake did not expect the surge of hope and happiness that flooded her frame when she heard his words.

This is all a terrible mistake.

His expression was as sincere as any could be. "Will you give us a chance? We owe it to ourselves, do we not?"

Blake wanted to scream *no, no, no!*

She tried to.

But what came out of her mouth, out of her heart, were the catastrophic words, "Yes. We do."

Stefan's head tilted. "You did not stutter."

Blake froze. "What?"

"You stuttered when you said 'whatever a woman brings into a marriage belongs to her husband' but after that, when you were expressing your own thoughts, your words were clear."

Blake's pulse surged and roared in her ears.

He was right.

"In fact…" Stefan's head tilted the other way. "You have been stuttering a lot less, lately."

"I had not thought about it," Blake admitted. "I only have trouble with a few letters, I think."

"B, D, and P. But not all the time." One corner of Stefan's mouth curved upwards. "Yes, I noticed. And when you just said 'we do' you did not stutter."

Blake dropped to a seat on the steps to the front porch, pondering this new information. "I wondered… when I was released from some of my terrible memories… if the stutter would go away."

Stefan sat beside her. "If you think about it, does it get better or worse?"

"I d-do not—well, now I know." She huffed. "Worse."

"Then the answer is simple." Stefan wrapped an arm around her. "Do not think about it."

Blake turned her head and gazed into his eyes. "How can I d-do that?"

"Like this." Stefan pulled her into his embrace and kissed her again. Very well.

May 23, 1845

Last night after a week of preparation, and while Blake was packing the last of her things, she found herself sitting on the rug in her bedroom staring at the floor.

What in God's name was she thinking?

For two months she endured the exhausting, filthy, frightening, dangerous, monotonous, wet, cold, windy, and seemingly endless journey. Her body ached every night. Her pallet atop her crates and boxes was never comfortable.

When she finally reached Santa Fe and took her first bath in this, her new home, she was overwhelmed with simple contentment—an emotion which had been missing from her life for years.

And scrubbing the embedded wagon trail dirt off her skin carried away all the negative emotions which had grasped at her for most of her previous life: the hopelessness, degradation, imprisonment, and worthlessness.

The effect on her soul made her giddy.

But now she was preparing to make the trip again. And not in the direction of a new life, but back in the direction of the life she hated and had happily left behind.

Even though she fully intended to make her stay brief and return to Santa Fe as quickly as possible, the niggling fear that she would be trapped there could not be shaken.

I cannot do this.

But she must. If she wanted to expand her options and her income by investing in the trading posts, she needed to retrieve some of the money she left with Mister Jackson Whittle.

And it was only sensible to see where the posts would be built along the way.

Blake Somersby you are a liar.

And you know it.

Blake heard Chenoa climbing the stairs. She stopped in the doorway when she saw Blake sitting on the floor.

"Is something amiss?"

Blake decided to be honest. "I do not know if I can stand to make this journey two more times."

Chenoa walked into the room and sat cross-legged on the floor in front of her.

"Why *are* you doing this?" Chenoa leaned forward and peered into her eyes. "Tell me the truth."

Blake faltered. "I—because—the trading p-posts are a very good idea."

"Yes they are. But that is not why."

No it is not.

"If I want to invest, I need to collect the money from my b-bank," Blake stated.

Chenoa frowned. "I talked to Leif. He says you could send a letter with Stefan and the bank would give him money."

Blake had not thought of that, but it was probably true. She threw one last gauntlet.

"If I do not go, you will not go," she said softly. "And Leif is the first good thing to come your way in ten years. I will not let my selfishness stand b-between you and a chance for happiness."

Chenoa's gaze dropped. "I am grateful for your friendship. But I do not believe that is why."

Blake's excuses were spent, but she was not ready to voice her truth.

Let someone else do it.

"What do you think it is then?"

Chenoa's pale eyes met hers. "Stefan Hansen."

There it was. But, "What do you mean by that?"

Chenoa's expression disarmed Blake's response. "You are in love with him. Why can you not say this?"

Because that makes it real.

"You must decide, Blake. Is he worth the journeys?" Chenoa climbed to her feet. "Once you decide, tell me if we are going."

With that she walked across the hall to her own room and closed the door.

After a night where the hours alternated between restless wakefulness and dream-disturbed slumber, Blake awoke this morning having come to a decision.

Stefan Hansen was definitely worth the effort.

Please God, do not let me be wrong.

*****

Today was pay day at last. Stefan and Leif went to the bank in Santa Fe along with the other men who worked the wagon train to collect their six hundred dollars each.

Though Blake spent the last several days preparing to head back across the prairie to the city she loathed, there were still tasks that she needed to accomplish.

First, she went to the landlord and paid the next six months of rent on the house as surety that she would return.

"I expect I will be back before that," she told him as she counted out the money. "And if the house is in the same condition as I left it, and none of the contents are missing, I will pay you an additional one hundred d-dollars at that time."

The man's eyes brightened. "I understand, Senorita. I will keep an eye on it myself."

Blake thanked him and went to the lumber yard to procure milled lumber. In spite of the promise of a reward for the landlord, she asked Stefan to put boards inside the shuttered windows on the ground floor.

"So no one can peek inside and take stock of what is in there," she explained.

She hated to leave her new cast iron cookware behind, not to mention her collection of spices and hardly-opened cookbooks. But on this journey they would be moving quickly, and all meals would be geared toward simplicity.

Even so, it was clear they needed to take Blake's little wagon, and she was very glad she had not sold it.

"We might want to consider doubling the team to four," Leif suggested. "They could pull faster and longer that way."

"It means packing along more grain," Stefan counseled the group at supper that night. "But I agree the speed would be worth it."

"We are not moving entire households this time," Blake reminded the men. "Besides the grain for the animals and food for us, all we need are b-bedrolls, extra clothing, and something to cook and eat with."

And to that end, Blake had washed and pressed all of her masculine clothing—which she never expected to wear ever again. But to be honest, those garments were far better suited to the journey than dresses could ever be.

With a resolute sigh, she closed the lid on her trunk.

*****

"How soon can we leave?" Tom-tom asked at supper that night.

"What still needs to be done?" Blake asked.

"Buy the grain and load it into the wagon." Stefan ticked the tasks on his long fingers. "Buy two more oxen. Attach a longer tongue for the wagon. Buy tack for a team of four."

He looked around the dinner table. "Not in that order, of course."

"Are the horses ready?" Chenoa asked.

Stefan nodded. "Reshod, rested, and fattened."

"What do we have for human food?" Leif asked Blake.

"I procured about thirty pounds of jerky, fifty pounds of masa, ten pounds of sugar, and three large canisters of lard. And—I am bringing the chickens for their eggs." Blake shrugged. "The food will not be fancy, but with adding in game and fish we will not starve."

"Do not forget that we will cross paths with other travelers this time," Tom-tom added. "We were on the first train of the season, but other trains have been leaving Independence about every two weeks."

Blake remembered that from the initial discussion regarding the trading posts. "And I imagine you three will not be the only ones heading back to work another train."

"True," Stefan confirmed. "In fact, two of the men left straight from the bank today."

"I will take the wagon to the waggoneer tomorrow," Leif

volunteered.

Stefan nodded. "I will go to the stockyard and select two oxen to complete the team."

Tom-tom smiled. "And I will take care of procuring adequate grain."

Blake looked at Chenoa. "Let's cook whatever food we have that cannot be packed with us, and then pack the rest."

"If we can complete these things tomorrow, will we leave the next day?" Leif looked around the table.

Blake's belly clenched.

So soon?

She drew a deep breath, but her mind was made up.

"I can be ready," she forced herself to say. "What about the rest of you?"

Inquisitive glances bounced around the supper table, and no one objected.

Stefan grinned. "I guess it is settled then."

May 27, 1845

"Our goal is to cover twenty miles a day and reach the fourth location for the posts on the eighth day..." Stefan frowned at Blake. "What are you wearing?"

She lifted her chin defiantly. "Clearly you have never worn a dress or you would understand that trousers are far more p-practical when traveling rough like we are."

"Are you saying that you will dress like a man for this journey, too?" Stefan's voice squeaked incongruously with his disbelief.

Blake detected a definite twinge of disappointment in his tone. "Yes. It makes sense, does it not?"

"I suppose," he conceded.

"How will you know how far we have traveled each day?" she asked. "Is the trail marked in some way?"

She had not paid attention on the way to Santa Fe, but

now being the only wagon traveling with a small group it occurred to her that she had no sense of how far they traveled daily with the train.

Leif looked puckish. "I met a man who was working on a way to tabulate the distance traveled by counting the rotations of the wagon's rear wheel. He gave me one of his designs to try and the waggoneer attached it under the wagon bed."

All five adults bent down to look.

"This tab here moves that wheel one notch with every rotation," Leif explained. "Then every twentieth notch moves the next wheel once. And every twentieth notch there moves the third wheel once."

Stefan looked at Leif. "That means each notch on the third wheel is four hundred rotations."

"Yep. And he measured the wheel and said four hundred rotations is very close to one mile."

"One mile for every notch on the third wheel." Blake was impressed. "That is brilliant."

"And a tool we can sell at the posts," Stefan added. "The settlers can definitely use this."

It took two more days than originally planned to get everything finished, but before the sun topped the mountains to the east on this, the third morning, Stefan led the team of four oxen across the wash and onto the end of the Santa Fe Trail.

Once they cleared the town, Blake drove the team and began training Chenoa to do the same. Because the hostlers and scout rode on horseback during the trip to Santa Fe, none of the men actually had the same amount of experience in driving the wagon as Blake had.

Driving four oxen required more arm and shoulder strength than driving two, but the animals understood their task and stuck to the worn paths without being directed to.

The quintet moved at a brisk pace and did not stop for a break until late afternoon. Leif checked the third wheel under the wagon, and the marker was one notch past the first one— where they started the day.

"Twenty-one miles!" he called out.

Stefan clapped his hands together. "Excellent. Let's set up camp for the night."

Supper that night was jerky and corncakes. Conversation was sparse. Blake was not certain whether that was because everyone was as tired as she was, or because the enormity of what they had embarked upon was hitting the rest of them the same way it was hitting her.

The two women's beds were made up inside the wagon and the three men would sleep underneath. Just as she did the very first night on the trail in March, Blake climbed into her bed and wondered if she could possibly survive the journey.

And she still had one more crossing after this one.

I will return.

I must return.

"Goodnight, Blake," Chenoa said softly. "And thank you."

"You are welcome," Blake whispered. "Sleep well."

As the roosting chickens clucked and settled in their cage at the back of the wagon, Blake lay on her back and stared at the canvas above her.

Chapter Twenty-Two

June 5, 1845

Leif checked the wheels under the wagon regularly and in the early afternoon of the seventh day announced that they were one hundred and forty-five miles from Santa Fe.

The party had traveled around the hilly southern edge of the mountains east of Santa Fe and out onto level land.

"There is a decent stream over there," Tom-tom pointed out. "And with the mountains as a barricade the wind is not quite as fierce here."

Stefan agreed that this location for a trading post was just what they had been hoping for. He collected the stakes from the wagon and, with Leif and Tom-tom's help, paced out an acre of land with one side set back from, but parallel with, the trail.

The men pounded the stakes into the corners of the plot, and then placed additional stakes at ten-pace intervals between them. Then they strung fencing wire from stake to stake.

When they finished, Stefan stood in the middle of the rectangle with his hands on his hips.

"This is it, Leif," he said to his brother. "The start of the line of Hansen Trading Posts."

Leif flashed a self-satisfied grin. "Wait until you see this."

He ducked inside the little wagon and came out with a wooden placard about three feet square.

Blake looked at Chenoa. "Where was that?"

She giggled—the first time Blake had ever heard her react to anything in such a manner since she met the woman. "It was under my bed."

This trip will be good for her.

Leif carried the sign to the center of the side of the plot that faced the trail before he flipped it around. In bold black lettering on a bright white background the words declared:

Future Site of a
Hansen Trading Post

Stefan was clearly taken by surprise—and happily so. "This was your idea?"

"Yep!" Leif looked like he was about burst with pride. "And there are three more in the wagon."

"This way, the wagon masters will know and plan to stop on subsequent journeys!" Stefan did a silly jig that make Blake laugh. "This is perfect, Leif!"

Blake walked over to Stefan and stood beside him. "This is good, Stefan. Very good."

He looked down at her, smiling. "I am glad you approve, Miss Somersby."

Blake slipped her arm around his waist and leaned her head against his shoulder, turning her attention to the staked claim in front of them. "I am imagining all the women who will stop here, wash with clean water from the stream, and enjoy a supper of hot b-beef stew and b-biscuits."

A grinning Stefan rested his hand on Blake's shoulder. "I think we will make a good team."

Blake smiled.

So do I.

June 11, 1845

Blake reined the oxen to a halt and considered the position of the sun directly above them. "Why are we stopping?"

Stefan rode Sterk to the side of the wagon while Leif dismounted. "For a couple of reasons. Leif wants to check the mileage. He thinks we have reached the next stopping point on the trail."

Blake looked around considering the land. This would then be the location for the second in the chain of four trading posts between Council Grove and Santa Fe. There was a nearby wooded area which might provide lumber for wagon repairs, plus a water source—two of their requirements.

"And the other reason?" Chenoa asked.

Stefan smiled and pointed to a pond. "Because that stream, which flows into one of those rivers, has been dammed."

"Beavers!" Chenoa looked pleased.

Blake did not understand why they were so excited about a beaver dam, but before she could ask Leif popped up from under the wagon, paper and graphite in hand.

"Two hundred and ninety-two miles," he announced. "This is the spot!"

That was good news but, "What about the b-beavers?"

"My father used to supplement his income by hunting beaver and selling their pelts," Stefan explained. "He said there was good money in it."

"And the meat is very good," Chenoa added.

"We have made pretty good time, so far," Leif stated. "I propose we take a couple of days to rest the animals and do some beaver hunting."

Blake had to admit she welcomed the proposition. This journey was every bit as hard as the first one, but for different reasons—mainly the speed at which they were moving, and reining four oxen instead of two.

"I will ride ahead and see if the next train is approaching," Tom-tom offered. "Settlers in the last one were eager to trade for eggs, so maybe we can get some coffee this time."

"Great idea." Stefan turned to Blake. "How many eggs can we spare?"

"Half a dozen, at the least," Blake replied. "More if we do not eat them for a couple days."

When the man claimed the hens were good layers, he told the truth. The five travelers enjoyed fresh eggs every morning and there were usually enough to cook with at supper as well.

"If you two shoot the beavers, I will clean the skins," Chenoa offered.

"Will you cook the meat?" Stefan asked Blake.

"Some of it," she agreed. "And I will dry the rest to take with us."

*****

Blake heard the rifles fire in quick succession. Several minutes later Stefan and Leif—both soaked to the thighs—walked back to the wagon dragging two large beavers with them. She and Chenoa had already hobbled the oxen and started a pair of fires.

Chenoa retrieved a hatchet from the wagon. "I will cut saplings for the drying frames while they skin the carcasses."

Blake walked over to where the brothers worked.

Stefan looked up from the task. "Once we get the skin off and remove the castor glands and oil sacks, we can start butchering the meat."

"I have the fires started and a pot of water heating," she replied. "I plan to treat the meat like a pot roast—simmer it for a few hours and throw in potatoes and onions toward the end."

Stefan nodded and returned to his gruesome job. "That sounds good."

Chenoa returned dragging green and flexible lengths of young trees. Blake helped her untwist some rope so Chenoa could use the five smaller strands to tie the wood into circular frames.

"I can use the twine we brought to tie the pelts to the racks," she stated as she built the five-foot diameter frames. "But this requires something stronger."

By the time the sun hung low in the western sky the two beaver pelts were stretched on the drying frames and Chenoa had them nearly scraped clean.

Blake boiled the beaver meat for six hours to assure it was tender. While it cooked slowly over a low fire, she sliced the remaining meat into thin strips and trimmed away all the fat. She rolled the strips in salt then hung them to dry over a second low fire. Stefan and Leif were tasked with turning the salted meat regularly to ensure they dried well.

The first chunks of beaver meat, which were now simmering with the potatoes and onions, smelled delicious and broke apart easily when Blake prodded them with a fork. The sound of horse hooves pulled her attention to the trail, and she smiled when Tom-tom rode into view. But her smile faded when she saw the expression on his face.

Tom-tom reined his horse to a stop and jumped from the saddle.

"What did you find?" Stefan's tone proved he noticed Tom-tom's somber demeanor as well.

"I do not have good news," the Negro scout stated. "There is trouble ahead."

Chapter Twenty-Three

"What is it?" Stefan asked.

"Cholera." Tom-tom looked sickened by what he had discovered. "The train coming has been decimated by it."

Chenoa's pale eyes rounded. "What is cholera?"

"Cholera is an infection of the gut," Leif explained. "It causes pain, nausea, and violent diarrhea."

Chenoa frowned. "And people die from this?"

Stefan nodded grimly. "If they do not have enough clean drinking water, they turn feverish, have seizures, and die."

"Clean drinking water is hard to maintain on the trail," Blake murmured. She looked up at Stefan. "What should we do?"

Stefan wished he had a better answer than, "There is nothing we can do, I am afraid."

"We must stay away from them," Chenoa declared. "We cannot risk the evils spirits seeing us and sickening us."

This was the first time Stefan heard Chenoa espouse the Fox thoughts about diseases and their source. While it was true that no one knew how the disease was spread, he did not believe evil spirits had anything to do with it.

"I agree we should stay away." Stefan hated to be selfish

and not offer what little aid they might, but the truth was undeniable. "Once a single person succumbs, those around them often fall as well."

"Many on the train believe that cholera was brought by the new Irish immigrants," Tom-tom relayed. "The disease is new to our continent, so they might be right."

"Are there Irishmen on the train?" Blake asked.

"There were." Tom-tom's consternation was clear. "They were *accidentally* shot once the disease broke out."

A terrible thought poked Stefan. "How close did you get?"

Tom-tom put up his hands. "I did not touch anyone. Nor did I accept the food and drink they offered."

"How far ahead are they?" Stefan pressed.

"I estimate about ten miles."

"And they are headed this way?" Leif asked.

Tom-tom shook his head. "They are not moving anywhere at this point."

Stefan looked at Leif. "We will need to circle around them."

Leif nodded his agreement. "And up wind, just in case."

That is a very wise suggestion.

Stefan returned his attention to Tom-tom. "Can you lead us around the stalled wagons and be able to find the trail again when we are safely past them?"

"I can." All eyes turned to Chenoa. "I know this land," she continued. "It is how I knew where to find the wagons when I escaped."

Stefan made the decision. "We will stay here for a couple days as planned. Then Chenoa will take the head and lead us around the danger and back to the trail."

He pointed at the scout. "Tom-tom will keep an eye on the train and let us know if they start moving in this direction before that."

"Agreed," Leif seconded and rubbed his belly. "And now—can we eat supper? It smells wonderful."

June 14, 1845

Blake packed the dried beaver meat in salt. Chenoa and Leif devised a way to attach the huge round sapling frames with the beaver pelts to the back of the wagon so they could drag behind it and continue to dry in the sun.

Chenoa rode Sterk. Her life with the Fox was filled with horses so she was not cowed by the big stallion. And though she was accustomed to riding bareback, Stefan convinced her that Sterk was not.

"He will not understand your commands," he explained as he gave Chenoa a leg up into the saddle. "Just be gentle on the reins and you two will get along fine."

With his mount claimed by another, Stefan sat on the wagon's bench beside Blake. He smiled at her.

This worked out well.

The group decided to stick to the trail until they could see the stalled wagon train ahead of them. Stefan sat beside Blake as she drove the team, his admiration for the unconventional woman growing daily.

"You seem to be stuttering even less than before," he observed. "Perhaps your new way to consider what happened to you really is affecting it."

"Or perhaps I have not been as upset." Blake smiled shyly up at him from under her wide-brimmed hat. "Perhaps I have reasons to be happy."

Stefan lifted her chin and gave her a quick kiss on the lips. "I am happy as well."

He looked at his brother. Leif and Chenoa rode side by side rode in front of the wagon so their backs were turned and they did not notice the kiss. Tom-tom rode nearby, always on the alert.

Stefan watched Leif. His head was always turned toward Chenoa. And he smiled a lot. Snippets of conversation floating back and Stefan figured out they were speaking in Fox half the time. He wondered if he should try and learn the language.

It might come in handy with the posts.

Tom-tom rode up next to the wagon. "There they are."

Stefan squinted his eyes against the morning sun and peered forward. The wagons formed a square, but several of the animals grazed outside of it.

"They have stalled long enough for the livestock to have eaten all of the grass inside," Stefan said. "This is not good."

Chenoa stopped Sterk and looked back at Stefan.

He threw his left arm to the side and pointed.

She nodded and reined the stallion off the trail.

*****

The little wagon's progress was slowed by the rougher terrain, and without a trail to follow Blake had to work harder to direct the oxen. Tom-tom and Chenoa rode ahead, looking for the easiest path through the wild prairie which was riddled with hillocks and prairie dog holes.

"I am glad I was not the first to traverse this land," Blake told Stefan. "It must have taken three or four months to cover what now takes but two."

"Do you want me to drive for a while?" he asked.

She seriously considered it. Her upper arms burned and her shoulders ached.

"After we cross the stream," she conceded.

The stream was small and judging by the look of its banks was merely a wash for rainfall.

"Looks like it rained here," Stefan said, confirming her thoughts. "And we did not get any where we were."

"Just clouds and wind." That was good, considering the meat and pelts that were drying. Blake caught a whiff of something vile and covered her nose. "Ooh. What is that?"

Stefan winced. "Death."

As the group circled around the wagons at a half-a-mile distance, they had moved from upwind to downwind of the train. Sterk and Heder pranced nervously with the change of wind and its tragic warning.

Blake gagged.

"Do you have a kerchief to tie over your face?" Stefan asked.

She nodded and handed him the reins. Then she climbed back into the wagon to retrieve it.

"Get it wet," Stefan instructed. "That will help."

He handed her his kerchief. Blake dipped both into the pitcher of drinking water, then rung them out through the wagon's back opening. Then she returned to the front and climbed onto the driver's bench.

Stefan accepted his wet kerchief and tied it over the bridge of his nose so it covered his mouth. Blake did the same.

It helped. A little.

"When can we get back on the trail?" she asked.

"I believe we are headed there now." Stefan stared past her toward the open prairie. "Blazes!"

*****

Stefan handed the reins to Blake and faced Chenoa, twenty yards ahead. He cupped his hands around his mouth and blew a warbling whistle. Sterk stopped, whirled around, and trotted to Stefan, ignoring Chenoa's commands.

"What's going on?" Blake demanded.

"Indians." Stefan leapt to the ground and grabbed Sterk's reins.

"What—"

"Indians." Stefan cut Chenoa off. "Get inside the wagon and hide."

Clearly he did not need to repeat the order. Chenoa was already on the ground and running to the wagon's back opening.

Stefan pulled himself into his stallion's saddle as Leif and Tom-tom met up with him.

"Do you see them?" Stefan asked. "What tribe?"

"This is Fox and Sauk land," Tom-tom answered.

"Let me do the talking," Leif said sternly. "And tell Blake to keep Chenoa out of sight!"

I do believe both women already know that.

"You stay with the wagon," Tom-tom instructed Stefan. "I will go with Leif. To be honest, a Negro will be trusted more easily than a white man."

Stefan grimaced, knowing that was true and why.

Tom-tom threw a thumb in Leif's direction. "But a white man who can speak their language, even rudimentarily, will impress them."

"You will warn them about the cholera and tell them to stay away from the wagons?" Stefan pressed. "For their own safety?"

"Of course." Leif looked at Tom-tom. "Let's go."

Stefan watched the two unarmed men ride out to meet the Indian party of six, praying that their warning was successful, and that the Indians would not feel as though they needed to come closer or inspect the wagon.

Then, so he did not appear either defensive or aggressive, he reined Sterk around and rode back to the wagon's side.

*****

Blake watched the scene play out in front of her with the reins gripped tightly to stop her shaking hands.

"Leif and Tom-tom are riding out to meet the party," she said softly, letting Chenoa know what was happening.

"How many?" Chenoa asked.

"Six."

"That is good." Chenoa sounded relieved. "Not a war party. They will want to know why we are not staying on the trail."

"At least we have a very good reason," Blake replied.

"Now Stefan is riding back to us."

The look on his face was grimly hopeful.

"Tom-tom suggested I stay back," he explained once he was by Blake's side. "White men are not trusted, but Negroes understand how the red man has been treated."

Though the point was valid, Blake wondered if Stefan explained so that she would not think of him as a coward. Under less fraught circumstances she might smile at that.

"But Leif speaks Sauk, so that shows respect," Chenoa offered from.

"That is what Tom-tom said." Stefan looked at the group of men gathered about fifty yards away. "Leif is speaking now, and he is using his hands quite a bit."

Chenoa chuckled from her hiding place. "Is that not what anyone does when their language is limited?"

Blake did smile at that. "It is true."

"I wish they would stop pointing at the wagon," Stefan grumbled.

Blake's pulse pounded in her ears. "Do you think they will want to look inside?"

"I am afraid so." Stefan faced the women. "Hide yourself, Chenoa. Blake, stay right where you are."

Blake watched out of the corner of her eye as Chenoa climbed behind an unopened bag of oats and covered herself with the one open that was only partially full.

If she does not move, she will be undetectable.

"Here they come," Stefan warned.

Blake was so frightened she felt like she was going to wet herself.

She must have looked frightened because Stefan leaned toward her. "Remember you are a man."

Blake gasped. She had forgotten about her own disguise.

"Do not speak," Stefan continued. "I will speak for you if necessary."

Blake nodded mutely.

Leif was smiling as the group approached. That had to be good. Tom-tom was not, but he did not appear overly concerned either.

Please God, protect us.

"Blake!" Leif called out and she nearly fainted in fear when he did. "I have promised our friends a chicken in exchange for allowing us to travel on their land."

Oh!

Blake nodded and moved through the wagon past Chenoa to the cage at the back.

Am I supposed to pick one?

Leif appeared in the opening with one of the Indians and said something to him in his language.

The man answered and pointed at Blake.

She felt wetness between her legs and knew she had lost control. Her face flamed in humiliation.

Leif turned to face her. "He asks you to give him the white one."

Blake opened the top of the cage and reached inside. She grasped the white chicken, lifted it out, and leaned over to hand it to Leif. She kept her legs together, hoping the wet spot was not visible.

Leif handed the chicken to the Indian and spoke to him again while Blake closed the cage and fastened the latch with trembling fingers.

Thankfully, Leif and the man rode away.

Blake closed the back flap and made her way back to the front of the wagon, wondering what she should do next.

Change her underclothes and trousers for certain. And as soon as possible.

She sat backwards on the driver's bench and waited. After several minutes of conversation, the Indians turned their horses around and galloped off.

Blake sucked a huge sigh of relief. "They are leaving," she said quietly. "You can come out now."

Chenoa pushed the feed sack aside. "We are safe?"

"Yes."

Stephan addressed her from the same spot he stood in before she went to get the chicken. "Are you ladies well?"

How was she going to explain that she needed a minute to change clothes? By not revealing too much.

"We are, but we need a moment." Blake slid off the wagon's seat and through the opening, then she closed the front flap.

Chenoa gave her a puzzled look.

"I think I wet myself," Blake whispered sadly. "I need to change."

As she unfastened her trousers, the truth was exposed. But in a six-week journey, there was no way to avoid it.

She groaned and looked at Chenoa. "My cycle has started."

Chapter Twenty-Four

"Is everything all right?" Stefan asked when Blake opened the flap.

"Yes. We are fine." Blake reclaimed her seat on the bench while Chenoa opened the back flap and climbed down.

"That was close," Leif said. "They did not believe me about the other wagons being dangerous."

"They wanted to raid the horses since the wagons were not moving," Tom-tom added.

Stefan climbed down from Sterk and gave Chenoa a leg up into the saddle. "How did you convince them otherwise?"

Leif grinned. "I asked them if they could not smell the decay, because I was choking from it."

A laugh broke from Chenoa. "They would never admit a white man scented the wind better than they did."

"I counted on it." Leif shrugged. "And before they could argue, I offered them a chicken as a sort of toll in exchange for permission to rejoin the trail once we passed the contaminated wagons."

"He was brilliant," Tom-tom effused. "I could not understand what they were saying, but I watched their faces and they were impressed."

Chenoa beamed at Leif. "You did well."

He beamed back. "Thank you."

Stefan climbed up and sat next to Blake. "Let's get moving before we overstay our welcome, shall we?"

Blake handed Stefan the reins. "Will you drive for a while?"

He accepted them, his face etched with concern. "Are you certain you are well?"

"It is nothing."

"Why will you not tell me, then?"

Blake glared at him. "It is not your concern."

Stefan was clearly irritated. He slapped the reins and shouted, "Step up!"

As the wagon began to roll he growled, "I believed us to be able to speak honestly to one another."

"We are. About most things," Blake qualified.

Stefan shot her a glance. "What can we not speak of?"

Blake knew her face must be red as the kerchief Stefan wore. "Personal things."

"I have no secrets from you," he pressed. "I will tell you anything you want to know."

Blake found her opening. "Then what do you know about women's bodies?"

Stefan's expression showed his shock and embarrassment. "What—what do you mean?"

This was not going well. "I mean about how their bodies function?"

He was still clearly both confused and alarmed. "Function?"

She huffed her frustration. "Monthly!"

Stefan's mouth opened, then snapped shut. He turned to look straight ahead, his gaze fixed on the unmarked prairie.

"I am sorry I pushed for your answer," he murmured after several minutes. "Especially after what happened on the way to Santa Fe."

"You *should* be sorry," Blake grumbled. "B-but to be honest, there is no way to keep it secret. Not with such a small group and a single wagon."

Stefan's regard returned to hers. "I promise not to press you for answers in the future."

"Thank you."

"Can I ask you one thing, though?"

Blake narrowed her eyes and glared at him. "What?"

"What did you do with the rags?"

"I had to bury the rags at night so I was not d-discovered."

Stefan's expression shifted to one of admiration. "You are amazing."

"No," she huffed. "I was desperate."

*****

As Blake lay on her bedroll in the quiet darkness, she could not get the memory of the death stench on the wind out of her head. She had never experienced any sort of epidemic so had nothing to compare it to. But the idea that the wagons were stuck in the middle of the prairie several hundreds of miles from help, and with a virulent disease sweeping through the settlers was the stuff of nightmares.

The trading posts should offer medical help.

Blake's eyes widened at that idea. Why hadn't she thought of that before? It was an obvious need.

With the posts placed approximately one hundred and forty miles from each other, help would never be more than seventy miles away.

And more likely closer.

A fast rider could reach a post in three days or less.

The medical person would not necessarily have to be a doctor, but someone with basic knowledge of common ailments and their cures. The key would be a sure supply of herbs and medicines.

Herbs would be easy—simply plant a garden of those most often used to treat infections and injuries at each post.

And medicines would be delivered along with other supplies on a regular basis.

Blake decided to talk to Stefan about that the first thing in the morning.

*****

"That is a great idea," Stefan agreed over his eggs and coffee.

"I think so, too." Leif sat on the ground by the fire. "So *now* how many people are going to live at each post?"

"One person could have more than one responsibility," Blake pointed out. "For example, the cook could also provide the medical help."

That made sense to Stefan. "The posts will be very busy for a few days, but in between trains will be very quiet. We do not need to pay more workers than necessary."

"You are giving them free housing and food, are you not?" Blake asked. "Plus there is land for a garden. Or goats and chickens. You will not have to pay anyone too much beyond that."

"True." Stefan spooned the last bit of eggs into his mouth and considered another possibility.

He looked at Leif. "Let's say a husband and wife live at the post, and she sews blankets between the trains' arrivals. She could sell them and keep the money—right? And that sort of thing could become their compensation beyond the room and board."

"Sure. Do we offer the possibility of generating whatever income they can in lieu of a salary?" Leif smiled a little. "I do like that."

Blake handed the dirty pan to Chenoa who was washing the breakfast dishes. "Anything that can be done to make the p-posts self-supporting will make you more money in the end."

Once again, Stefan was impressed by Blake's business mind. He looked up at her as he handed her his empty dish. With the morning sun shining through her lengthening halo of red curls she looked angelic.

Damn but she is beautiful.

For more times than he could count he wondered how firmly she would resist marriage. Up until now Stefan did not consider himself a marrying sort of man, but his father's ultimatum shook him to his core.

But since making this journey, and coming up with the idea of the trading posts, Stefan felt reborn. He not only had a purpose and a plan, but he now recognized Blake as the perfect partner. Not only for business, but for the softer sides of life.

Home. Wife. Children.

Growing old together.

He was stunned to realize that he never wanted anything more than he wanted Blake to marry him.

I will need to tread carefully so I do not turn her away.

What did women want?

The kind of women Stefan was used to dealing with wanted money. Blake was definitely in a different category.

She wanted her independence.

And she wants to accomplish something, he mused. Something important. Something lasting.

"What are you thinking so hard on?" she asked. "You are miles away."

Stefan looked up at her again. "I am thinking about how very smart and capable you are."

Blake's cheeks flushed violently. "Oh! Um, thank you."

Stefan stood and now he looked down at her. "And you are a beautiful woman, even with short hair and dressed in men's clothing."

Blake glanced sideways at Leif and Chenoa, but they were not paying attention to Stefan's words.

Her large brown eyes returned to his. "Thank you, again."

Stefan saw no reason to beat around any bush. "I *have*

fallen in love with you, Blake. I think you should know that."

She did not express the same sentiment, but she did smile and lift her mouth and invite his kiss.

Stefan obliged. Happily.

June 27, 1845

Stefan, Leif, and Tom-tom marked out the fourth plot for the trading posts—the first stop for the wagon trains after leaving Council Grove. To celebrate that night the men fished in the Arkansas River and Blake fried the breaded fish fillets in lard. She also made biscuits and fried potatoes.

Stefan patted his belly when the meal was finished. "I do not know when I have eaten so well."

Blake was pleased with the compliment. "When will we reach Council Grove?"

"Six or seven days," he answered. "Then another eight and we will be in Kansas City."

That news was a mixed blessing.

"I would offer you all to stay in my house," Blake said. "But I expect it to be occupied."

"Your house?" Leif sounded surprised. "You still have a house there?"

Blake groaned inwardly. She had become so comfortable with these men that she forgot her resolve to keep her finances a secret.

"I did not have time to sell my father's house before I left, so I engaged a rental agent," she explained. "I thought once I was established in Santa Fe that I would instruct him to sell it and send me the money."

"And rent it in the meantime." Stefan nodded. "That was a sensible idea."

"Thank you. Who wants the last biscuit?"

Stefan held out his hand. "If you sell these at the posts, they will become famous."

"These and stew will be the staples." Blake handed him the biscuit. "The biscuits are quick and simple to make, and the stew can be stretched if the demand is high."

Stefan looked at her approvingly. "You have been thinking about all of this without stopping."

She laughed. "Of course I have. I will not hand my money over to just anyone."

"Money from the sale of your father's house, I assume," he said with his mouth full of biscuit.

Blake pressed her lips together and nodded. That was the safest response.

July 10, 1845
Kansas City, Missouri

Forty-one days after leaving Santa Fe, the little wagon pulled into the plot of land where the Kansas City wagons met up with the trains which originated their journeys in Independence, ten miles to the east.

"From now on, as long as we are in Missouri, Tom-tom will masquerade as our slave for his own protection." Stefan's expression clearly displayed his feelings about that unhappy circumstance.

He faced the Negro. "Please know that anything I say to you in that capacity is only to maintain the charade."

Tom-tom shook Stefan's shoulder in a good-natured gesture. "I understand, my friend. It is well worth the act if I am reunited with my mother and father in the end."

"I need to drive the wagon to the waggoneer's," Blake reminded the men. "It needs new wheels and other repairs before I d-drive it back to Santa Fe."

Stefan did not look pleased by that. "And the oxen?"

Blake had her mind made up. "I will sell them and buy a new team when I am ready to leave."

"Will you join another train?" Chenoa asked.

Blake wanted to travel more quickly than that but, "All I know is that I cannot travel alone. I suppose I will have to wait and see."

"Perhaps we will be ready to start building the first post," Stefan stated. "And you could travel with us."

Blake considered him thoughtfully and wondered how soon that might happen. "Yes. We shall see."

Blake drove the wagon through the streets to the same waggoneer she bought it from. Stefan and Leif unhooked the four oxen and headed for the stockyards to sell them on Blake's behalf.

As they did, the waggoneer approached, looking confused. He obviously remembered the bachelor, Blake Somersby, and was surprised to see him again so soon.

"You came back?"

"I had business to attend to," Blake rasped, trying to sound more manly. "But I am leaving again, and the wagon needs repairs first."

The waggoneer's gaze moved over the sturdy little vehicle. "How soon?"

"I am not sure," Blake admitted. She was pondering whether she should accompany Stefan to Cheltenham, or simply make her investment and head back.

"I might need to travel to eastern Missouri before I go."

He nodded. "Pay me in advance. I will make the repairs, and then store it here until you return."

That was fair.

After paying the man and leaving the shop, Blake led Chenoa and Tom-tom to a hotel she knew that had reasonable rates and clean rooms.

When they entered the lobby, Blake removed her hat and fluffed her short curls with her fingers. At this moment, she needed to be recognized as a woman.

"We require two rooms," she told the desk clerk.

The man's gaze moved coolly to Tom-tom. "He cannot stay in a room. He will be housed in the stable with the other animals."

Blake knew this would be the case. "I understand. But we still require two rooms. One for her and me." Blake indicated herself and Chenoa. "And one with two beds for the brothers who traveled with us."

The clerk grunted and turned the registration book around so she could sign it. "The rate is two bits a night per room. How long will you be staying?"

"I plan to be here for two weeks at this point." Blake filled out all of the names, including Tom-tom's. "But that could change."

When she finished signing the register, the clerk checked it over. Then he reached behind him and retrieved the keys for two rooms. "Second floor. Stairs are over there. And the stable is out back."

"Thank you." Blake smiled. "The four of us will also need baths. Can you please see to that?"

*****

Once again, the luxury of a hot bath soothed Blake's body and soul. She decided that her house in Santa Fe needed a permanently installed tub—with a drain—that was close to the kitchen so hot water was always at hand.

Just like this.

Rather than drag a tin tub upstairs, along with multiple buckets of hot water which were subsequently dumped out the windows before the tub was taken back down the two or three sets of stairs, this hotel had added a bathing room near the kitchen.

It was brilliant in Blake's mind.

After she dried off and wrapped herself in a robe, she took the back set of stairs up to the room she was sharing with Chenoa. "Your turn."

When Chenoa left the room, Blake sat at the dressing table to take a hard look at herself in the mirror for the first time since the last day of February, when she chopped off her hair, and rubbed shoe polish into it.

Four-and-a-half months ago.

Her hair had grown over two inches in that time, and Blake could not see how anyone would take her for a man anymore. She expected the waggoneer did because he had seen her with shorn hair. Either that, or he was very good at pretending.

That did not matter any longer. Now that she had traveled the Santa Fe Trail in both directions, she knew how easy the path was to follow. She would organize her own traveling party if necessary.

More likely she would travel with Stefan and Leif for the first three hundred miles and then join a train for the rest of the way. She did not think any wagon master would deny her, not after she told him she was making the trip for the third time.

Blake leaned closer to the mirror.

In spite of the hardships of the journey—cooking in the open, sleeping in a wagon, driving a team from morning to night, and being exposed to wind and sun on a daily basis— she looked far healthier than she did when she began this adventure.

I look happy.

The visage that stared back at her was truly alive. Her brow was smooth and her eyes crinkled at the corners. Her lips curved softly upward.

Stefan thinks I am beautiful.

Now the smile sculpted her entire face.

And he loves me.

For the first time in her life, Blake pondered the idea of living with a man without marrying him.

Surely, it would be shocking. But life in the Republic of Texas was not as sophisticated as life in Missouri. She saw plenty of women in Santa Fe who ignored eastern societal norms. Why couldn't she?

After living for a quarter of a century under her father's harsh control Blake was done with that sort of existence. And if she never married, then no man could take her fortune from her. She would be able to make her own decisions, and bend her will to her lover's on her own terms.

She wondered if Stefan would be scandalized by the idea. Based on his admittedly wild life, though, he might be relieved by the freedom she offered him.

Would he be willing to live in Santa Fe?

She would ask him again when the time came, and until then she would freely express her affection for him—or more honestly, her love for him. Blake was completely captivated by the big, charming, and attractive man.

She knew she was taking a risk, but if she had to head off to Santa Fe alone and with a broken heart, so be it. With that decided, she got up from the little table and its mirror to dress for supper.

Like a woman.

Chapter Twenty-Five

"We need to make a trip to the Westward Wagons office in Independence tomorrow," Stefan declared at supper in the hotel's dining room.

"Why?" Chenoa stared at Leif. "Will you work another train?"

"No, my love." Leif laid his hand over hers. "I will not leave your side."

"Except," Stefan clarified. "For the day, as he and I travel to Independence and back."

Blake faced him and, once again, her beauty claimed his breath. In her blue cotton dress, with its scooped décolletage, he could see the upper swells of her unbound breasts.

He forced his eyes up to meet hers and noticed how they were pinched at the corners with amusement.

"Why *are* you going?" she asked.

Stefan almost lost his train of thought. "To—to tell them about the trade posts we will build along the route."

"In order for the wagon masters to plan accordingly," Leif clarified. "We will tell them that the posts will be built and stocked by the end of March of next year."

Blake's eyes lit up. "Is that true? Can we accomplish it

that quickly?"

She said we.

"If we can raise the money quickly enough, then I believe we can." Stefan had full confidence in that statement. "Building during the winter months will be difficult, but not impossible."

Blake smiled. "That is good news."

Leif squeezed Chenoa's hand. "How will you ladies occupy your time while we are gone?"

The woman looked embarrassed. "I need to find some appropriate clothing. I cannot continue to appear as a half-breed."

Blake turned to face her. "I need to check on my house before I visit the rental agent. I left a trunk of clothes in the attic and I am sure something there will fit you. You are welcome to anything that does."

Chenoa's relief was palpable. "Thank you."

"So, tomorrow's plans are set," Stefan said. "We should return from Independence well before supper, so we can all dine together again tomorrow night."

He waved for the waiter. "Will you put the remainder of our meals on a plate? I want to take it to my man in the stables."

July 11, 1845

Blake stood in front of her house the next morning with her stomach in knots. "I never thought I would come back here."

Chenoa stood beside her and her gaze moved over the structure. "It is a nice house."

"On the outside." Blake drew a deep breath and tried to loosen the bands that squeezed her chest. "But my life inside those walls was anything but."

"You do not need to do this..." Chenoa turned pale blue

eyes on Blake. "We can leave."

"No. It will be fine." She regarded Chenoa and made a decision. "I will instruct the agent to sell it though. I will never live in it again, so there is no reason to keep it."

"And you need the money for your investment." Chenoa's eyes narrowed. "Do you not?"

Oops.

Blake smiled nervously. "Yes. Of course."

She walked up to the front door and knocked firmly.

A woman about five years older than Blake answered. Her gaze moved from Blake to Chenoa and back. "May I help you ladies?"

Blake heard a strong Irish accent. She gave the woman a friendly smile. "I am Blake Somersby and I own this house."

The woman's eyes rounded. "We pay rent! Every month!"

"That is good to know, but it is not why I am here."

The woman relaxed a little. "Why then?"

"I left a trunk of clothes in the attic," Blake said. "Are they still there?"

The woman nodded. "We did not ever go up there, so it must be."

Blake nodded, still smiling. "May we come in?"

*****

Even though she had only been gone a few months, Blake was glad to see that the house was still neat and clean, and the furnishings were in as good a condition as when she left. On the other hand, she steeled herself for whatever onslaught of emotions might pummel her now that she was inside the dwelling once again.

This house had not been a happy home since her mother died, but looking back at it now, time and distance had shone an entirely different light on her little family.

The shocking realization that her father was never a nice

man suddenly became clear. It was not her mother's death that changed him—it was the removal of her mother's protection which allowed his vitriol to find a new target in his daughter.

Blake felt another layer of pain strip away with that revelation, but it was immediately replaced by righteous anger. She was his only child. It was his duty to love and care for her.

Her resolve to be both independent and successful in business surged to an even higher level.

I will care very well for myself *now.*

And I shall do it with the money you left me to manage.

There was both revenge and victory in those thoughts. And as Blake led Chenoa up the stairs to the second floor and the door to the attic, she felt as though she was scaling the tallest mountain in the world with ease.

"It is this way." Blake walked down the hall to the little room with the attic door in it.

The door was not locked. The hinges creaked as Blake pulled the paneled door open and she climbed the narrow, dusty steps. The attic was dimly lit by screened openings under the eaves, but they provided enough light for Blake to find her way.

The last trunk she packed still sat in the middle of the attic floor. Blake lifted the lid and the scent of cedar filled her nostrils. Inside, the heaps of silks and cottons made Chenoa gasp.

"So pretty!" she breathed.

Blake lifted the top dress and shook it out. The orange silk was wrinkled, but otherwise the dress was in good condition. She handed it to Chenoa, who held it up to her own body.

Blake nodded approvingly. "It might be a little too long, but it should fit you."

Chenoa looked up at her and smiled. "I have not worn silk for so many years."

Blake turned back to the trunk and dug down to find the light blue dress that she knew was there. "This color will match your eyes."

It did.

All in all, Blake gave Chenoa five dresses. Then on a whim, she retrieved one for herself—a buttery yellow gown with white lace trim and blue piping. The colors complemented her red hair and brown eyes and she felt pretty on the few times she had a chance to wear it.

I will wear it while I am here.

After that she would decide what to do with it, since it was too fine for Santa Fe.

Blake closed the half-empty trunk and decided to tell the Irish woman to help herself to anything she wanted from what was stored up here.

"I do not expect to return agian," Blake explained to her tenant. "And because I plan to put this house up for sale, it is best if the things that are in the attic do not go to waste."

The woman was clearly stunned. "Thank you, ma'am."

Blake and Chenoa walked back to the hotel with their load of finery. "I will ask the hotel laundress if she is able to press these," Blake stated. "Then you can change out of your costume."

"And have it burned," Chenoa said with surprising venom. "The leathers served me well on my journey, but I have my life returned to me now and I wish to dispose of the past."

Blake smiled.

As do I.

"I forgot what cities were like." Chenoa's tone was wistful as the women walked back to the hotel. "I forgot how big the buildings were, and how wide the streets."

Blake looked around as if seeing the bustle with fresh eyes. "There are a lot of people. And so many carriages."

"The city feels alive." She peered up at Blake. "Is that an odd thing to say?"

Blake understood that Chenoa's view of Kansas City was completely different from hers, and she did not wish to squelch the woman's reaction. "No. It is not. I think it is the perfect thing for you to say."

"I hope we can stay here for a little while." Chenoa

flashed a small, apologetic smile. "But I know you do not feel the same way."

Blake shrugged a little. "My life will soon be in Santa Fe. I can bide for now."

*****

Stefan and Leif took a carriage to Independence and walked the two blocks to the Westward Wagons office. Inside, the same thin man who registered them in February was once again behind the desk, but today there was a nameplate facing them.

He looked up and his gaze showed no sign of recognition. "May I help you?"

Stefan removed his hat. "Good day, Mister Smithworthy. I am Stefan Hansen, this is my brother Leif. We worked the March first wagon train to Santa Fe."

"And you wish to be employed again?" The man opened a ledger and picked up a steel-nibbed pen. "How soon can you leave?"

"No, that is not why we are here." Stefan pointed at the chairs in front of the desk with his hat. "Might we sit?"

Smithworthy looked a little annoyed. "Were you both paid in Santa Fe?"

Leif chuckled. "Yes, sir. We are not here to lodge any complaints. Far from it, in fact."

The thin man closed his ledger and clasped his hands on the cover. He sighed heavily. "Go on."

Stefan sat in one of the two plain wooden chairs in front of the man's desk. Leif took the other. Then Stefan faced the man and adopted a pleasant expression.

He opened their interview with, "Have you, yourself, ever traveled to Santa Fe, Mister Smithworthy?"

"No." He cocked one eyebrow. "Why?"

"If you had, then I think you would be surprised at how

many valuable items are discarded along the trail."

Smithworthy scowled. "What are you talking about?"

"Settlers overload their wagons, sir," Leif explained. "They are inexperienced and believe that there are household items that they simply cannot do without."

"Like a piano," Stefan interjected. "Which ended up in the Arkansas River."

"You are joking."

"We are not," Leif countered. "And once they have traveled a few hundred miles and their teams are tiring, and they are running out of grain, they start abandoning those heavy, but still valuable items, on the side of the trail."

Stefan picked up narrative. "Where they are destroyed by the elements and become useless to anyone."

Smithworthy was obviously confused. "Well? What do you want me to do about that? Impose weight limits?"

Stefan waved his hands in front of his chest. "No, not at all. That is not practical and too hard to enforce."

"Then what is your point, gentlemen?" the man was clearly losing patience.

Stefan leaned forward and tapped the ledger. "What if we offered a way for Westward Wagons to profit from that waste and increase bookings at the same time?"

Though he looked skeptical, Smithworthy leaned back in his seat and steepled his fingers. "I am listening."

Stefan explained the origin of their idea as a string of posts where the settlers could buy, sell, or trade their discards for supplies.

"But then we realized, the posts could be so much more than that," Leif stated.

Smithworthy's position did not change, but his eyes narrowed. "More? How?"

Stefan painted the picture. "Imagine you are a city dweller who has been riding for endless days, sleeping in a crowded wagon, and cooking over a fire. You are tired, hungry, and dirty."

"And perhaps," Leif added. "You find you did not pack

enough flour, or salt, or dried meat, for example."

"But once you have passed Council Grove," Stefan said. "There is not one single chance to re-supply for the next seven hundred and twenty miles—until you reach Santa Fe."

The thin man leaned forward again. "What are you proposing?"

This time it was Leif who explained the placement of the posts and their proximity to the wagon trains on any given day.

"How will you make this happen?" Smithworthy asked.

"We have permission from the Republic of Texas to purchase the land, and on our return to Missouri we staked out and mapped the four locations." Stefan smiled. "Now we begin building."

Smithworthy frowned. "So how, exactly, is Westward Wagons going to 'make a profit and increase bookings at the same time'?"

"Not every settler who heads west books with your company," Leif stated. "Many unwary men hook up with anyone who claims to be a competent wagon master and then pays him to lead them west. True?"

The man behind the desk nodded slowly.

"Obviously we will not turn away any trains that stop at our posts, that would be inhumane," Stefan said carefully. "Instead, we will give the settlers an incentive to book with you."

"What sort of incentive?"

Leif gave the man the idea he and Stefan had come up with on the carriage ride here. "Free wagon wheel repair or replacements at any of our posts, but *only* if they are with a Westward Wagons operated train."

"If you advertise this, then those who are nervous to begin with will know that Westward Wagons assures that they will not be stranded on the prairie," Stefan continued.

Smithworthy looked skeptical. "How can you do this?"

"The staff at our posts will repair the wheels for reuse in between trains," Leif said.

"And of course, Westward Wagons will pay us for the materials." Stefan kept his tone casual. "The cost can be offset by a minor price increase on your part."

Smithworthy appeared to be on the edge of agreeing, so Stefan added another benefit. "When Westward Wagons advertises the wheel replacements—which are exclusively for *your* trains—then you will also list the other services we will offer at our four locations."

Leif shifted in his seat, catching Smithworthy's attention. "Everyone who sees the advertisement will assume those additional services are exclusive to Western Wagons as well.," he pointed out. "And they will book with you because of it."

"I see your point." Smithworthy nodded slowly. "What are the other services?"

Leif ticked them on his fingers. "First of all, we will stock grain for the oxen and horses, as well as tack repair supplies. Secondly, we will have basic foodstuffs available for purchase—including the option to purchase hot, prepared meals which will be available every day."

"Really?" Clearly the man was impressed.

"And third, we will have someone at each post with medical knowledge and supplies." Leif shot Stefan a concerned glance. "That need became very clear on our return trip here."

Stefan faced Smithworthy. "I do not think you could know this, but one train suffered a cholera outbreak halfway to Santa Fe."

The man paled. "Are you certain?"

"Yes. We left the trail to circle around them, and when the wind shifted, we could smell them." Stefan wrinkled his nose. "They were not moving and we do not know how many died—or if anyone survived."

Leif leaned forward, his voice gentle. "Was it one of yours?"

Smithworthy checked his ledger and calendar. He looked stricken. "Did you pass another train in close proximity?"

Stefan shook his head. "No, sir."

"Then I am afraid it was our May fifteenth departure." The man's shoulders slumped. "Damn."

Stefan hated to profit from the tragedy but, "When people hear of that and see that there will soon be medical help at the posts, they will want to book with you."

Smithworthy nodded, his expression grim. "Because, as you said, when we advertise the free wheel replacement, we will mention everything else you offer."

"Yes, sir."

Smithworthy stood and held out his hand. "You gentleman have a deal."

Stefan and Leif did likewise.

"Thank you," Stefan said. "This will be advantageous for us all."

"We will provide you with a pamphlet outlining what the posts will have available for purchase, sale, or trade," Leif promised. "And we will keep you informed as to our progress."

"Thank you, Mister—Hansen was it?"

"Yes. I am Leif and my brother is—"

"Stefan?" Smithworthy wagged a pointed finger. "I know why that sounded familiar."

He opened a desk drawer and shuffled through some papers.

"Here it is." He held out an envelope. "This arrived about a week ago, addressed to you. I held on to it, in case you ever came back."

Stefan accepted the envelope. "This is my mother's writing."

Leif's brows pulled together in concern. "I hope everything is well."

"We shall soon see." Stefan returned his attention to Mister Smithworthy. "Thank you again, sir. Expect to hear from us soon."

As soon as the brothers exited the office, Stefan opened the envelope. He hoped Leif could not see his hands shaking.

Chapter Twenty-Six

June 16, 1845
Washington D.C.

Dear Stefan and Leif,

I am writing to you both to tell you that your father suffered a heart attack two days ago, which was brought on by a stressful shock which I shall not outline in this letter. He is resting at home, which the doctor says is all that can be done for him.

The doctor has informed me that the best course of action at this point is for us to return to Cheltenham to continue your father's recuperation there, far away from the stress of politics. Your sister will be returning with us as well.

At this time, I cannot say whether your father will resume his position in the Senate, or whether he will retire. That remains to be seen once his health is restored.

I cannot know if, or when, you will receive this letter, but I do hope that, once Nicolas's condition is made known to you, that you will both come home to Cheltenham as quickly as possible.

It does not matter how you have fared since you left us, Stefan. You will be welcomed with open arms by both your father and I.

With all my love, your mother,
Sydney

Stefan stared at Leif. "We were headed there anyway, but now we need to hasten our departure."

"Agreed."

The men climbed into the carriage for the ten-mile journey back to Kansas City.

"Pappa is strong, He will recover," Stefan said as much to assure himself as Leif.

"But he is still leaving his Senate post to travel back home." Leif was clearly worried. "He did look a bit peaked when we saw him in January."

"My *bestefar* lived to be sixty-nine," Stefan argued. "Pappa is only fifty-seven."

Leif rubbed his chin. "I am sure Nicolas will be greatly heartened by the news of our endeavor."

Stefan agreed. "Mister Smithworthy will do our advertising for us. I would not be surprised if more people are willing to move west as a result."

"Even if the wagon trains break off and take the northern trail to Bent's Old Fort, they will have passed two of our posts beforehand."

"True."

The brothers fell silent for several minutes before Leif spoke again. "I will ask Chenoa to marry me again before we go. And, even if she says no, I will ask her to come to

Cheltenham with me."

Stefan said nothing. He had been wrestling with what to say to Blake ever since he read his mother's distressing letter.

He already resolved to ask her to marry him and come to Cheltenham with him, using her potential investment in the trading posts as an excuse. It made sense for her to meet his Uncle Rickard, if he agreed to invest as well.

But he could not show up at Hansen Estate with a woman whom he had traveled with for four months, but had not married.

His father would assume the worst—that he was still living a loose lifestyle with regards to the female sex—and no matter how he might argue to the contrary, the fact remained that he and Blake were not wedded.

"I will ask Blake as well," he confessed. "But I have no assurances of her answer."

Leif did not seem surprised. "How did we end up this way, Stef? In love with two women who are in no hurry to marry? And at our rapidly advancing ages."

Stefan snorted. "Rapidly?"

"Remember, I turned thirty-seven out on the Texas plains, somewhere between Council Grove and Santa Fe." Leif shook his head. "I do not even know which day, only that my birthday has passed."

"And I will be thirty-two in September." Stefan blew a sigh. "Perhaps we are reaping what we have spent so many years sowing, brother. It would serve us right to be on the other side now. To own the hearts that were broken."

"Speak for yourself," Leif grumbled. "I never played as fast and loose with the ladies' affections as you did."

Stefan shot him an apologetic look. "Guilty by proximity, I suppose."

*****

Once the carriage pulled to a stop in Kansas City the brothers climbed out. The day had turned cloudy and was spitting rain as if undecided whether to let loose its bounty or be stingy with it.

As they turned toward the hotel Stefan told Leif, "I am going to take Mamma's letter to Tom-tom and let him read it."

"Good idea." Leif matched his pace to Stefan's. "How soon do you think we will be able to leave?"

Stefan answered honestly. "I suppose we can decide as soon as we know if any weddings need to take place first."

Leif clapped Stefan on the back. "Good luck."

Stefan flashed a crooked grin. "And to you, as well."

When they reached the hotel, Leif went inside while Stefan went around back to the stables. He found Tom-tom grooming Heder.

He walked up and patted Leif's mount. "He looks good. How are his shoes?"

"I recommend re-shoeing all three of our horses," Tom-tom replied. "It's time, and the trail was rough on them."

Stefan nodded and turned his head to consider Sterk, contentedly munching grain in his stall. "How has it been out here for you?"

Tom-tom shrugged. "I am well accustomed to the smell of manure, and the horses are quite good company."

Stefan returned his attention to Tom-tom. "Are there slaves working here?"

Tom-tom nodded. "They will not speak to me. They believe me to be a spy."

Stefan huffed a laugh. "A spy? For who?"

Tom-tom stopping currying Heder in mid-brush and met Stefan's gaze.

"The railroad we spoke of briefly," he said softly. "Or rather, those who wish to stop its expansion."

Stefan grasped the meaning of Tom-tom's coded words. He referred to the underground railroad—the secret overland routes for escaping slaves.

"Well, as it turns out, we are leaving Kansas City sooner

than we planned." He handed Tom-tom Sydney's letter. "This was waiting for us at the Western Wagons office in Independence."

Tom-tom put the curry brush down and unfolded the letter. His expression grew more determined as he read.

"Not only do I want to meet my parents," he said as he refolded the missive. "But I want to thank the man who saved them both."

He gave the letter back to Stefan, his eyes wet. "Without your father's actions on their behalf, not only would I remain an orphan for the rest of my life, but my mother and father would never have seen each other again."

At that moment, Stefan was indescribably proud of his father. It had been a long time since he allowed himself to feel that way. He tucked the letter inside his shirt, momentarily unable to speak.

"When will we leave?" Tom-tom asked. "And how will we travel?"

Stefan and Leif decided that on the way back from Independence. "That depends on how the next days go…"

The Negro looked rightfully puzzled. "What does that mean?"

"Leif is asking Chenoa, once more, to marry him. Even if she says no to the proposal, he will ask her to come to Cheltenham with him anyway."

"Because if he leaves her behind, he thinks she will disappear." Tom-tom lips twisted in a rueful smile. "I think she cares for him more than he knows. But unless you have lived at the whim of someone with power, as both she and I have, it is hard to understand how fearsome that situation is."

Stefan had not ever put the kidnapped woman and the freed slave in the same category before this, but Tom-tom was exactly right.

He drew a deep breath. "In addition to Leif's repeated proposal to Chenoa, I plan to propose to Blake myself."

Tom-tom's eyes widened. "I wish you luck. She is a worthy adversary."

Stefan found that an odd choice of words. "Adversary?"

Tom-tom laughed. "She is a strong woman—stronger than she knows. You will always want her on your side, not across the field."

I am beginning to realize that.

"In any case, if the women are coming, then we will take a carriage to Saint Louis." Stefan shrugged and tried to look unconcerned. "And if they are not, then we will be three bachelors on horseback."

*****

Blake dressed for supper in the yellow dress from her previous life. As she stood in front of the tall mirror in her hotel room, she was pleased with the woman who gazed back at her.

There was not much she could do with her curly hair, but even its short length seemed to complement her appearance tonight. She smiled, and the image brightened even further.

It is because I am happy.

She gasped in surprise when she met Chenoa in the hallway. "You look beautiful!"

The other woman blushed furiously and did a slow turn in the light blue dress. "I do believe it fits well, even if the hem drags a bit. I will shorten all the dresses later."

"And the color does match your eyes, just as I thought." Blake looped her arm through Chenoa's. "We shall now go down to the dining room and impress our gentlemen friends!"

Judging by the brothers' twin expressions, they were more than impressed—they were gobsmacked.

Stefan wordlessly held Blake's chair with the oddest, almost strained, expression. Once the four were settled around the table and their supper orders placed, Stefan finally spoke.

"When Leif and I went to the Western Wagons office in Independence, there was a letter waiting for us there." He handed it to Blake. "Our father has fallen ill and our parents and sister have returned to the Hansen estate in Cheltenham."

Blake read the letter silently and passed it to Chenoa. "You were already planning to go to Cheltenham to speak with your uncle, were you not?"

"Yes," Leif answered. "But now we must make the journey immediately and not dawdle here in Kansas City."

Of course.

Blake looked at Stefan, dreading his answer. "How soon will you leave?"

His gaze was troubled. "We have a couple of things we need to accomplish first, but hope to be on our way in a day or two."

So soon.

Chenoa's hands sank to the tabletop and she looked stricken. The letter she held shook slightly.

Blake gripped her wineglass and lifted it to her lips. She took a slow sip. The thought of Stefan riding off on his own was unsettling.

Should she withdraw the money for her investment in the trading posts tomorrow, and then leave for Santa Fe while Stefen was in Cheltenham—trusting that he would do as he said with the trading posts—and reconnect with him once the posts were under construction?

Or should she wait here to travel with him on his return— which might come too late in the year for her to be able to journey back to Santa Fe before winter?

Help me, Father.

I do not know what to do.

"We understand that this news was unexpected, and it does change how we will need to handle things," Stefan said carefully. "But we do not have a choice about it."

Blake set her wineglass down and frowned. "No, of course not."

Stefan and Leif exchanged heavy glances. "The thing is…" Stefan's voice trailed off.

"The thing is," Leif picked it up. "We are wondering if

you two might want to come with us."

Chenoa brightened at that suggestion. "Perhaps…"

Stefan turned to Blake. "You could meet my Uncle Rickard. I know he would be so impressed with your business mind that he would be happy to invest."

Blake was not sure how to accept that statement. "You want me to come with you because I will be your business partner?"

Stefan looked horrified. "No! Well, yes. But not only for that."

"Then why?" she pressed.

"I, uh, I want my parents to meet you." He flashed a clearly forced smile. "But we can talk about that later."

What is going on with him?

Their supper arrived and conversation shifted when Stefan asked about the women's visit to Blake's house.

"I have decided to put the house up for sale," Blake stated before she remembered that was where Stefan believed her investment money was coming from.

"Of course, you already knew that," she covered quickly. "But because of your news I will visit the rental agent tomorrow and get that process started immediately."

*****

Stefan asked Blake to take a walk with him after supper. Since receiving his mother's letter today, every aspect of his life had become urgent, including proposing to Blake.

That did not assuage his nerves, however.

Proposing marriage was unsettling enough for a long-time bachelor living loosely, but his intended had already declared that she would never marry because she did not want to lose the things she owned.

But she stated tonight at supper that she was selling the house to invest in their business venture, so what else could there be? Spices and cookbooks, pots and pans, and the money she would receive when she sold her team of oxen.

Not exactly a fortune.

It must be the principle of the thing.

"Shall we sit?" he asked when they reached a small park. He indicated a wooden bench centered in the glow from an oil lamp on a nearby pole.

Blake sat wordlessly, her dark eyes focused on his.

Stefan decided to start with a kiss. He cupped her chin and gave her a long, slow, and tender kiss which stirred him deep in his belly and shuddered his breath. When he leaned away, her eyes fluttered open and her lips remained parted.

"I love you, Blake," he whispered.

"And I love you," she answered in kind.

He smiled. "Will you come to Cheltenham with me?"

"I have decided that I will," she stated softly. "As long as I can return to Kansas City in time to travel back to Santa Fe with the last train of the season."

Stefan was not pleased to hear that, but then Blake had not yet heard everything he was about to say.

"We have spent every day together since the first of March," he began. "And in the last two months we have been very close companions, have we not?"

Blake swallowed thickly. "Yes."

"Once my mother realizes this, I cannot take you home and not be married to you." He lifted one shoulder. "She would skin me alive."

Blake's eyes widened. "Are you asking me to marry you?"

Stefan smiled. "In my very awkward way, yes."

Her expression crumpled. "But I already told you—I will never marry."

"But you said you love me," Stefan objected.

She gave a little nod. "More than you can imagine."

This made no sense. "Then I do not understand your reasons."

"I told you—the law strips me of everything that I own and gives it to my husband." Blake waved spayed hands in front of her chest. "I cannot allow that to happen."

Stefan jutted his hands through his hair. "You said you are selling your house to raise the investment funds. Are you afraid that if you marry me that your portion of the business will become mine?"

Blake blinked. "Well, there is that too."

Too?

He had no interests in her household goods.

Stefan grabbed her hands. "We can draw up a contract which gives you a specific percentage of the business. We can protect your portion that way."

Blake stared at him. "Is that possible? Would such a document hold up in court?"

"I cannot see why it would not."

"Could it include everything that is mine today?" she pressed. "Even the café in Santa Fe?"

Stefan scowled. "I would assume so."

Her interest in having a contract made Stefan feel like she did not trust him, but he was willing to sign one even so. He would have plenty of time for the rest of their lives to assure her he would never undermine her or her finances.

Blake's gaze darted around the park and the people strolling through it on this mild summer's evening. Fireflies decorated the night, their blinking phosphorescent spheres dancing around the bushes and trees.

Then she closed her eyes, squeezed his hands, and heaved a shaky sigh.

When she opened her eyes again, she lifted her chin and looked into his. "I have a lawyer. We can visit him tomorrow afternoon."

He recoiled. "You have a—"

She cut him off. "If he confirms that my inheritance could remain mine with a signed agreement, and you are willing to sign that agreement, then my answer is yes. I will gladly marry you."

Now Stefan blinked.

"Just to be clear," he said slowly. "If you are guaranteed

that I have no rights to any funds, or any property that you own today, before the vows are spoken, then you will marry me?"

Blake's expression was a mix of hope and fear. She chewed her bottom lip, stared into his eyes, and nodded.

A smile spread over Stefan's face until his cheeks hurt. "So now we are engaged?"

"I suppose we are," she breathed.

He pulled her into his embrace and kissed her until passersby coughed and grunted their disapproval.

Blake chuckled and looked into his eyes. "Never mind them." Her voice was husky with desire. "I certainly do not."

Stefan kissed her again, wondering how in the world he had gotten so lucky.

*****

"Congratulations." Leif downed a shot of whiskey in the hotel's bar.

"How did it go with Chenoa?" Stefan asked before gulping his own celebratory shot.

Leif stared at the empty glass. "She still refuses marriage."

"I am so sorry, brother." Stefan signaled the bartender for two more drinks."

Leif turned his head toward Stefan. "That said however, she *is* willing to accompany me to Cheltenham."

Stefan was surprised to hear that, though he was pleased by the news. "Mamma will have something to say about you traveling with an unmarried woman."

"She will have less to say to me, than she would if it were you," he declared with an apologetic shrug. "You know *that* is true."

It was. Stefan pushed down the resentment the statement stirred, knowing that his parents would see his transformed situation for themselves once he was back in Cheltenham.

"There was one caveat to Blake's acceptance, however." Stefan accepted the refilled whiskeys from the bartender and slid one in front of Stefan.

Leif's brows jumped toward his hairline. "And that is?"

"She wants an ironclad contract which says I have no rights to any assets which she owned previous to our marriage."

"What is hers remains hers?" Leif's brows remained in their elevated position. "So that refers to the house—or the money from its sale?"

"Yes, and from the café in Santa Fe. But more specifically, that her investment in our trading posts from the sale of the house *remains* hers," Stefan explained. "Her percentage of ownership does not shift to me."

Leif's brows relaxed. "That does seem fair, actually."

"It is unconventional, but I also agree." Stefan lifted his glass and clinked it against Leif's. "To a swift and safe journey to Pappa's side."

Leif laughed. "With a wife, a refugee, and a freed slave in tow."

Chapter Twenty-Seven

July 12, 1845

Blake left the hotel right after breakfast. She had much to accomplish today and wanted to be certain that she had time to do everything the way she needed to do.

She had passed a sleepless night, her emotions bouncing from euphoria at the prospect of marrying Stefan, to despair at the possibility of not being able to return to Santa Fe. She and he had much to discuss about that particular situation, and Blake wondered which dream she would give up if forced to make a choice.

For now, she knew for certain that she would need to travel to Cheltenham with him and Leif, not only for their future business partnership, but to meet the family in the event that this engagement resulted in marriage.

She had no worries about continuing to travel with Stefan as an unmarried woman, but she did wonder what his parents might think. His history with the female sex was far from exemplary, and Blake would not blame them for thinking the worst.

But at nearly twenty-nine and thirty-two years of age, neither of them fell under anyone else's rule.

We will do what we know is right and move forward with clear consciences.

Her first stop this morning was to consult with Mister Fitzwilliam, the rental agent. He was obviously surprised to see her again so soon.

"Hello again, Miss Somersby." He held the chair for her while she sat facing his desk. "What can I do for you today?"

"I have decided to sell my house," Blake stated. "I found Santa Fe to be quite satisfactory all in all, and I will return there to live."

Fitzwilliam did not seem to know what to say. "Would you, uh, would you like me to arrange the sale?"

"Yes, please. And as quickly as possible." Blake smiled sweetly. "I'll be traveling to Saint Louis this week, and when I return, I would like the sale to be completed and the funds available."

The agent pulled out a sheet of paper and a pen. "How long will that be?"

"Six weeks at the most. I will need to leave Kansas City by the first of September, I believe."

Fitzwilliam nodded while he made notes. "And the deed to the property?"

"I will have my lawyer provide that once the sale is made and he has the full payment in hand." Blake dipped her chin. "Less your commission, of course."

He flashed a quick smile. "Of course."

Fitzwilliam wrote for another minute or so, then slid the paper across the desktop. "Will you look this over and the sign the bottom?"

Blake read the simple agreement which stated that she was engaging Fitzwilliam as her representative in the sale of the home, which became wholly hers upon the death of her father.

His commission was listed as ten percent.

Blake's gaze lifted to the agent's. "If this business is completed and all of the money is in my lawyer's hand by August fifteenth, then I will pay you a five percent bonus on the sale."

The man smiled broadly. "I will do my best, Miss Somersby. Thank you."

Blake added the August fifteenth date and five percent bonus to the bottom of the agreement and then signed and dated it. She handed it back to Fitzwilliam and watched him countersign the document.

Then she stood and extended her hand. "Thank you, sir. I look forward to a successful resolution."

He stood as well and shook her hand. "It is a pleasure doing business with you, Miss Somersby."

*****

Blake's next stop was her lawyer, Mister Jackson Whittle. She had not asked Stefan to join her at his office because she needed to have a blunt conversation with the man about her situation, and she needed to do it before Stefan got involved.

"This situation is not as unusual as you might believe, Miss Somersby," the lawyer said. "There is a precedent for a woman holding on to her own fortune separate from her husband, especially in England."

"But we are in America," Blake countered.

"True," he admitted. "But we often refer to their laws as a guideline. The general consensus is that as long as the husband does not contest the arrangement at a later date, then there is no problem."

That was not completely comforting.

While Blake did not imagine Stefan ever *would* contest it, she still asked, "What if he does?"

"Then we must structure the language so that there is no ambiguity." Just like the rental agent, Mister Whittle pulled out a sheet of paper and took notes. "And we must have witnesses for the signatures, in addition to a notary."

That sounded more encouraging.

The lawyer looked up from his paper.

"What exactly are the conditions that you are asking for?"

Blake had already thought this through quite thoroughly.

"That every penny which is in my accounts as of today, and every bit of property which I own on the day that we are married, plus any income derived from the rent or sale of that property, will remain mine. My husband will have no access to any of it as long as I am alive."

Whittle was writing furiously as he spoke to Blake. "The cash in my safe, and the principle amount of the invested monies—plus interest earned at this point—will be specified."

"Does it have to be?"

He looked up from his paper. "What do you mean?"

Blake chose her words carefully. "Can the contract simply say something to the effect of 'all cash on hand plus all monies currently invested and earned interest'? Does the exact amount need to be written down?"

The lawyer considered the idea. "Listing the specific assets is the normal procedure, and that is for your protection. But I suppose the broader language would suffice."

That was a relief. "Then let's do that."

Mister Whittle tapped the end of his pen against his chin. "I am guessing that your fiancé does not know exactly how wealthy you are, and that you do not wish for him to know."

Blake smiled a little. "That is correct. At least not as yet."

"And you do not want him to know, because..." the lawyer let the sentence fade off.

Blake decided to offer the easiest reason. "I do not ever want to think he married me for my money."

Mister Whittle looked smugly satisfied and Blake believed he might be silently congratulating himself on correctly guessing that reason.

"Fine, then." He looked at his paper. "What about the interest which your investments accrue in the future? Would you like that to be available to him?"

Blake had not thought of that. "You mean as a steady income?"

The lawyer nodded. "If not, I will continue to reinvest it

as I have."

Blake sighed her indecision, then stated, "Reinvest it for now, I suppose."

Mister Whittle wrote on his paper. "What about the house?"

Blake explained the arrangements she had just made with the rental agent.

"I will list the house as an asset for the purpose of today's contract, and then what is done with it afterwards is covered." The lawyer made more notes. "And when do you need the contract ready for signatures?"

"How soon *can* it be ready?" Blake asked. "We plan to leave Kansas City the day after tomorrow."

Mister Whittle looked up in surprise. "When is the wedding?"

That question caught Blake off her guard. "I honestly do not know."

"Will you marry before you depart from Kansas City?"

"I had not expected to," Blake admitted, concerned. "Does that change anything?"

Whittle shook his head. "No, this document is a pre-nuptial agreement. After it is signed by both parties, it will be valid whenever the vows are spoken, whether today or ten years from today."

Blake smiled her relief. "That is good to know."

"However, if you both are leaving Kansas City, then the document and its copy will need to be written and signed today. Will your fiancé be available?"

"I—may we sign it first thing tomorrow morning?" Blake hedged. "I d-do need to confirm our plans."

Mister Whittles shoulders relaxed. "Yes, I suppose that will be acceptable."

"After I return to Kansas City, I will open a bank account and put half of what you are holding for me in there, so it's available to me when I return to Santa Fe," Blake added. "Will you please make a third copy of the agreement for me to leave with them as well?"

*****

Stefan waited in the hotel's dining room for Blake to join him for lunch. He had battled with himself all night, trying to decide which was the better path: marrying Blake before leaving Kansas City and showing up at Hansen Estate with a wife, or showing up with a fiancée and letting his mother watch him exchange his marriage vows.

It would mean the world to Sydney to be at his wedding, considering how he had been living his life for the past decade or so.

Not to mention his father.

In many ways, Stefan was the definition of a prodigal son. He had been sowing his oats for years and living off his father's money. But now that he was pushed to fend for himself, he had risen to the task. The business plan he and Leif devised was a solid one.

Wagon trains heading west, as far as California and the Pacific Ocean, were increasing every year. Not only that, but there was an excellent chance that small communities would grow up around the trading posts as opportunities expanded.

And there was still the rumor of statehood for Texas.

Stefan knew the answer to his situation. He needed to ask Blake to wait to be married until they reached Cheltenham.

Please, God, do not let that ruin everything.

*****

Blake saw Stefan sitting at a table by one of the tall six-paned windows. She straightened her shoulders, smiled confidently, and walked toward him.

"There you are." A grinning Stefan stood to pull out her chair. "How did everything go?"

Blake took the proffered seat and looked up at her fiancé.

Fiancé!

Their change of status was still so new, that it shocked her a little every time she though of Stefan that way.

"All is in place," she assured him as he left her side and regained his chair opposite hers. "The agreement will be ready for both of us to sign when Mister Whittle's office opens in the morning."

A waiter approached and took their orders for luncheon, momentarily interrupting the conversation.

"And the sale of your house?" Stefan asked when the waiter departed.

Blake reminded herself that Stefan believed that was the sole source of her investment, so of course he was concerned about it.

"Yes, that is all settled as well. In fact, I offered him a five percent bonus to complete the sale in four weeks."

Stefan chuckled, visibly relieved. "You are indeed a formidable business woman, Miss Somersby."

Blake's cheeks warmed. "I do believe that is the best compliment a woman could ever receive. Thank you."

"You are very welcome, my love." Stefan's smile faded and he looked nervous. "There is something else I do need to discuss with you."

Blake held her breath for a brief moment. "And I also have something to d-discuss with you."

"You go first, then," Stefan urged, looking like he had just received a stay of execution.

That reaction set Blake nerves on edge. "No, you. I insist."

Stefan drew a deep breath and reached for her hand. "Have I told you today how very much I love you?"

"Yes, at breakfast." Blake forced a reassuring smile. "But a woman never tires of hearing it."

"I do love you, Blake. With all my heart."

"And I, you."

Where is this leading?

"That said…" Stefan squeezed her hand. "I wonder if you would object to postponing our wedding until we reach

Cheltenham?"

A surge of relief washed over Blake. "That is *precisely* what I was going to ask you!"

"Really?" Stefan's expression was incredulous. "Why?"

"I imagine for the very same reason as you," Blake posited. "So that your parents—more specifically, your mother—could be present."

Stefan nodded. "It would mean so much to her."

A lump thickened in Blake's throat and tears stung her eyes. "To be honest, my motives are selfish as well."

Stefan squeezed her hand again, his brow furrowing. "What is amiss?"

Blake felt foolish that what she was about to say was moving her to tears, but there was no help for it. "I am an orphan with no siblings. Having your family stand with us as we make our vows makes all the difference to me."

"Oh, my darling, I had not considered that." Stefan slid off his chair and knelt beside her. He firmly kissed the back of the hand which he still held in his much larger, much rougher grasp.

"I promise you, Blake, we will have the wedding of your dreams. I know Sydney well—she will happily rise to the occasion and everything will be perfect."

Blake used her free hand to wipe tears that did not seem likely to stop. "As long as you are my husband by the end of that day, it *will* be perfect."

Then she leaned down and kissed him well, unconcerned about who might be watching.

July 22, 1845
Cheltenham, Missouri

As she was remaking the bed with clean sheets, Sydney Hansen heard the rhythmic clop of horse's hooves and the jangle of tack through the open window of the bedroom. She peered into the early dusk and saw a large, four-horse carriage pulling into the circular drive. Her spirits sank a little.

If Stefan and Leif had gotten her letter, they would be arriving on horseback, not in a six-person coach.

I wonder who this could be, then?

Leaving her task unfinished, Sydney hurried to the top of the staircase.

"Anne! We have guests arriving!" she called to her housekeeper as she hurried down the steps.

When she reached the bottom, she popped her head into Nicolas's office. "Were you expecting anyone?"

Her husband was on his feet and buttoning his waistcoat, which hung loose on his narrowed build. "No. And it's rather late to be arriving unexpectedly, don't you think?"

Anne McCain strode from the kitchen into the entry way. "It is a good thing we washed sheets today, I reckon."

Sydney grabbed the brass handle and yanked the heavy front door open. As she walked out onto the front porch, it took her a moment to realize who she was looking at.

"Stefan?" Her son's skin was darkened by the sun and his frame was leaner than the last time she saw him, but more muscular at the same time. Clearly whatever physical work he had been doing had been good for him.

"Mamma!" Stefan walked toward the house with his arms wide.

Sydney nearly leapt down the stone steps from the front porch and ran into his embrace.

"And Leif!" she cried as the older brother stepped out if the carriage.

"We came as soon as we got your letter," Leif stated as he hugged her tightly. "We have been traveling for eight days."

Nicolas appeared beside Sydney and he shook Stefan's hand without letting go. "It is good to see you, son. You look well."

Stefan beamed. "I am Pappa. And how are you?"

"Fit as a Hardanger fiddle," he lied, and shifted his hand to Leif's.

Sydney let the misstatement pass for now. "Why did you engage such a large carriage?"

"We have brought some people with us." Stefan looked like the proverbial cat who'd eaten all the canaries.

He moved his attention to the front porch. "Anne? Would you please summon Jack and Sarah as quickly as you can?"

"I will send Forrest straight away!" Anne disappeared into the house.

"Why do you need them?" Nicolas asked.

"You will see." Stefan's smile widened. "Shall we begin the introductions?"

He turned to Leif. "You first."

Leif nodded mysteriously and walked back to the still-open carriage door. Anne's son Forrest bolted past them toward the foreman's cabin in the woods before Anne reappeared and stood by Sydney's side.

Leif reached out his hand and guided a strikingly beautiful woman with black hair and pale blue eyes out of the conveyance. He tucked her hand in his arm and approached Sydney.

"Mamma, this is Chenoa, the woman I am courting."

Courting?

At last!

Tears sprung to Sydney's eyes. "Welcome, my dear. I am so glad to meet you."

As Leif introduce Chenoa to Nicolas, however, Sydney noticed that Chenoa kept looking at Anne with the strangest expression: curiosity tinged with fear.

"Mamma?"

Stefan's voice pulled her attention back. He walked toward her with a woman on his arm as well. What under God's good Heaven had these men been doing for the last six months?

"This is Blake Somersby, my fiancée."

Sydney's jaw dropped. "Your—Stefan!"

Stunned, Sydney held out her hands toward the tall woman with cropped, curling red hair. "I never thought I would see the day!"

"I am very glad to meet you, Mistress Hansen." Blake grasped both of Sydney's hands. "I hope we will b-be friends."

Sydney noticed the slight stutter, marked it up to nerves, and smiled warmly. "Call me Sydney, please."

Blake squeezed her hands. "Thank you. Sydney."

Stefan pulled Blake over to Nicolas to introduce them. Sydney looked toward the woods and saw Jack and Sarah hurrying towards the big house, with Forrest urging them on. As the couple drew closer, Sydney saw their expressions ease when it became obvious that Nicolas was not stricken.

"What is it Sydney?" Jack asked. "What is amiss?"

"I am not sure," she answered honestly. Was it only to introduce the women? "Stefan insisted that the two of you be summoned posthaste."

"Jack! Sarah!" Stefan cried. "We have a very important surprise for the two of you—one which I believe you never expected."

Chapter Twenty-Eight

Leif was walking back toward the carriage. He waved one hand, beckoning whomever remained inside to exit the conveyance.

A well-dressed Negro man, who appeared to be in his mid-twenties, stepped out. He faced Jack and Sarah looking as if he was seeing a dead man risen from the grave.

Sydney glanced at Stefan.

He had tears in his eyes.

Leif pulled the Negro toward the waiting pair, his expression tender. "Jack, Sarah, this is Tom-tom—"

Before Leif said another word, Sarah screamed, "*Espoir!*"

Jack looked like he had been punched. "Can it be?"

Leif shot Sydney a confused look.

Sarah threw her arms around Tom-tom, sobbing loudly. "My boy! Espoir! My lost boy!"

Jack grabbed them both in a bear hug, and the beefy, middle-aged former slave succumbed to tears as well.

Sydney turned to Anne. "Espoir?"

"It means 'to have high hopes' in French," Anne explained. "She told me she had named her son that many years ago, but I forgot about it until this moment."

"And how…?" Sydney looked at Stefan, gobsmacked. "You boys certainly have a story to tell!"

"More than that, Mamma. Much, much more." Stefan looked at Nicolas. "Pappa, Leif and I are going into business."

*****

After the carriage was unloaded and dismissed, the gathering moved indoors and clustered in the stone house's large and well-lit entryway. Blake waited silently, deeply annoyed that she stuttered when she met Stefan's adored mother for the first time, and tried unsuccessfully to tamp down her embarrassment.

Sydney and Anne consulted, Sydney nodded, and then addressed the small crowd while Anne disappeared toward the back of the house.

"First we will all gather in the dining room for pie with coffee, tea, or Akevitt." Sydney's eyes sparkled along with her grin. "After that, Chenoa and Blake shall occupy what once was Stefan and Leif's room."

She pointed at the luggage. "Please let Forrest know which bags are yours."

Chenoa saved her from speaking and indicated the bags which needed to go up to that room. Forrest gathered them and climbed the stairs.

"Tom-tom, Espoir, I believe you would like to stay with your parents in their cabin?"

Tom-tom had not let go of either Jack or Sarah. "Only if they are amenable."

Jack scoffed but he was grinning. "Try and stay elsewhere, boy, and we will drag you back by your heels!"

Sarah looked beatific, as if angels were speaking to her.

"That puts Leif and I in the apartments in the stables," Stefan observed. Blake noticed he did not look upset by their diminished situation. "By the way, where is Kacy?"

"*Kirstie* is in Saint Louis," Nicolas growled, surprising Blake. She had never heard Stefan and Leif's little sister referred to by another name.

"Pappa..." Leif's tone was patient. "There are battles to fight, and there are battles which are not worth the effort."

Blake realized at that moment that Leif's long-held position in the family was to keep the peace between the willful Stefan and his stubborn father.

How will I fit in?

"Her initials *are* K.C.," Stefan offered. "She says it sounds more like a grown woman—which, of course, she *is*."

Blake watched the interaction carefully, learning so much about the family she was marrying into in the process.

Sydney slipped her arm through Nicolas's and the look she gave him dripped with warning. Obviously, the wife was concerned that her husband might suffer another episode of the heart if he became overly agitated.

"Kacy is what our daughter—who, by the way, has inherited *your* Nordic stubbornness—wishes to be called," she said softly. "Please let this go, Nick. It is not worth risking your health over."

Nicolas drew a deep, chest-expanding breath. He blew it out with a resigned expression. "You are right, *min presang*. I shall concede."

"Good." Sydney stood on her toes and kissed his cheek. "Now let's all have pie."

*****

Anne's husband, Jeremy McCain, joined the group, while Jack, Sarah, and Tom-tom politely declined, before retreating to their cabin to begin the process of getting reacquainted.

Over pie and Akevitt-laced coffees, Stefan and Leif entertained them all with stories about the wagon train: how they were hired and what happened along the way.

"And then this person here," Stefan hooked thumb in Blake's direction, sending a shock through her frame. "Turned out not to be what 'he' seemed."

Sydney's eyes widened. "He?"

Stefan smiled encouragingly at Blake, who had not spoken since meeting Sydney. "Tell them your story, my love."

Blake took a stalling sip of coffee, deciding to talk directly to Sydney.

Pretend she is your loving mother.
Pretend she will understand.

Blake set her cup down and focused her gaze on her soon-to-be mother-in-law.

"I was born in Kansas City in eighteen-twenty-six, and do not have any siblings. When my p-parents and I had visited Saint Louis, and were traveling back to Kansas City," Blake pulled a fortifying breath, "we were attacked by group of Sauk, who were angry about b-being moved out of Missouri."

Anne was pouring coffee, but she froze at Blake's words. The housekeeper's sudden and somber stillness pulled Blake's attention, making her certain her suspicions were correct.

Blake forced her gaze back to Sydney's. "My mother tried to fight them, b-but one of them sliced her throat."

Sydney gasped. "Oh! You poor thing…"

Blake pinned Anne with a stark gaze. "You are Sauk."

"Half." Anne set the coffee pot on the table with a slight tremble. "My father was French."

Chenoa stood suddenly and left the room.

Leif stood as well. "I will see to her."

Then he quickly followed her out.

Sydney frowned. "What is going on?"

"Chenoa was kidnapped by the Sauk when she was fourteen, and then forced into marriage to a very bad man for the next ten years or so," Stefan said quietly. "We found her half dead by the side of a river."

"Like I found your mother," Nicolas stated, his deep voice filling the room.

Stefan nodded. "Believe me, Pappa, the significance of

that was not lost on Leif."

Anne sank onto an unused chair, her expression somber and her eyes welling. "I am so, *so* sorry, Blake."

Her sincerely expressed contrition lifted away yet another layer of Blake's grief. "It is not your fault, Anne. It was a shock, is all. Neither Chenoa, nor I, were warned."

Stefan shifted in his chair and cleared his throat. "I apologize, Blake. We truly did not think of it. Anne has been a part of the family for so long, we forget her heritage."

Blake understood that.

Even so, it would have helped to be prepared.

"Anehka. That is my Sauk name. And Chenoa means *dove*." Anne looked toward the doorway. "I wondered when I heard that, and saw her... Her hair is so dark..."

Anne returned her gaze to Blake's. "I thought she might be like me."

Blake suddenly remembered the obvious connection. "You taught Leif to speak Sauk."

"I did."

"Because he could speak to her as she re-learned English, her transition back was greatly eased," Blake offered. "She is still healing, I am afraid. But she gets better every day."

"Tell them the rest," Stefan urged, clearly hoping the conversation would shift back. "Tell them why you were on the wagon train. And how."

*****

Stefan watched Blake as she recounted her life with her father, and her subsequent decision to travel to Santa Fe and open a café. She talked about altering her father's clothes and chopping off her hair, touching her short curls when she did.

She seemed to stumble over some of the details, specifically in reference to financing the trip, but the more she spoke, the less she stuttered.

"It was hard, exhausting work, driving the wagon," Blake admitted, grinning ruefully at Stefan. "And keeping my gender a secret was difficult because Stefan took an interest in the 'young city boy' who was clearly in d-deeper water than 'he' expected."

"Why did you return to Kansas City, then?" Nicolas asked.

Stefan took a hard look at his father. His deep voice was still strong, but he had lost significant weight in the last six months. His color was less robust. As was his stride.

Blake nudged Stefan out of his musings. "Answer your father."

Stefan smiled softly at Nicolas. "Leif and I returned to Kansas City to start a much-needed business. That is when we received Mamma's letter, and hastened our trip onward to Cheltenham."

Nicolas cocked one brow. "Hastened?"

"We were coming anyway. I want to talk to Uncle Rickard about investing." Stefan hoped his tone sounded as casual as he tried to make it, and he changed the subject to ward off his father's expected negativity. "And—there is one other *very* important reason."

"What?" Nicolas grunted.

Stefan grasped Blake's hand under the table and lifted their interlocked hands in the air. "Our wedding, of course!"

Sydney gasped again. "Of course! How wonderful!"

Stefan pointed at his mother. "Send a message to Kacy that she is needed at home immediately. She must help you with the preparations."

"Why the rush?" Nicolas sounded suspicious.

Stefan knew his father had every reason to be, based on his previous escapades. "We must get back to Kansas City, and put our business into action. Before winter hits too hard."

"What *is* this business, Stefan?" Sydney pressed.

"Tomorrow, Mamma." Stefan glanced at Nicolas. "To be truthful, we have been traveling for eight days, and we are too exhausted to explain everything tonight."

"He speaks honestly," Blake confirmed. "I can hardly keep my eyes open."

Sydney stood. "In that case, go make your preparations for bed. We will see you in the morning, whenever you are fully rested."

Stefan stood and pulled out Blake's chair. When she rose, he offered to see her upstairs to her room.

"I am well acquainted with its location," he teased.

Blake glanced at his parents, but neither were paying them any attention. "That would be nice."

Stefan led Blake to the staircase. As they climbed in step with each other she asked him, "What does *min presang* mean?"

Stefan felt a wash of warmth when his father spoke those words to his mother. "It's 'my gift' in Norwegian. And it has been my father's nickname for my mother for as long as I can remember."

"So then she was *his* best gift as well?" Blake grabbed his hand and squeezed it. "I hope I can be yours."

When they reached the top of the stairs, Stefan turned her to face him squarely. "You already are."

He kissed her well enough and long enough that she was certainly completely convinced.

*****

Chenoa was already in the room, in her nightdress, and brushing her hair.

Blake walked up behind her and met her eyes in the mirror. "How are you feeling?"

Chenoa lifted one shoulder and turned around to face Blake. The hand holding the brush fell to her lap.

"Leif told me how Anne came to be here."

"How?" Blake prodded.

"Back in eighteen-twenty-one, Nicolas advertised for a

new foreman, because his foreman, John Spencer, needed to retire." Chenoa's voice was soft but steady. "Jeremy applied and was hired."

"Was he married to Anne at the time?"

Chenoa nodded. "That was why he was out of work. No one wanted to hire a white man who was married to a half breed."

"But Nicolas was willing to." That spoke volumes about the man. "Plus, he freed Jack and Sarah, and then paid them a salary."

"I think he is a remarkable man, Blake, even if he and Stefan have butted heads."

Blake sat on one of the two narrow beds in the erstwhile 'boys' room. "I agree. But I do wish one of the brothers had the forethought to warn us that a Sauk woman was part of the household."

"That is what I said to Leif." Chenoa rolled her eyes. "In between sobs."

Blake chuffed. "I said the same to Stefan. He said that she had been a member of the family for so long, that he honestly forgot her heritage."

Chenoa ran her hands through her hair and set the brush aside before she spoke again. "To be honest, after seeing this family, I do think I believe him."

*****

Stefan found Leif on the back porch after he said his final goodnight to Blake. "Were you waiting for me?"

"I was." Leif stood. "Our bags have already been taken to the stable."

The brothers fell in step for the walk across the back yard to the tall stone-bottomed, wooden-topped outbuilding.

"How does Pappa look to you?" Stefan ventured.

Leif's gaze remained fixed on the stable. "Honestly?"

"Yes. Brutally."

Leif rubbed his chin, rasping his eight days of beard growth. "I believe his days of being a Senator are finished."

Sadly, Stefan thought so, too. "Do you think he knows that? I mean, he has been in politics for twenty-three years. That's a long career. Do you think he would be willing to step down?"

"Or be his stubborn self?" Leif countered. "And say he is as 'fit as a Hardanger' when clearly he is not?"

"We will need to talk to Mamma, alone, and figure out what he is thinking."

"Agreed." Leif slid the stable door open. Stefan stepped inside, Leif followed, and slid the door closed behind them.

A lamp had been lit for them by the apartment's door. Stefan took it from its hook, and Leif opened the door.

Nicolas built the two-room dwelling for Jack and Sarah after he bought them, freed them, and moved them onto his property. Now that Jeremy and Anne lived in the former foreman and housekeeper's rooms in the main house, Jack and Sarah lived in the cabin Jeremy built.

Stefan hung the lamp in the front room, relieved to smell soap, not dust. "I do not believe these rooms get much use anymore. But I am very glad they are still kept up, just in case of days like today."

Leif lit a second lamp and carried it into the second room. "Let's get some sleep. I have a feeling that tomorrow is going to be a tough day."

Stefan sat and pulled off his boots.

To put it mildly.

*****

Sydney stood behind Nicolas and massaged his neck as he pulled off his boots. "How are you feeling?"

"I feel fine," he stated. "Do not worry about me."

"I mean about Stefan and Leif," she clarified. "Showing up with women on their arms, and a business plan in their pockets."

"The business plan has yet to be seen," he grumbled.

Sydney stopped her ministrations and pulled a chair close to her husband. "Tomorrow, they will explain it. And then Stefan will get married. And I do hope Leif will follow closely behind."

Nicolas smiled softly. "You like them, don't you? Blake and Chenoa?"

Sydney smiled back. "I like the way Stefan and Leif look at them. Our sons are smitten. And yes, I do like them."

Nicolas, nodded. "It seems I did the right thing by cutting Stefan loose."

"You did, indeed." Sydney laid her palm on his thigh. "Might we talk about your plans now?"

Nicolas deflated. "I do not want to quit the Senate."

"I know. But I worry about you." Sydney squeezed Nicolas's thigh. "I do not want to lose you, husband. And it was so unbelievably dreadful when I thought I might."

Nicolas slid a stunned gaze to hers. "I had not considered that."

Sydney wiped a tear. "I beg you—*please* consider it now."

He frowned. "Someone will have to replace me."

Sydney scooted her chair to face him more squarely. "I have an idea about that. What about Richard?"

"Rickard's son?" Nicolas scoffed. "He is just a boy."

"Nicolas," Sydney cajoled. "Richard Atherton is a twenty-two-year-old Harvard honors graduate with a degree in business law."

Nicolas narrowed his eyes, but said nothing.

"You know he came home after his graduation to talk to Rickard about what path to pursue next," Sydney pressed.

Nicolas shook his head. "But I do not know if he has any political aspirations…"

"Ask him," Sydney urged. "It is not a six-year full term, only the remainder of yours. He could use the next two-and-a-half years as an entry to his future career, whatever that is."

Nicolas scuttled his gnarled fingers through his graying hair. Sydney knew him well enough after over their quarter of a century together to wait for him to come to the conclusion himself.

He heaved a deep sigh, then returned his attention to her. "You have made a good suggestion, I will admit that."

Sydney gave a small nod. "Thank you."

"And, I also admit that I never considered how you might be worried about losing me." He laid his hand over hers and squeezed it. "I only thought of my Norse pride at being considered frail."

Sydney lifted his hand to her lips and kissed it. "Your mind is sharp, Nicolas. Think of all that you could teach Richard. The knowledge and insight that you can offer him is invaluable."

Nicolas smiled crookedly. "It is, isn't it."

Sydney's spirit rose. "Does that mean you will think about doing this?"

Nicolas's expression grew resigned. "Yes, *min presang*. I will think about it."

Chapter Twenty-Nine

July 23, 1845

Late the next morning, Blake and Chenoa sat at the dining room table finishing their breakfast with Sydney. It was clear that Sydney wanted to get to know her sons' women, and Blake was glad for that.

She liked Sydney. A lot. As Stefan had said, Sydney was a strong woman who clearly did not stand on convention, and she congratulated Blake on her bravery in executing her plans for Santa Fe.

Blake chuckled to herself.

I wonder how that independent attitude was accepted in Washington?

As the women talked, the conversation eventually grew more intimate, until Sydney faced Chenoa and flat-out asked, "Why are you hesitant to marry Leif?"

Chenoa blanched and looked like a traitor facing a firing squad. "What?"

"You obviously love him," Sydney said tenderly. "What holds you back?"

Blake tried to come to her friend's aid. "Stefan told you last night that her first husband was not kind."

"Is that it, Chenoa?" Sydney's voice dropped to a whisper. "Do you fear the marriage bed?"

Chenoa's cheeks turned violently red. She swallowed audibly and nodded, wide-eyed and pale.

Sydney glanced around, as if to be certain their conversation could not be overheard, before she said, "I am going to tell you a story about Nicolas's mother. But it is a story that my husband does not know."

Blake shot Chenoa a surprised look, but Chenoa only stared at Sydney.

"His mother, Kirsten, was the granddaughter of King Christian the Sixth of Norway and Denmark..."

Blake's jaw dropped. "She was?"

Sydney nodded and waved an unconcerned hand. "Do not worry, this will not affect your marriage as it did ours."

Blake wanted to ask more about that particular revelation, but now was clearly not the time to do so.

Later, though.

I will ask Stefan later.

"And because she was a princess, her parents sent her to Copenhagen to, hopefully, find a suitable husband," Sydney explained. "But she was American born, and the nobility there did not accept her. They saw her as... I suppose you would say, lower class."

Chenoa nodded. "I was seen that way by the Sauk. Their women resented my husband marrying a white woman, even though I fought against the marriage."

Sydney's expression darkened. "Did the other men rape you?"

"No," Chenoa whispered. "Only my husband."

"Well..." Sydney drew a sad sigh. "Kirsten was not so fortunate."

Blake choked a sob, and slapped her hand over her mouth to hold back any more.

Nicolas's poor mother!

"One night, she was brutally raped by half-a-dozen men, and then left to fend for herself," Sydney said quietly. "The next morning, torn and bleeding, she boarded a ship to start her journey back to Philadelphia."

"But Nicolas does not know any of this?" Blake clarified, stunned by the horrific story.

Sydney shook her head slowly. "No. And neither did her parents. Not until long after she married Nicolas's father."

Chenoa's expression was grim. "Why do you tell me this?"

"To let you know that there are good men, loving men, patient men, who will never hurt you." Sydney reached for Chenoa's hand. "Reid Hansen was just such a man. And so is Leif."

Tears began to roll down Chenoa's cheeks. "Was the marriage a good one?

"Very. And though Kirsten believed she was too damaged to either enjoy her physical union with Reid, or ever bear him children, she did both."

Sydney squeezed Chenoa's hand. "Reid went to extraordinary lengths to prove his steadfast love and gain Kirsten's trust. Clearly Leif has done enough to keep you by his side thus far."

"He has," Chenoa murmured. "But I am still scared."

"From what I have seen, he loves you so deeply," Blake offered. "And he knows *why* you are scared. He would never, ever, press you to do anything that you were not ready for."

Chenoa sat quietly, her gaze moving erratically over the lace tablecloth.

"Kirsten was scared, but she trusted Reid." Blake asked her friend gently, "Do you trust Leif?"

After a moment, Chenoa nodded.

"Then please talk to him," Sydney urged. "Because clearly you are as deeply in love with him, as he is with you."

*****

Stefan and Leif, now bathed and clean-shaven, appeared in the dining room bringing an abrupt end to the women's conversation.

"Is there any food left?" Stefan asked when he saw Blake and Chenoa's empty plates.

"Of course!" Sydney smiled brightly as she stood. "Don't you boys look nice!"

"We are not *boys*." Stefan's tone was exasperated. "Stop calling us that!"

Sydney shrugged. "Old habits die hard, son. Take a seat and I will tell Anne to make your plates."

Stefan moved to the chair next to Blake. "Where is Pappa?"

Sydney froze and a trill of fear snaked through her frame. "I—I do not know."

"Is he still in bed?" Leif asked.

"No, he got up when I did." Her heartbeat stuttered. "Did you see him in the stable?"

Stefan and Leif exchanged glances.

"I heard someone, but I assumed it was Jeremy," Stefan said. "Then I went back to sleep."

"That was hours ago." Leif added. "No one else was there when we left to come to the house."

Where is he?

"I am sure he is fine, Mamma," Stefan assured her. "He is probably out talking with Jack or Jeremy about some urgent issue which cannot wait another moment to be dealt with. You know how he is."

Sydney prayed silently that he was right. "That has not been his habit since the—since we returned home."

The front door of the house opened.

All five adults scrambled into the hallway.

Nicolas stilled and faced them with a bemused expression. "What is amiss?"

"Where were you?" Sydney yelped.

"I decided to go for a morning ride."

"Where?" she demanded.

"Atherton's. I had breakfast there." Nicolas spread his hands, confusion sculpting his features. "What is going on?"

"You did not tell Mamma you were leaving, and she was worried," Stefan scolded. "Did you lift the saddle by yourself?"

"No. I rode bare back." Nicolas raised his hands higher, palms forward. "And before you ask, no gait faster than an easy trot, I swear."

Though Sydney figured she knew why Nicolas had ridden to see their neighbors, she still took him to task. "The next time you decide to go rogue, you need to tell someone!"

Nicolas laid a contrite hand against his chest. "I apologize. But everyone else was sleeping, and I did not wish to disturb them."

"I was not asleep," she grumbled.

"True. But I wanted to invite Rick to come over later and hear Stefan and Leif's proposal," Nicolas explained. "I thought, why not have him hear it when I do?"

Stefan's skeptical look indicated that he saw something in his mother's reaction, and might have figured out that his father had another motive for his disappearance, so she spoke quickly to head off any inquiries.

"That sounds like a very good plan, don't you agree?"

"What time is Uncle Rickard coming?" Stefan asked Nicolas.

Nicolas faced him. "Two o'clock. Can you be ready?"

The insinuation obviously stung, judging by the irritated set of Stefan's jaw. "We are ready now."

"Good. Now I am going to wash up."

As he headed up the stairs, Stefan turned back to his mother. "Did you write to Kacy?"

Sydney felt calmer than moments ago, now that she knew where Nicolas had gone and why. "I did, but I have not taken it into town to the post office. Would you like to take it?"

Stefan patted his midsection. "After we eat breakfast, I would be happy to."

*****

After all introductions were made, Stefan, Leif, Nicolas, and Rickard, with his son Richard in tow, initially tried to hold their meeting in Nicolas's office, but Sydney, Blake, and Chenoa objected.

"Every one of us will be impacted by the decision, so we all wish to be present as the proposal is explained," Sydney stated, much to Blake's relief.

Blake knew that Stefan knew that she planned to invest, but she had not yet named a number. What happened in the next few hours would determine how large, or small, her portion of the business would be.

As the eight adults settled into the large drawing room, Sydney helped Anne serve tea and sweet biscuits, while Nicolas poured Akevitt for those who wanted to fortify their beverages.

"I saw Jack and Sarah with a young man today," Rickard mentioned after sipping his enhanced tea. "Who was that?"

Leif pointed at his uncle. "Now *that* is a story, Uncle Rick."

"Let's hear it!" Rickard grinned. "We have time."

Stefan began the startling tale. "It turns out that Rosie knew where Jack and Sarah's boy was after Nicolas bought Sarah and brought her to Cheltenham."

Rickard gaped at him. "No! Is that—"

"Patience, please!" Stefan beamed at his uncle. "So Rosie sent a letter to the owner offering to buy the boy."

"But—" Leif injected. "She did not receive a reply for almost twenty years. Not until the man was dying."

Stefan nodded eagerly. "His son found Rosie's letter in his father's papers, and sent a reply saying he was selling off everything to pay his father's debts, and asked Rosie if she was still interested."

"The letter stated that the boy, well, man now, was *strong and knew how to read*." Leif chuckled. "I suspect he was asking for more money because of it."

"Long story short, Rosie went to that man's farm—about fifteen miles west of St. Louis—and paid two hundred dollars for the slave they called Tom-tom."

Rickard's incredulous regard was bouncing between the two brothers. "But how—"

"We met Tom-tom while we were working the wagon train," Stefan continued. "And when we mentioned we were from Cheltenham all the pieces fell into place."

"He traveled through Missouri as our 'slave' so he could come with us and be reunited with his parents," Leif concluded the tale.

"Wagon train?" Rickard's confusion sculpted his aged features. "You two worked a wagon train?"

Blake decided it was time to jump into the rapid exchange before she was forgotten about altogether. "That is where I met Stefan. I was disguised as a man and driving a wagon to Santa Fe."

The room fell silent, and all eyes moved to her.

"And then Stefan and Leif rescued Chenoa along the way, when they found her half-dead beside a river," she continued.

A visibly stunned Rickard looked at Nicolas. "Just like—"

He grinned. "That has been noted."

Stefan frowned a little at Blake and retook the floor. "Leif and I got the inspiration for our business while we were traveling to Santa Fe and back."

"Are you ready to hear it?" Leif asked Nicolas and Rickard.

"Hold on." Rickard drained his teacup. "All right, go ahead."

Blake listened quietly while the brothers outlined their inspiration for the trading posts, how the posts would be built and where, plus how they would be staffed. She decided not to interrupt unless her idea of hot meals was not mentioned.

"And to top it off," Stefan paused and smiled at Blake, "my beautiful fiancée is planning to arrange for hot meals to be ready for purchase at each stop, thereby giving the women in each wagon a much-needed break from cooking over a fire."

Blake smiled her thanks. Stefan winked charmingly at her, making her cheeks warm pleasantly.

Nicolas leaned forward and pinned Stefan with a hard gaze. "This all sounds fine, but how will you procure the land for the posts?"

"We already arranged that with the Texas land agent in Santa Fe," Stefan stated. "Then on the way back to Council Grove we marked out the acre plots and posted signs saying *future home of a Hansen Trading Post.*"

"Have you paid for the land?" Nicolas pressed.

"Not yet. We did not have the money, obviously."

"The land agent agreed to take payment and give us the deeds when we return to build." Leif sounded confident. "And now we are looking for investors."

"How much?" Rickard asked.

Leif explained that they figured it would take a thousand dollars to build and stock each of the four posts. "But we plan to raise five thousand, just to be safe."

Rickard nodded. "How much are you putting in?"

"All we have to hand at the moment," Stefan answered. "One thousand dollars."

Blake chewed her tongue and forced herself to remain quiet while she watched Nicolas and Rickard's reactions.

"*You* have a thousand dollars?" Nicolas demanded.

Stefan's jaw flexed. "We were paid six hundred each for working the train. So yes, we do."

"Not only that," Leif jumped in, once again deflecting father and son conflict, "we have struck an agreement with Westward Wagons to promote our trading posts by offering their travelers free wheel repair or replacement along the way."

"*Only* their wagons," Stefan clarified. "That will bring them more business."

Now.

"And they will mention all of the other services offered at

the trading posts as well. Though those are not exclusive to Westward Wagons," Blake related. "In addition to hot meals, there will be medical attention at all posts. Plus, the ability to trade, buy, or sell any furnishings."

"Most settlers overpack their wagons," Leif added. "We would give them a chance to get something in return for what they might otherwise discard along the trail."

"Won't you simply end up with piles of unwanted furniture?" Nicolas asked.

Stefan's startled gaze jumped to Leif before Blake decided to answer that question.

"The furniture can be dismantled and the parts reused," she offered. "Hardware, obviously, and glass for windows."

Stefan caught on and he faced his father again. "There will be a constant need for lumber, both to build and to burn, until the trees we plant are mature."

"And the trades we make will not cost us any money, we will be certain of that," Leif added.

Nicolas nodded pensively, seemingly satisfied with the explanations.

Rickard's eyes narrowed. "What would I get for my investment?"

"We are actually asking for a loan, Uncle Rick," Stefan replied. "We promise a ten percent return within three years or less."

Leif nodded. "That way, Stefan and I retain control of the business."

"This is brilliant."

Blake turned to young Richard Atherton in surprise. Rickard's son had not said a single word throughout the entire discussion, but now his eyes lit up.

"A loan is what I would have advised, if I had been asked," he said with no trace of malice. "And for exactly the reason you stated."

Blake opened her mouth, but Stefan spoke before she could. "The loan structure was Blake's idea."

All eyes moved to her, yet again.

"Good for you!" Sydney effused.

Richard leaned forward. "You will need contracts written. I can help you with that."

Stefan smiled at his younger cousin. "That would be much appreciated. Thank you."

Rickard looked at Nicolas. "How much are you putting in, Nick?"

"We are not asking him to invest," Stefan demurred. "My father challenged me with making my own way, so that would defeat his purpose."

"Well, then, I will meet your thousand," Rickard stated. "I believe you boys are on to something."

Blake bit back her smile at the men in their mid-thirties once again referred to as boys.

"Thank you, Uncle." Leif stood and shook Rickard's hand.

"What if I decided I *wanted* to invest?" Nicolas challenged. "Would you turn my money down?"

Stefan looked at Leif. "What do you think?"

Leif shrugged and his eyes were twinkling. "I suppose we could allow it. But not more than a thousand dollars."

Stefan addressed Nicolas. "Is that satisfactory?"

Nicolas looked happier than he had since Blake met him. "Yes. That will do."

Stefan crossed the room to shake his father's hand. Both men held on longer than was necessary, and Blake thought she detected moisture in Nicolas's eyes.

"That makes three thousand dollars," Leif observed, smiling at Chenoa. "Only two more to go."

The time had come.

"I will put in the remaining two thousand dollars," Blake said firmly. "But not as a loan. I will be an equal partner with the two of you."

Chapter Thirty

Stefan looked at Blake, concerned and condescending at the same time. "You do not have to do that, darling."

"I know I do not *have* to…" Blake's tone was calm and controlled. "But I *want* to. I believe in this scheme, and I want to be a partner."

Stefan sank into his seat his brows pulling together in his confusion. "But what if your father's house has not sold yet?"

"That has nothing to do with anything," she claimed. "I have the money now."

Stefan was gobsmacked by that revelation. "How much do you have?"

Blake's cheeks flamed and her gaze moved around the room. "May we speak of this privately?"

"Yes. Of course, you can," Sydney interrupted.

She turned to Nicolas. "Nicolas, please refresh everyone's cup. We shall all toast to the success of the Hansen Trading Posts along the Santa Fe Trail."

Stefan could not wait to speak with Blake, so when his father shooed everyone except Uncle Rickard and Richard out of the office, he was too relieved to consider what his father's motives might be for the private conversation.

He took Blake's arm. "Let's go outside and talk. There is a bench under the maple tree in front of the house."

Blake nodded and smiled awkwardly. "Of course."

Stefan shifted his grip to Blake's hand and forced himself not to hurry her to the spot. When they reached the bench, Blake pointed at the tiny tombstones that rested in the shade of the big, broad tree.

"Oh, dear." She looked at Stefan. "Whose babies died?"

Stefan had forgotten about the graves. They had been there since he was six.

"Sydney was married once before. She got a divorce and married my father," he explained. "She had two stillborn boys with her first husband who were buried somewhere else."

"How sad." Blake heaved a sigh and regarded the twin plots. "But how are they here now?"

"My father moved them here as a wedding gift for Sydney." Stefan easily recalled the day that his father marched the entire household out to see the new graves. "He told her that all of her children were with her now."

"Your father is a romantic at heart," she observed.

Stefan wondered about that. "If you think so."

Blake looked at Stefan while she pointed at the graves. "That is the most romantic thing a husband could ever do for his wife. Trust me on this, Stefan. It was incredibly thoughtful."

Her declaration gave Stefan pause, and made him consider his father in that startling light. Was she right?

Blake sat on the bench and looked up at Stefan. "Ready?"

Stefan sat beside her, and turned to face her. "Yes."

Blake pulled a deep breath. "I will go straight to the heart of it. As of this moment, I have almost eleven thousand dollars in the bank."

Stefan jumped to his feet, momentarily shocked out of his senses. "*WHAT?*"

Blake simply stared at him.

"I thought—I mean, the way you dressed—your wagon was so small—" Stefan scuttled his hands through his hair and stumbled in a tight circle. "Where did you—how did you—"

Then the lamp lit in his mind.

"That is why you wanted the contract?" he yelped. "The one that stated that what you bring into the marriage remains yours?"

"Yes. It is." Blake stood and faced him. "I lived my entire life at the whim of a man, and I will never do that again."

"I would never take advantage of you! And I would never be unkind!" Stefan shouted. "I am not your father!"

"No, you are not," she said softly.

The contrast between her tone and his was disconcerting, and Stefan lowered his voice. "Why do you mistrust me so?"

Blake said nothing and sat back down.

Stefan hesitated, then did the same.

"If I mistrusted you, would I invest twice as much in the business as you and Leif?" she asked. "Of course not! I trust you with my whole heart. With my whole life. I would never agree to marry you otherwise."

Stefan shook his head, trying to wrap his thoughts around the fact that his future wife was a wealthy woman. "It does not feel like trust."

Blake's eyes pooled. "Just because the assets are mine to control, does not mean I will withhold anything from you. You will be my husband, and what is good for you is good for me as well."

"When I agreed to sign the contract, I had no idea you were rich. None whatsoever." He pulled a steadying breath. "It will take me a pace to come to grips with it."

"I understand." Blake swiped a tear from her cheek. "But think of this—we will not need to live in the café with strangers. We can build a nice house in Santa Fe. One which might accommodate children someday."

Santa Fe?

Stefan had achieved good standing with his father at long last. He assumed that meant he would need to move back to Missouri to run this estate once his father had recovered enough to return to Washington for the remainder of his

Senatorial term.

"My circumstances with my father have changed," he said carefully. "When he reinstates me as heir, I might need to remain in Missouri to watch over the estate until he completes his time in the Senate."

The blood drained from Blake's face. "Missouri? What about the trading posts?"

"I suppose I could live in Kansas City and manage both," he offered. "Leif could live in Santa Fe."

"I will not live in Kansas City again."

That was a surprise. "You would prefer Cheltenham?"

"No!" Blake declared. "I prefer Santa Fe!"

This conversation was taking a terrible turn. "What about me? What about our engagement?"

She grabbed his hand tightly in hers. "I love you with all my heart, Stefan. I do. I want to marry you and raise a family with you. I want live my life by your side."

"Then we are in one accord," Stefan stated.

"Not entirely." She pulled a shuddering breath. "If I am forced to spend the rest of my life trapped in Kansas City, I will not live long. That city will surely kill me."

*****

Blake left Stefan's side, claiming a headache, and retreated to the cool darkness of the bedroom she was sharing with Chenoa. She stretched out on the narrow bed and let her tears of disappointment flow.

She would be part of the trading post business, no matter what. That was just good business.

But if she had to choose between marrying Stefan and remaining in Missouri, or returning to Santa Fe alone to fulfill her dream of starting a new life there, she knew which path she would ultimately choose.

Santa Fe.

*****

Chenoa came into the room to get ready for supper and woke Blake from a fitful nap.

"Are you ill?" she asked, her voice heavy with concern.

Blake sat up and rubbed her eyes, deciding not to say too much just yet. "I had a small fight with Stefan about my bank account."

"I was thinking that, when he asked how much money you had, it was a little rude." Chenoa sat on the other bed. "Are you still fighting?"

"I do not believe so," Blake answered honestly.

At least, not about that.

"I believe he understands my feelings and why I asked him to sign that contract."

Chenoa nodded. "It is good for a woman to be able to hold on to what is hers."

Blake stretched her arms and flexed her neck. "What about you?"

Chenoa's shoulders slumped. "Leif talks of returning to Santa Fe, because he believes Stefan will be required to stay in Missouri."

"And you do not want to return there?" Blake was deeply disappointed by that idea. "I had hoped you would help me with the café."

"I am sorry, Blake." Chenoa's expression reflected her regret. "But after talking with Sydney this morning, I had a very serious conversation with Leif. A very honest one."

"And?" Blake prompted.

"And I think I will agree to marry him."

"That is wonderful news!" Blake moved to the other bed and hugged her friend. "But what does that have to do with moving to Santa Fe?"

Chenoa looked stricken. "I have fallen in love with Missouri. I feel safe here."

"Oh." That was a fair point, considering that the Sauk had

been moved out of the state.

"I know you never want to return to Kansas City, but I do. I have never lived in a city, and I think it is wonderful there." Chenoa smiled softly and shrugged. "I hoped Leif and I could stay here."

Blake flopped back on the bed. Both of their futures had taken a very bleak turn, indeed.

"It appears that Stefan, as heir, needs to stay in Missouri, so Leif will need to go back to Santa Fe." She heaved a heavy sigh. "Oh, Chenoa. We are in love with the wrong men."

*****

As Stefan and Leif entered the main house through the kitchen door, the clock on the drawing room mantle chimed seven-thirty. The brothers wound their way through the busy and delicious smelling kitchen, and headed that direction.

After Stefan returned from his upsetting talk with Blake, he and Leif had stationed themselves in the drawing room where they could see the door to Nicolas's office across the entryway.

When the secretive meeting was completed, they wanted to ask Richard about the contracts he offered to help with, and set a time to meet with him.

After that, they spent the rest of the afternoon talking about, and making lists for, the trading posts.

Stefan poured two small glasses of Akevitt and handed one to Leif. "Here's to a productive day."

Leif flashed a crooked smile. "In more ways than one."

"What do you—"

Stefan was interrupted by the sound of horse hoofs approaching the house. He went to the open window and pulled back the gauzy curtains to try and see who was approaching.

"Single rider, riding astride," Stefan stated. "Wait, is

that—"

Stefan set down his glass, ran to the front door, and swung the portal wide open. "It *is* you!"

Stefan rushed across the porch, leapt over the stone steps to the drive, and grabbed his little sister in a big bear hug. He swung her in a full circle before setting her on somewhat unsteady feet.

"I cannot believe you came so quickly!" Leif reached Stefan's side and hugged Kacy with a bit more decorum. "We posted the letter only this morning."

"I received Mamma's letter at one o'clock and rode out before three." She punched Stefan in the arm. Hard. But he noticed that something in her expression was off. "I could not wait another minute to meet the woman who finally tamed this crazy stallion."

"I wish you could have seen it, Kacy," Leif said, grinning. "When he fell, he fell hard."

Stefan regarded Kacy's trousers, realizing of a sudden that there was a definite pattern in the way the most important women in life dressed.

First Sydney when she worked with the horses, then Kacy who rebelled at most conventions, and lastly Blake who wore her father's clothes to sneak onto the wagon train.

Independent women, one and all.

"Do you want to run upstairs and wash for supper?" he asked. "Leif and I can take care of the mare."

"That would be wonderful, thank you." Kacy took two steps toward the porch steps, then turned around. "Do not worry, brother. I will change my clothes as well. No point in scaring her off right away."

Stefan chuckled.

If you only knew.

*****

Blake and Chenoa heard a bit of a ruckus downstairs and exchanged curious glances.

Blake pushed herself upright. "I suppose we should get dressed and go see what is happening."

Bootsteps moved past their closed door to the other end of the hallway.

"That was neither Sydney nor Nicolas's stride," Chenoa observed. "Do you think the sister has returned?"

"Oh! Yes! She must have." Blake stood and crossed to the dressing table. "Ugh. I look like I have been crying and sleeping all afternoon."

Chenoa stepped up behind her. "What have you been doing?"

"Crying and sleeping. But I do not wish to look like it." Blake grabbed a towel. "If I scrub with cold water, perhaps I will look less like I am decomposing."

Chenoa laughed. "Yes. That is just the thing."

Half an hour later the two women exited their shared room properly dressed for diner. Blake had nervously changed her dress three times, in the event it *was* Kacy who strode past their door, glad that her short hair required very little attention.

She had one chance to make a good impressed on the adored younger sister, and she put her efforts in that direction.

Blake braided Chenoa's hair and wove the braids around the woman's head, pinning them in place. "You look lovely. Perfect for the announcement of an engagement."

Chenoa tilted her head from side to side to get a good look in the mirror. "I wonder if that is what Leif has planned."

"I believe it is bound to come up. Sydney did summon Kacy home to help plan a wedding, remember." Blake rested her hands on her friend's shoulders. "Perhaps it will be a double ceremony."

Chenoa stared at Blake in the mirror, her pale eyes as wide as saucers. "I am both thrilled and terrified by that idea."

Blake chuckled and kissed the top of Chenoa's head. "Let's go find out, shall we?"

The woman talking to Stefan and Leif with her back to the

drawing room door was as tall as Blake.

Not surprising, if Nicolas was her father.

Her hair was light brown with golden streaks. When she turned around, her Nordic features declared her to be Nicolas's daughter, while the green of her eyes reflected Sydney's input.

"You must be Kacy." Blake stuck out her hand. "I am Blake Somersby."

Kacy grasped it and smiled softly. "I love your hair."

Blake touched it self-consciously, as she always did when her unusual style was mentioned. "I had to cut it about five months ago, so I could p-pass as a man on the wagon train."

Kacy's eyes widened. "Now *that* is an interesting story, one which I cannot wait to hear."

Stefan moved to Blake's side and slid his arm around her waist. "Blake is a lot like you, little sister. I think you two will get along famously."

"And this beauty is Chenoa." Leif pulled the reticent woman out from behind Blake. "I am happy to say that she has finally accepted my proposal as well."

Kacy's surprised gaze bounced between her brothers. "Will it be a double wedding then?"

"It will need to be," Stefan said. "We do not have time to plan two events."

Kacy's brows pulled together. "Why? Are you leaving again?"

Stefan nodded and launched a shortened version of the brother's plans.

Kacy's frown did not ease. "What about Pappa?"

*****

That conversation was cut off by the appearance of Nicolas and Sydney at the bottom of the stairs.

"I see you women have met our daughter," Sydney said as she walked into the drawing room. She stopped at Kacy's side and kissed her daughter's cheek.

Kacy lifted one accusing brow. "You did not tell me they are both getting married."

Sydney gasped and turned to Leif. "Is that true?"

"Is what true?" Nicolas asked, joining the circle.

Leif still held Chenoa's hand. "Chenoa has agreed to become my wife."

"We will have a double wedding before we head back to Kansas City." Stefan grinned at Kacy. "You can plan two weddings as easily as one, can you not?"

Kacy looked stunned. "Are you expecting *me* to plan the wedding? Weddings?"

Stefan was confused. "Did Mamma not tell you? In the letter?"

"No!" Kacy placed the fingers of her splayed hands against her temples. "The letter only said the boys are here, and Stefan is engaged. Come home."

Judging from the look she threw Sydney, Kacy was not at all happy to hear of her expected role.

Stefan touched her arm. "Is everything well, Kacy?"

Her tepid smile was unconvincing. "Yes. Of course."

"Let's go into the dining room, shall we?" Sydney announced. "I, for one, am famished."

Stefan bent one elbow and Blake slid her arm through his.

"What were you doing in Saint Louis?" Blake asked Kacy as the trio walked down the hall to the dining room.

"I am thinking of opening a dress shop," she replied flatly.

"Will you make the gowns?"

Kacy slid her arm through Stefan's free one. "No, I will design them and then hire seamstresses."

"Did you design the dress you are wearing?" Blake spoke past Stefan as if he was not there.

Kacy smoothed her skirt. "No. This is one I already had."

"Do you care where we sit, Mamma?" Stefan asked, intentionally interrupting the pair as they approached the table. "Or is it every man for himself?"

Chapter Thirty-One

Stefan watched his father as the meal progressed, wondering what he had discussed so secretively with the Athertons this afternoon. Whatever it was, it seemed to lift his spirits quite a bit. Nicolas looked less haggard now than he did when he came back from their neighbor's house this morning.

Kacy, on the other hand, had completely lost the zest which she displayed when he saw her in January. There was an underlying sadness in her eyes which none of her polite smiles managed to erase.

"Pappa was elected to his first term in the Senate in eighteen-thirty-six," Kacy was explaining to Blake and Chenoa. "I was seventeen and finished with school here, so I went with them to Washington for the swearing in."

Blake's eyes brightened. "Was it as stirring as I imagine?"

"It was. Of course, we were also there for President Van Buren's inauguration, so that was thrilling." Kacy glanced at Sydney, her expression puckish. "By the time we returned home for the Christmas recess, I had convinced my parents to let me escape from Cheltenham to continue my schooling in Philadelphia, and live with my Uncle Gunnar and Aunt Brigid."

Blake looked surprised. "Is there a college there which enrolls women?"

Kacy shook her head. "Sadly, no. But they do employ them. It is amazing what you can learn by telling a professor you are taking notes for a dean."

Blake laughed and grinned at Stefan. "Your sister is very resourceful."

"I am very proud of her, to be honest," he complimented.

Kacy's smile did reach her eyes that time.

"When did you come back to Cheltenham?" Blake asked.

"In the spring of forty-three." Kacy's expression sobered. "I know Pappa hates for me to say anything, but I was worried about him."

Nicolas growled. "I was fine."

"Even so, Pappa, someone needed to be here and oversee things," she stated firmly. "You and Mamma spent most of your time in Washington."

Stefan's gut clenched with guilt. "I should have been here."

"Yes, you should have." Sydney's voice held no detectible animosity in spite of her words. "But you were not ready. You had to get the wildness out of your system first."

"And now it is replaced with solid ambition," Leif offered on Stefan's behalf. "And soon, the stability of a wife."

And a very wealthy one at that.

Stop it.

"Will you return to Washington when Pappa does?" Stefan asked Kacy, wondering what her role in the family would be going forward from here. "Or move to Saint Louis and open your dress shop?"

Kacy's gaze fell to her plate and she fidgeted with a chunk of bread. "I—no."

Stefan shot a concerned look at Sydney, but his mother's eyes were fixed on Nicolas.

"Tell them," she urged.

Nicolas nodded. He wiped his mouth with his linen napkin and cleared his throat. Then he rested a fist on either side of his dinner plate. His gaze moved around the table and landed on each person present.

"I am not going back."

"What?" Stefan blurted.

"Why not?"

"Really, Pappa?" Kacy exclaimed, obviously stunned by the revelation. "You are not?"

Nicolas lifted one huge, gnarled hand to quiet the room. When everyone stilled, he continued.

"My wife has pled her case and won. To preserve both my health, and my marriage, I will not return to Washington to complete my Senate term."

"Will you appoint someone to serve in your stead?" Stefan asked, terrified that his father might suggest him. Or worse, Leif.

Either choice would ruin absolutely everything.

"Is that how these things are handled?" Leif asked, looking every bit as apprehensive as Stefan felt.

Nicolas nodded solemnly. "In a manner of sorts. I wrote to Governor Edwards a little over a week ago and asked him to appoint the man whom I put forth to replace me. Both the Governor and the man I suggested have agreed."

A wash of relief flushed Stefan's veins a moment before he realized the answer. "You asked Uncle Rick."

Nicolas smiled and wagged his head. "No. I asked his *son*."

Of course. The Harvard grad with a business law degree and nothing else to do at the moment. That made all kinds of sense.

"I assume he accepted?" Leif prompted.

"He did. This afternoon in my office." Nicolas's chest expanded and shrunk before he spoke the final words confirming the shift in his own future. "The letter has already been written, signed, addressed, and posted. It should arrive at the Capitol building over a week before Richard does."

If Pappa is not going back...

"Then you will stay here and manage the estate?" Stefan

clarified. "So that Leif and I can start building the trading posts as planned?"

"Yes." Nicolas reached for Sydney's hand. "You *men*, go and make your fortunes. I will be here, with your mother, determinedly enjoying a retirement worthy of a country lord."

*****

Blake sat up straight in her chair as a lightning bolt of an idea zinged through her.

She stared at Chenoa across the table. "They can switch!"

Chenoa's features lifted with relieved joy. "Yes! They can."

"Switch what?" Stefan frowned at her. "What are you talking about?"

Blake clasped her hands together, her interlaced fingers pressed to her lips and savoring the moment, praying that her suggestion would not be shot down.

Choose your words carefully.

She faced Stefan. "Your father is retiring here, to the estate. Neither you nor Leif will be required to live here."

"We were not going to live here anyway. At least, not full time," he hedged.

"Right." Leif was clearly as confused as his brother. "Stefan is going to live in Kansas City, and I am returning to Santa Fe."

Stefan slapped his forehead and his eyes lit up like gas lamps. "*Switch!* Of course! It is the perfect solution!"

"Solution?" Leif's gaze bounced from Stefan to Blake and back. "To what problem?"

Chenoa laid her hand on Leif's. "I love Missouri, and I love Kansas City. I do not want to go back through Indian land and live in Santa Fe."

"The Sauk were all moved out of Missouri, Leif," Blake reminded him softly. "Chenoa feels safe here."

"And Blake hates Kansas City, because it holds so many unpleasant memories for her," Stefan told his parents. "Her dream was to move to Santa Fe and open a café and a guest house."

"Switching your locations sounds perfect, under those circumstances." Sydney looked happy and sad at the same time. "Leif and Chenoa can stay in Kansas City, and Stefan can join Blake in Santa Fe."

Blake guessed why the obvious ambivalence. "Sydney, we promise we will come back to visit."

Stefan wisely continued, "And train tracks are being built as we speak, Mamma. They come as far as Missouri from the eastern seaboard already."

Sydney nodded. "That is a very good point, Stefan. And our journey from Washington was cut from eight weeks to two as a result."

Stefan lifted his glass. "There is only one thing left to do now, right Kacy?"

His sister startled, as if her mind had been miles away from Cheltenham. "Right. Um, what?"

Stefan looped his free arm around Blake's shoulders. His smile was seductive and his eyes glowed like blue flames.

"Get your brothers good and married, of course!"

August 2, 1845

Nine days later, on the first of August, Stefan and Leif pledged their troths to Blake and Chenoa. And this morning Blake opened her eyes to the big, auburn-haired man, with the bluest eyes she had ever seen, smiling at her.

"Good morning, wife."

Blake smiled back. "Good morning, husband."

Her naked body tingled when she thought of what occurred the night before. Stefan was both gentle and assertive as he aroused sensations and reactions in her that she never dreamed were possible.

I want to do it again.

Blake turned on her side. "It was a lovely wedding, don't you think?"

Stefan smiled crookedly. "I am not a good judge of these things, but I would say Kacy outdid herself."

Blake agreed. The ceremony in the Lutheran church in the center of Cheltenham was simple, but the decorations were not. Ribbons, flowers, and candles made the sanctuary look positively ethereal. The discarded dress which Kacy had embellished for Blake was draped over a chair in the room that once was Stefan and Leif's.

"Your sister is quite talented, you know," Blake stated, prompted by the sight of the gown. "Her idea to find one blue dress to match Chenoa's eyes, and one to complement my hair, was inspired. Then adding the same silver lace and white silk roses to both, meant that both were equally stunning."

"I do hope Kacy finds love and gets her own wedding someday," Stefan murmured. "But if you think she has talent, then at the least she will be able to support herself in the meantime."

"She does Stefan," Blake insisted. "Did you not see how beautiful Chenoa looked? I noticed that Leif wiped his eyes when he looked at her."

Stefan ran the back of one long finger down her cheek. "She was not as beautiful as you, my love. God's honest truth."

"Good answer." Blake's cheeks warmed at his touch. "I do believe you will make a suitable husband."

Stefan chuckled softly. "Well, you are stuck with me now."

Blake leaned close and kissed him. "Can we do it again?"

"Make love?"

A thrill snaked through her belly. "Yes."

Stefan's hand slid up her thigh. "Are you sore?"

In answer, Blake pulled him on top of her. "Please?"

He answered with his body.

Though tender from her deflowering the night before, Blake's responses were more intense, now that she understood what was happening. Her culmination left her shaking and unable to move.

"I love you," she whispered.

Stefan lay panting beside her. "And I you."

Kacy had planned a wedding brunch for eleven o'clock that morning, and invited the Athertons to join them, so Stefan forced himself from his marriage bed to wash and get dressed.

Blake's responsiveness last night was a pleasant surprise, but this morning he was left breathless and boneless.

This was looking to be a very good marriage.

Very good, indeed.

*****

Sydney adjusted the table settings yet again as she anxiously waited for her newlywed sons and their wives to appear. She figured Stefan and Blake would have worked things out satisfactorily, and really did not expect anything earth-shattering from Leif and Chenoa.

Even so, she was dying of curiosity to see how the couples acted the morning after their wedding nights.

"Sydney, calm down." Nicolas stepped up behind her and took a gentle hold of her arms. "Why are you so nervous?"

Sydney looked up and back at her husband. "I just want their marriages to be off to good starts. That is all."

Nicolas turned her around. "Our sons are grown and, frankly, experienced in the arts of bedding a woman. They will do well, I promise you."

"And their wives?" Sydney prompted. "What do you think?"

"I do not believe Blake has ever met a challenge she did not rise to and conquer." Nicolas smiled softly "She reminds me of you, you know. And the fact that Stefan chose her should let you know how much he loves you."

Sydney loved hearing that, more than she could express. "And Chenoa?"

"Leif has the patience of a saint. You know that."

She did. "He *has* been a steadying influence for Stefan ever since they met in Norway."

"And now, he will gentle Chenoa like a highly-strung filly," Nicolas observed. "She will come around. And probably sooner than later."

The front door opened. "Nick? Sydney?"

"Come in!" Sydney kissed Nicolas's cheek, then hurried into the hallway.

Kacy was descending the stairs, looking more rested and serene than she had in weeks.

Finally.

"The married couples have not yet appeared," Sydney said. "We will wait in the drawing room until they do."

"I need to speak with Anne," Kacy deferred. "I will join you all shortly."

While Kacy headed toward the kitchen, Rickard and Bronwyn Atherton followed Sydney with their youngest son James Reid right behind them.

"Where is Richard?" Sydney asked.

"Richard is right behind us with a small wagon. He's on his way to Saint Louis right after this." Bronnie's smile was sad. "I am so, *so* proud of him, but Washington DC is such a long way away."

Nicolas draped a consoling arm around her shoulders. "It is only two weeks by train now, and I expect that time to be cut in half in my lifetime."

Bronnie looked up at him. "Thank you for asking him to be your replacement, Nicolas. It really is quite an honor for the Atherton family."

Nicolas squeezed her shoulder and stepped away to shake nineteen-year-old James Reid's hand. "With Glynnis married and living in Saint Louis, you will be the next lord of the Atherton manor. Are you ready?"

He grinned. "Yes, sir."

The front door opened and Richard stepped inside. "Hello?"

"Drawing room!" Rickard called out.

Nicolas was passing out glasses of champagne when Kacy reappeared. "Thank you, Pappa."

When she smiled at Nicolas, Sydney noticed the coldness in her daughter's regard of her father was gone.

Thank goodness.

Now maybe we can move on.

"I am sorry Glynnis and Rhys could not come," Nicolas said to Richard, handing him a glass. "Will you see them in Saint Louis before you embark on your journey?"

Richard shrugged. "I suppose that depends on whether the babe is in the process of being born or not."

"My poor daughter is so miserable. Missouri's hot, humid summers are impossible for women so near their time." Bronnie looked imploringly at Rickard. "I should be there."

He nodded his agreement. "Now that Richard is prepared to leave, and the weddings are past, I will take you tomorrow afternoon when I retrieve the wagon. Will that do?"

"Yes." Bronnie smiled lovingly at her husband of twenty-five years. "Thank you."

Footfalls on the stairs announced the imminent arrival of Stefan and Blake.

"Drawing room!" Rickard called out, again.

*****

Stefan saw that Leif and Chenoa had not yet appeared. But then, they had spent the night in the stable apartment and did not have the benefit of the main house's chiming grandfather clock to keep them on track.

"I see the wagon out front. Are you leaving today?" Stefan shook Richard's hand.

"I am." Richard shifted his attention to Blake. "Good morning, Mistress Hansen."

Blake gasped a little and looked wide-eyed at Stefan. "I am Blake Somersby Hansen, now."

Stefan chuckled. "Since yesterday, I believe."

Leif and Chenoa entered the drawing room holding hands. Stefan thought that was a good sign.

"Why are we are gathering in here?" Leif asked.

Nicolas handed each of them a glass of champagne. "To toast the new Hansen women, of course, and to send Richard off in style."

Rickard grinned and lifted his glass. "Hear, hear!"

*****

Once everyone relocated to the heavily laden dining room table, conversations moved through the group as they always did in the two close families. Families who were brought together by a chance meeting, and a pair of land grants, nearly eighty years earlier.

Stefan noticed a definite change in Kacy today. It was a change for the better, and that was good, but he wondered what prompted it.

And why she was so distressed to begin with.

When he caught her eye and opened his mouth to speak, she flicked a tiny shake of her head and moved her attention to Blake.

"When will you head back to Kansas City?"

Blake looked at Stefan, then Leif. "Tomorrow?"

"So soon?" Sydney cried.

Stefan took control of that conversation. "We must, Mamma. We have already been here longer than we expected to, though for the best of all reasons, of course."

"It will take us a week to get there by carriage," Leif explained, obviously in agreement. "And we need to get wagons, lumber, and supplies readied."

"And hire the men—"

"And their wives," Blake interrupted. "Do not forget that component."

"Right." Stefan flashed an apologetic grin and returned his attention to Sydney. "We need to be on our way before the end of this month."

Sydney's shoulders slumped and she sighed. "I will miss you Stefan. And Leif. And my new daughters—we have had so little time together."

"Blake and I will come back to visit," Stefan promised. "And Leif and Chenoa will still be in Missouri, remember."

"And once the trains start running, we can be to Saint Louis in less than two full days." Leif was sitting close enough to Sydney to reach for her hand. "We plan to spend Christmas with you every year."

That statement poked Stefan, and for a brief moment he regretted his decision to move to Santa Fe. But when he looked at Blake, and saw how happy she was, that regret evaporated like cold raindrops on hot paving stones.

"Well then, I suppose the time has come for me to make my announcement as well."

Stefan stared at Kacy. "What announcement?"

Kacy drew a deep breath. "I am also leaving Cheltenham. In fact, Jack should have my trunk loaded in Richard's wagon by now."

Sydney's brows pulled together. "Are you moving to Saint Louis already?"

Kacy gave her mother a kind look. "No, Mamma. I am traveling back to Washington with Richard."

Stefan was not sure if he saw anger in his sister's expression, but he sure as hell saw her determination.

"Are you two eloping?" Stefan blurted, finding that idea *very* hard to believe. But why else would Kacy return to Washington when their parents were not?

"Oh, good Lord, no!" Kacy yelped. Then she quickly addressed Richard. "I meant no offense. But you are like a little cousin to me, even though we do not actually share any blood ties."

Richard was clearly trying to hold back his mirth with one hand as he waved the other hand toward Kacy. "No offense, taken, I assure you."

"Washington?" Nicolas growled the word, his expression thunderous. "I—"

"Stop." Kacy interrupted and pointed a stiff finger in his direction, her green eyes flashing like flames. "Pappa, I love you and Mamma very much. I do. But after what happened in June, you no longer have the right to say anything to me about what I do with my life."

Kacy's hand fell and her tone softened. "I am a fully grown, twenty-five-year-old, unmarried woman..." She gestured toward Stefan. "And now, I have no inheritance to sustain me—but I do have a business there to run."

Stefan was completely confused by her words—obviously, there was a big chunk of story missing in this exchange. "A business to run? Isn't that in Saint Louis?"

Leif, looking equally confused, nodded his agreement. "Then why are you going back to Washington, Kacy?"

Kacy rose to her feet. She pulled three business cards out of her pocket and dropped them in the center of the dining room table.

"I am going back to Washington to try my very hardest to salvage whatever I can of the life I *almost* had there."

Almost?

What the hell had happened to her?

Kacy's intense gaze moved first to Nicolas, and then Sydney. "And if I cannot, I will create an entirely new life there. In either case, I choose to not live my life here."

She pointed at the business cards. "You will all know where to reach me."

Kacy kissed Sydney's cheek, then Nicolas's. She rounded the table and hugged Chenoa and Leif, then Blake and Stefan.

"I love you all, and I will pray for you every night." She flashed a trembling smile. "Until we meet again."

Kacy spun on her heel and walked out the front door.

Rickard and Bronwyn, joined by James Reid, hurried after her.

All the Hansens—new and old—brought up the rear. Once they had all waved Kacy and Richard out of sight, Stefan turned to his parents.

"What did Kacy mean by salvage whatever she can of the life she *almost* had?" he demanded. "What are you not telling us?"

Nicolas and Sydney exchanged a somber look.

"Go on," Nicolas urged his wife.

Sydney faced the crowd filling the front porch. "Kacy swore us to secrecy. She did not want to have to answer your questions. Or worse, endure your pity."

"Pity?" Leif snapped. "Why would we pity her?"

"Let's go back inside," Rickard suggested. "It's a rather long story."

"Wait!" Stefan barked, not moving from his spot. "What is the story about?"

Rickard met his gaze with a stern one of his own. "It is about what happened to cause your father's heart attack."

Volume 20 of
The Hansen Series:
The Rogue and the Rose

REDESIGNED

Book Two:
Kacy & Twain

Kris Tualla

Chapter One

January 10, 1845
Cheltenham, Missouri

Kacy heard familiar voices from upstairs.

Could it be?

She stopped packing her things and ran from her room. As she hurried down the stairs, she heard her father's deep voice.

"Arrested?"

Oh no.

Kacy slipped inside the doorway of Nicolas's office and stood unmoving, hoping not to attract any attention.

Nicolas glared at her brother Stefan from across his battered oak desk. "For what?"

Stefan attempted to sound unconcerned. "For murder—"

"Murder!" their father bellowed.

Sydney gasped softly in her upholstered seat nearby. Her hand covered her mouth and her eyes widened. She shot a startled gaze at Kacy.

Oh, Stefan. What have you done now?

As much as Kacy deeply loved and adored her big brother, she wasn't blind to his faults. Stefan had always been stubborn and strong-willed just like their father, but he had a reckless and impulsive streak that had never been completely contained.

"I was innocent, of course! It was a misunderstanding!" Stefan turned to their adopted older brother. "Leif! Tell him!"

Leif faced Nicolas with an apologetic expression that Kacy recognized as: *you know how he is*. "Someone tried to pin the murder of a working girl on Stefan by leaving a bloody dress next to him when he was asleep."

Nicolas scuttled his hand through his thick but fading blond hair. "Where in the hell were you sleeping?"

Stefan's face flushed. "Outdoors. By a river."

"In December?" Nicolas snorted. "Are you daft?"

"He—we—didn't want to bed down in the brothel," Leif offered. Judging by the cautious look on his face he knew the declaration would bring more questions.

Nicolas's brow lowered and his dark blue eyes turned stormy. "So you were whoring?"

Stefan scoffed. "Like *you* never did?"

Oh, no.

Stefan, think before you speak for once.

Kacy leaned back and waited for the explosion she knew was coming.

Nicolas recoiled. "*What?*"

"He has you there, Nicolas," Sydney softly reminded her husband.

Stefan leapt through that opening. "Exactly! And Aunt Rosie is like a member of the family now."

Nicolas's fists hit the top of the desk. "We aren't talking about me!"

Sydney stood, her hands clasped in front of her waist, and quickly changed the subject. "Is that why you boys weren't here for Christmas?"

Boys?

Kacy pinned her lips between her teeth to keep from laughing. Stefan was thirty-one and Leif was thirty-six. They had not been counted as boys for nearly a decade and a half.

Stefan smiled sadly at Sydney. "Yes, *Mamma*. I am really sorry."

"We came as soon as we could," Leif confirmed. He turned toward Kacy and smiled. "At least we are here in time for Kacy's birthday tomorrow."

He remembered.

She smiled back at Leif, so glad that both of her big brothers were unexpectedly here.

"Her name is not Kacy," Nicolas growled.

Here we go again.

"Pappa, stop." Kacy stepped further into the room. "I like the nickname—I always have. Those are my initials and the name honors both of my grandmothers' names: Kirsten and Ciara."

Nicolas snorted.

"In fact…" Kacy paused, wondering how her next statement would be taken. "I used it the whole time I was in Philadelphia."

She shifted her gaze briefly to Stefan before she gave Nicolas an apologetic shrug. "And before you say anything else, I plan to use it in Washington as well."

Stefan startled visibly. "Washington?"

Kacy faced him fully now. "I am moving to the Capitol with Pappa and Mamma when Pappa returns to the Senate."

Obviously Stefan was taken by surprise. "Why?"

While Kacy lived with their Uncle Gunnar and Aunt Brigid in Philadelphia to augment her schooling there, she made the trip to Washington DC twice a year to visit Nicolas and Sydney. But Stefan had not seen their parents for several years—not since before Nicolas was elected as Missouri State Senator and they moved to Washington.

Both of them had aged during that time. Their father's face was heavily lined and their mother's black hair had turned solidly gray.

Kacy was worried about Nicolas—the strain of their political life in Washington was much more intense than in Missouri. That was one of the reasons she insisted on accompanying her parents when they returned after the holiday break.

"I have an education that is wasted here, to be honest," Kacy continued, talking more to her parents than to her brothers. "And I want to do more with my life than sit out here in the west with no prospects."

And that was the other reason.

If I am going to be an old maid, then I am going to be an independent one.

Finding the expected husband had eluded Kacy thus far. Not that she had ever worked at it, of course. Her illicit studies had been so interesting—particularly in business—that she stayed in Philadelphia for an extra year. Most of the men she met were put off by her keen intelligence and her refusal to downplay her capabilities.

But living back in Cheltenham for the last year and a half had been so stiflingly dull that Kacy was determined to create an interesting life somewhere else, whatever that life entailed.

"Well I am glad you are here now." Sydney's statement jerked Kacy's thoughts back into the office. Her mother stretched her arms toward Stefan. "I've missed you both."

Stefan stepped into her embrace. At six-foot-three just like their father, Sydney's head tucked neatly under her brother's chin. "I love you, Mamma."

"I love you too Stefan, you know that." She released him and reached for Leif.

Leif wasn't as tall as Stefan so his cheek pressed against Sydney's tied-up hair. "I love you, Sydney."

"And I love you." When she stepped back, she looked pointedly at Nicolas. "Will you greet your sons?"

Nicolas rose slowly. And Kacy noticed. She feared it was more age than reluctance that affected their father's movements. Nicolas rounded the ancient desk and held out his hand.

"I'm glad to see you both, do not mistake me."

Stefan nodded as he gripped Pappa's hand. "Yes, sir."

Nicolas shook Leif's hand, but his eyes were still fixed on Stefan. "And this conversation is not finished."

January 13, 1845

"I understand." Kacy stopped her own preparations for departure and hugged Stefan tightly. "I am so glad that I got to see you, brother. I miss you so much when we are apart."

"When do you leave?" he asked when she let go of him.

"Two more days. It will take less than two weeks by train to get there."

"To be honest, I am glad you are going with them," Stefan said carefully. "Keep an eye on Pappa. He has gotten... older."

"I know. I see it, too." Kacy's knowing smile was sad. "But I intend to take this chance to make more out of my life than I have been able to thus far, being stuck out here in the woods."

Kacy moved her embrace to Leif. "I love you too, brother. Take good care of him, will you?"

Leif mumbled into her hair, "Always."

Thank you for reading my book(s)! I hope you enjoyed the characters and their stories.

Please consider leaving a review on Amazon.

And follow me on Amazon for an email notice about the next Hansen story release:

1. Go to any of my book pages on Amazon and click on "Kris Tualla" by the title. This will take you to my Author Page.

2. Once there, click **+Follow** under my photo. It's that easy!

Thank you for your support!

HANSEN FAMLY TREE

Sveyn Hansen* (b. 1035 ~ Arendal, Norway)

***

Rydar Hansen (b. 1324 ~ Arendal, Norway)
Grier MacInnes (b. 1328 ~ Durness, Scotland)

Eryndal Bell Hansen (b. 1327 ~ Bedford, England)
Andrew Drummond (b. 1325 ~ Falkirk, Scotland)

***

Jakob Petter Hansen (b. 1485 ~ Arendal, Norway)
Avery Galaviz de Mendoza (b. 1483 ~ Madrid, Spain)

***

Brander Hansen (b. 1689 ~ Arendal, Norway)
Regin Kildahl (b. 1693 ~ Hamar, Norway)

Symon Karlsen (b. 1705 ~ Christiania, Norway)
Skagi Karlsen (b. 1707 ~ Christiania, Norway)

***

Martin Hansen (b. 1721 ~ Arendal, Norway)
Dagne Sivertsen (b. 1725 ~ Ljan, Norway)

Reidar Hansen (b. 1750 ~ Boston, Massachusetts)
Kristen Sven (b. 1754 ~ Philadelphia, Pennsylvania)

Nicolas Hansen (b. 1787 ~ Cheltenham, Missouri Territory)
Siobhan Sydney Bell (b. 1789 ~ Shelbyville, Kentucky)

Stefan Hansen (b. 1813 ~ Cheltenham, Missouri)
Blake Somersby (b. 1818 ~ Kansas City, Missouri)

Kirsten Hansen (b. 1820 ~ Cheltenham, Missouri)
Twain Kensington (b. 1822 ~ Cheltenham, Missouri)

Leif Fredericksen Hansen (b. 1809 ~ Norway)
Chenoa (b. 1821 ~ Unknown)

***

WORLD WAR II

Holten Hansen (b. 1904 ~ Oshkosh, Wisconsin)
Raleigh Burns (b. 1912 ~ Berlin, Wisconsin)

Tor Hansen (b. 1913 ~ Arendal, Norway)
Kyle Solberg (b. 1919 ~ Viking, Minnesota)

Teigen Hansen (b. 1915 ~ Arendal, Norway)
Selby Hovland (b. 1914 ~ Trondheim, Norway)

Lucas Thor Hansen (b. 1918 ~ Sabetha Kansas)
Parker Williamson (b. 1917 ~ Denver, Colorado)

***

*Hollis McKenna Hansen (b. Sparta, Wisconsin)

Kris Tualla is a dynamic, award-winning, and internationally published author of historical romance and suspense. She started in 2006 with nothing but a nugget of a character in mind, and has created a dynasty with The Hansen Series. Find out more at: www.KrisTualla.com

In 2019, Kris was inducted into the **Colorado Authors Hall of Fame** for her *Camp Hale Series* of World War II novels. Two of those novels, *Sempre Avanti: Always Forward* and *Ice and Granite* have been optioned for a screen project.

Made in the USA
Middletown, DE
22 June 2021